Praise for the novels of Jim R. Woolard

Cold Moon

Read

"In *Cold Moon*, the ▨▨▨
James Fenimore C▨▨▨
at last." —Lo▨▨

D0870212

"Jim Woolard's *Co*▨▨▨
Shawnee war of 17▨▨▨
death lurked at every bend in the dark forest trails
and neither side offered any quarter."
—Elmer Kelton, author of *Cloudy in the West*

"Jim R. Woolard has done it again . . . A 'must read'
for every historical fiction fan!"
—Ellen Recknor, author of *Leaving Missouri*

Thunder in the Valley

"A must-read for those who crave an exciting tale of
American frontier fiction."
—Cameron Judd, author of
The Overmountain Men and *Timber Creek*

"Before there were fur trappers . . . there were the
long hunters like Matthan Hannar. It took someone
with the sizable talent of Jim Woolard to bring the
drama and passion of that early era to the pages of
America's historical novel."
—Terry C. Johnston, bestselling author of
The Cry of the Hawk and *Carry the Wind*

"Jim Woolard pulls back the curtain of time to give
readers a vivid look at an exciting era of American
history." —Robert Vaughan, author of
the *American Chronicles*

Titles by Jim R. Woolard

COLD MOON

THUNDER IN THE VALLEY

THE WINDS OF AUTUMN

COLD
MOON

Jim R. Woolard

BERKLEY BOOKS, NEW YORK

COLD MOON

A Berkley Book / published by arrangement with
the author

PRINTING HISTORY
Berkley edition / December 1998

The Penguin Putnam Inc. World Wide Web site address is
http://www.penguinputnam.com

ISBN: 0-425-16082-3

BERKLEY®
Berkley Books are published by The Berkley Publishing Group,
a member of Penguin Putnam Inc.,
375 Hudson Street, New York, New York 10014.
BERKLEY and the "B" logo
are trademarks belonging to Berkley Publishing Corporation.

PRINTED IN THE UNITED STATES OF AMERICA

10 9 8 7 6 5 4 3 2 1

For support above and beyond sincere friendship, the author thanks Shirley Justice, Jim and Doris Allen, Wm. Fisk, Lorle Porter, Steve and Sue Kokovich, Bill and Cherie Holland, Joe and Teresa Jones, Zoe Bechtol, Jerry and Sally Garst, George Robinson, Fern Wilson, and the Arizona cowboy, John Duncklee.

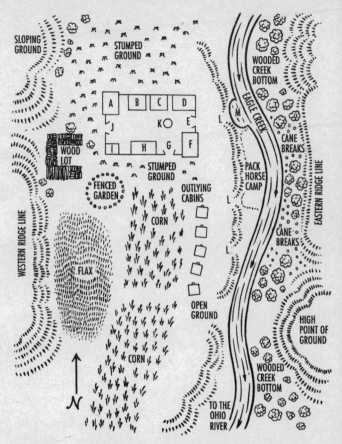

BRANDON STATION & ENVIRONS

A. NORTHWEST BLOCKHOUSE

B. LAYTON CABIN

C. PROVISION CABIN

D. FOWLER CABIN

E. WATER GATE

F. BRANDON BLOCKHOUSE

G. MAIN GATE

H. HORSE STABLE

I. BLACKSMITH FORGE

J. WOOD GATE

K. BAD WELL

L. CLEARED PATHWAYS

M. WATER GATHERING/ LAUNDRY AREA

RISING GROUND

PROLOGUE

Louisville, Kentucky

October 12, 1833

To the Honorable Judge Hickersby:

My letter, I trust, will be of some surprise, though I suspect your steadfast resolve has overcome the reluctance of many another old rifleman besides myself.

I will confess at the outset that not a day has come and gone without my recalling the earnest request you made of me the final night of your short visit. Please rest assured my initial refusal that bygone nightfall bore no disrespect for you or your proclaimed mission. Suffice it to say, the braggart receives no welcome at my door, and not being blessed with countless words as are the more learned about me, I ink the quill on every occasion with shameful but honest dread.

That I have endured a change of heart and will, henceforth, suffer my own shortcomings and fulfill your request, results from a recent incident here no man of conviction would dare ignore.

The whole of Louisville attended a week ago the twentieth anniversary commemoration of the 18 and 13 battle when we finally bested the hated Shawnee. As you are well aware, I am the sole living survivor of the infamous charge at the River Thames that swung the outcome in our favor and doomed to death the mighty Injun leader Tecumseh.

At the Black Rooster, Thursday evening last, howsomever, what you warned has become commonplace in your travels happened before my own eyes. The number of survivors of our charge at the Thames, the most renowned feat of arms in the annals of our fair state, grew with miraculous suddenness from one—yours truly—to a grand total of five, each toast of the tankard fetching yet another "dead" hero from the cold of the grave. And if that wasn't insult enough, other drunken revelers next regaled the crowd with fancified tales of helping me and my long departed companions, the great scout Nathan Breed and the fearless spy Hump Layton, defend Brandon Station during the Shawnee siege of that place clean back in the winter of 17 and 93. Never minding they would have been dressed in swaddling clothes at the time, not a few, by damned, had the utter gall to boast they had for certain more than once, thank you kindly, shaken the very hand of General Hugh Brandon his ownself.

I need not report none of these newly revealed, rumsotted, would-be heroes had ever before shared my company at a militia muster, let alone amidst the fright and bloodshed of our tussles with the Ohio Injuns.

It should please you, Your Honor, to know you were of help to me even in your absence, for though the false claims of my fellow drinkers sparked anger hot and fiery, I stayed tongue and fist by repeating over and over your parting admonition.

Never, I swear, have more telling words been spoken aloud.

We remaining few fully acquainted with the events of our fighting past must indeed step forward. If we do not, the current welter of lies and exaggeration circulating through tavern and meeting house will be acknowledged as the truth of how the Kentucky and Ohio country was conquered, thereby denying many brave souls actually having drawn bead on the red enemy the recognition and acclaim they so justly deserve.

It is not for myself I take up the quill: It is in memory of Nathan Breed and Hump Layton and their like, not forgetting along the way those few valiant women who stood tall beside us throughout our perilous struggle to raise and secure Brandon Station in the middle of the Ohio wilderness.

I will tell the story, as Hump was prone to say, with the bark on and hair side out, curses, ill feelings, scoundrels, and all. If you find my lines too raw or ungodly dull, you may treat them to the dust of the shelf or the flame of the hearth, though hopefully not before you finish your reading. After all, my dear judge, an old bounder consenting to toil without prospect of remuneration is entitled to some little indulgence, be he not.

More to follow . . .

Your obedient servant,
Fell Cooper

SNOW MOON

January 1793

1

We were ten miles above the Ohio's north bank, homeward bound for Kentucky and the warm fires of Limestone, when our scout, Nathan Breed, crossed the trail of the Shawnee.

Trust me, the sight of that clenched fist atop Breed's upraised arm sent a ripple of alarm through all of us lined out behind him, for the closed hand thrust high was the common signal among bordermen fresh Injun sign was present. And if Nathan Breed signaled so, you could bet your last powder charge there was no mistaking what he'd found.

The whole Brandon survey party halted stiff as dead trees in snow six inches deep, long-barreled guns filling hands suddenly shorn of mittens, eyeing and earing every which way at once. To say we feared the Shawnee and their red brethren was as certain as the clouding of our spent breath in the cold winter air.

At a come-hither sweep of Breed's lowered arm, Major Asa Fowler, commanding in General Brandon's absence, plowed forward and joined the kneeling scout on the high bank of the Indian Lick. The rest of us waited at the alert on the creek's frozen surface, anxious to learn how many of the red enemy were out and about, and in which direction they were traveling. More than just me, I reckoned, prayed the Shawnee tracks led off anywhere except toward our destination—Limestone on the far bank of the Ohio.

Hard trodden snow crunched behind me.

I neither started nor looked around, for if Nathan Breed was always in the lead, Hump Layton, General Brandon's spy, always marched at the rear of our party, guarding against any surprise from that quarter.

The big spy stepped alongside me and the packhorses in my charge, his towering bulk shading the late afternoon sun. A shaggy buffalo coat cloaked his massive shoulders. Nathan Breed had remarked over the supper fire that the spy's hide coat had taken all but the hooves and horns in the making, and I'd no call to believe otherwise. Hump Layton's chest and back side were so oversized his well-muscled lower half seemed small in comparison, and at any distance he appeared a two-legged buffalo, hence how he was called.

Layton's head, like his upper torso, rivaled that of his animal namesake, being wide across the forehead and narrow at the chin. Thick beard, brown and knotty as the hair on his hide coat, covered his cheeks and jaws. He wore without fail day and night a woven cap of striped vintage. Those in our party not particularly fond of the big spy argued, though never in his company I assure you, that the ever present cap hid the yawning scar of a Mingo scalping. Without his striped cap, his dislikers chided, Layton's ugly face stretched upward forever, exactly what the tough bastard deserved.

Such mouthings counted for naught with me. I cared not a whit what was under Hump Layton's cap. What he knew of Injuns and how he handled himself under threat of their attack, howsomever, concerned me greatly. Having just completed my twentieth year, I figured I'd a heap of living left undone. Hell's luck, I was so young that January afternoon I owned nothing outright except my rifle and hadn't yet kissed my first woman, pretty or ugly.

The big spy's massive shoulders turned slightly and hazel eyes missing part of the left brow centered on me. We were at the very rear of the column and Layton's deliberately softened voice didn't reach Cam Downing, the second packhorseman, standing scant feet ahead of us. "You hold yer horses and yer ownself good and steady, lad. Better'n most, I daresay."

His unexpected praise tied my tongue. He'd never before said anything solely for my ears. I pawed snow with a boot toe and bobbed my head, an awkward but passable acknowledgment of his kind words that reddened my ears; leastways they burned hot as the devil's pitchfork.

A knowing smile creased the big spy's bearded countenance. I swear his hazel eyes twinkled. He cradled his smoothbore musket in folded arms and asked, "You fought Injuns afore?"

I swallowed real fast and luckily avoided stammering like a brainless dolt. "Nary a one," I admitted truthfully. "But I can shoot a lick or two."

My honesty pleased the big spy. His smile widened and he chuckled. "Damn tickled you ain't no stranger to burnt powder," he said, nodding at the ongoing palaver twixt our scout and Major Fowler. "Breed appears worried, an' well he should be. Much as we've traipsed over the country, its a pure wonder the whole Shawnee nation ain't lurkin' yonder in full paint."

Right then Breed rose and disappeared into the bare trees beyond the high bank of the creek. Major Fowler, every eye fixed on him, wheeled, and half-stepped, half-slid down onto the frozen creek bed. He skirted the gray gelding tended by his servant Jaimie Crown, and slogged the length of the column, the heavy snow rough going for his short legs. He wended past surveyors John Block and Mason Welker, chainmen Bone Williams and Sam Moon, marker Noah Reem, and lastly, the bearskin-clad Telow brothers, Jacob and Askell. The major barked orders at each man in turn, and from how every soul stayed at attention, I determined the Injun sign located by Breed did indeed pose a serious threat to the column.

With the major still beyond earshot, Hump Layton straightened and talked from the corner of his mouth, his lips hardly moving at all. "Always remember, lad, a few gold coins and hundred free acres ain't payment enough for yer hair, poor though you be."

The wisdom of his statement was undeniable, and not questioning why I was suddenly worthy of his counsel, I spouted a hurried "Yes, sir!"

If the meanest sonofabitch in the hire of General Brandon was interested in helping me hang onto my scalp, so be it: The prideful and the foolhardy often warmed the same grave.

Major Fowler circled Cam Downing's packhorses, halted, and squared his shoulders with those of Hump Layton. The major stood no taller than the big spy's chest, but there was no question who was in command. Fowler's piercing blue eyes and stark gray hair fit perfectly with the solid jaw he scraped clean of whiskers each dawn. Gold braid traced the brim of his tricorn hat and the lapels of his tailored woolen greatcoat. From his left hip dangled a cavalry broadsword, its metal scabbard decorated with the Fowler family crest. Silver spurs studded the heels of black riding boots whose tops capped his knees. While the balance of the survey party traveled afoot, Major Asa Fowler, long accustomed to the trappings and privileges of rank, never ventured afield without his personal mount and his body servant.

From prior training and old habit, Hump Layton waited for his former superior to speak first. "Mister Breed has discovered the tracks of three Shawnee warriors," the major announced. "He is bothered that they didn't flee on our appearance as one would expect. They spent much time observing our approach, perhaps confirming our numbers and weapons. They then departed northwesterly. Breed is convinced they're not stray hunters. He claims they're scouts for a larger party intending to ambush us.''

"An' you, sir?'' Layton inquired.

Fowler's answer was quick and precise. "Far as we are from the Ohio, we've no choice but to heed his notion. Breed will trail the Shawnee, discern their true intentions, and report back by midnight, if not sooner.'' The major scanned the western horizon through the leafless forest. "With what daylight remains, we'll follow the Indian Lick till we gain Eagle Creek and wait there for Breed's return.''

The big spy beside me proved no less decisive in his thinking. "Was I you, sir,'' he offered, confident he could speak openly after years of service with Fowler, "I'd detail the point to the Telow brothers. They've tromped the country hereabouts much as Breed an' won't tarry. I'll hawk the rear with young Cooper here.''

Major Fowler silently weighed Layton's suggestion, his stern gaze in the meantime inspecting me from flop-brimmed hat down to stiff jackboots, as if even packhorsemen warranted a second looksee now that an encounter with the Shawnee loomed in the offing.

I readily acknowledge my garb wasn't of bragging quality. Briar snags and other rips and tears had frayed the sleeves of my ancient blanket coat, and below my coattail, fat drippings and horse slobber stained my leather leggins in numerous places. And the major couldn't miss the scruffy beard I'd grown for fear of frostbite. To my credit, his piercing gaze lingered longest on the pigskin shot pouch hanging at my right flank from its shoulder strap, the polled hatchet wedged behind my rope belt, and the worn stock of my flintlock rifle.

I was growing awfully uneasy under his close scrutiny, my nerves on the verge of fraying bad as my coat, when the major stomped snow from his riding boots and settled his attention on Hump Layton again. I sighed out wind I hadn't known I was holding, not so relieved, though, that I missed out on any of what Fowler next told the big spy.

"Jacob Telow will walk the point. Askell will join you and help guard the rear. We shan't stop for the night short of Eagle Creek, darkness or no, Mister Layton,'' the major ordered. His gaze sought me anew. ''Your horses are worn to a frazzle and hungry, Mister Cooper. But I'll abide no lagging or unnecessary commotion from them,'' he barked sternly. With that, he knuckled his forehead, spun abruptly on his heels, and retraced his path along the flank of the column, the tip of his sword scabbard furrowing the snow at each stride of his stubby legs.

His brusque manner rankled me plenty and my unseasoned temper loosed my tongue. ''I'll allow that squat pissdiddle sticks in yer craw now an' again,'' I blurted.

I regretted my slighting remark on the instant. Regardless of my sentiments toward Major Fowler, he commanded the survey party at the behest of General Brandon, and I understood from harsh experience the perils of faulting one's betters aloud: The tight-lipped sailed smoother waters than did the brashly outspoken.

I needn't have fretted any. Hump Layton, thank the Lord, took no offense on the major's behalf or of his own accord. Instead, his capped head tilted upward and he laughed deep in his throat, chest shaking with glee; then his head leveled, the laughter ceased, and his face sobered. ''I admire yer spunk, Fell Cooper. But Asa don't stick in yer craw none once you soldier with him awhile,'' he cautioned. ''I won't deny he ain't got any more warmth in him than day-old horse apples, yet he don't flog without just cause, an' he won't chew the same bone after the meat's gone. Never you fear, we commence tusslin' with the redsticks, he'll be plumb in the thick of it.''

Having been honestly and fairly chastised, my response was prompt and sincere. ''I'll bridle my jaw from here out, Mister Layton . . . sir!''

Another smile warmed the big spy's hazel eyes and he stuck forth an enormous paw. ''Hump, lad, just plain Hump. We'll let the officers call us 'Mister.' ''

Delighted with his show of friendship, I matched his smile without difficulty. His awesome grip I matched best I could, never minding he could crush my fingers like dry

twigs was he of such a bent. Still, my considerable strength
from months at the blacksmith forge surprised him. He
pried his hand free and his approving clap on my shoulder
almost broke bone.

"I'd be honored to tree the boar with you when we hit
Limestone, Fell, me lad," he proclaimed, "damned honored."

My shoulder hurt something fierce, but my swollen pride
offset most of the pain. Just the thought a mere packhorseman might actually pass muster with the infamous Hump
Layton teared my eyes. From what was said at the supper
fire, the general's spy was almighty choosy and embraced
few of his fellows, young or old.

Askell Telow interrupted us at that juncture, not an un-
fortunate turn of events since he spared me a second and
perhaps crippling clap on the same shoulder. Besides, I'd
have died of embarrassment if the likes of Hump Layton
caught me with my feelings smeared on my sleeve.

At Askell's overly loud "Reportin' as ordered, Captain!" I shortened my grip on the reins of the lead packhorse, for the younger Telow's lengthy bearskin coat and
furry headdress on occasion spooked the calmest of animals. A warning yip from Cam Downing alerted us Major
Fowler sat astride his gelding once more. His sword circled
twice above his head, and men and animals lurched forward
down the Indian Lick, the march for Eagle Creek finally
under way.

"Askell, hang twixt Cooper's horses an' my position,
equal distance if'n you please," Hump ordered. "First hint
of trouble, I'll rejoin you an' we'll fall back together, givin'
the others all the warnin' we can. Any questions?"

"Naw," Askell answered, "just so's me an' Jacob share
in any Shawnee scalps come a fight." He fingered wispy
hairpieces, hooped and dried, that decorated his waist sash.
"Jacob an' me's right slick with the knife, don't you know."

Hump's arms unfolded from about his musket. His empty
fist seized Askell's elbow and he jabbed the younger Te-

low's chest with the barrel of the musket. "Lessen they fall at our feet by chance, I ain't huntin' any scalps a-purpose. I aim to get every man jack of us safely to the Ohio. You keep close watch on me ever step or I'll leave you nose down in the snow for the Injuns to gloat over. You understand me?"

Askell withstood the big spy's stony glare for the briefest of moments, then gulped and nodded. Hump Layton returned Askell's nod, shouldered his musket, and set off upstream opposite the column's line of march, his bulk seeming to fill the Indian Lick from bank to bank. Askell never looked my way. He muttered curses, hawked and spat, but his eyes remained as ordered—locked on the retreating backside of Hump Layton.

The column was by now rounding a creek bend downstream. I tugged at Buck's reins and lit a shuck after them, anxious to catch up. Strong as Hump Layton was, and much as I trusted his toughness and courage, the safety of numbers never lost its appeal in Shawnee country.

The Indian Lick's narrow channel ran due south. The thick ice underfoot withstood the weight of men and horses without cracking, and the covering snow, while softened by sun warmth and toilsome for tired limbs, lay flat and free of drifts. Leery as we were of a Shawnee ambush, we favored the center of that frozen channel, the entire column endlessly searching the treed banks for any untoward movement or warning flash of painted skin. Let me tell you, a body wasn't firm with hisself, the jumps could lay hold of you and start you imagining redsticks where there was nothing but tall trunks and spindly brush.

An hour before twilight, the Lick's descent steepened, coursing over several flat shelves of stone. Each low waterfall was sheathed with ice slick and wet. The unsure footing further burdened horses already tired through, and both packhorse strings fell steadily behind the balance of the column. The Lick leveled after a half mile and Major Fowler waited for us to close up on him and the others, then determined we'd better blow the horses or risk breaking them down altogether.

The proper packhorseman, like the preacher overly devoted to his flock, worried constantly. Ignoring my own leaden feet, I checked each of my animals for loose straps, shifting loads, and the first hint of any swelling about the hocks and ankles. I knew without glancing his direction Cam Downing busied himself with the same chore.

Daylight waned rapidly. Tree shadow darkened the Lick's snowbound channel. I straightened beside the last animal of my four-horse string and, much to my surprise given Hump Layton's exacting orders, found Askell Telow watching me, his approach too silent for my ears. At the lift of my brow, he butted his rifle twixt moccasined feet and raised his free hand in a belaying gesture.

"Stand easy, I won't spook yer horses," he promised. "An' I ain't in no trouble with yer big captain friend neither. He wants I should ask why the delay, an' all's well, wait for him here . . . Ain't nothin' afoot, be there?"

"Naw, Major's given us a rest is all," I assured him.

"Praise the saints," Askell responded, sighing. "Maybe I rest awhile my skinny rump'll heal over."

"Hump did bite on you somethin' fierce," I conceded, ". . . an' maybe unfairly to boot."

Askell's pale eyes gleamed in the dwindling light. "Either way, there ain't nothin' gained was I to stay mad at the big bastard. Jacob says if'n Breed's right an' the Shawnee are out, we'll be damned grateful Captain Layton's travelin' with us no matter what."

"An' why's that?" I inquired.

"Jacob says other'n the captain and the major, the general's Virginians ain't trustworthy. Jacob says they parade in them fancy bluecoats totin' their new muskets an' cartridge boxes smart enough, but ain't none of 'em ever shot at anythin' with two legs, God forbid howlin' red heathens chargin' straight down their gullets. Their soldier'n amounts to shootin' at wood rounds an' drillin' twice a month. Jacob says thout ol' Hump hold 'em on the line, they'll shit green an' desert the major his ownself the first war whoop they hear. An' I damn well believe my brother,'' Askell concluded.

Cam Downing's familiar yip wafted from downstream and the column resumed its southward march. I hitched past horses and reclaimed Buck's lead rein, disappointed I'd no time to ask the younger Telow what Nathan Breed thought of Jacob's prediction. The last I saw of Askell in the gathering dusk he was still leaning on his rifle waiting for Hump Layton to make an appearance.

Jacob Telow's misgivings concerning the Virginians stuck in my head like a hammered peg and I was soon tallying up the fighting experience of the entire Brandon party. Hump Layton had fought Injuns on both slopes of the Alleghenies. Major Fowler had commanded continental troops in our war with the king's redcoats. The remaining six Virginians—the surveyors, the chainmen, and Jaimie Crown—Jacob Telow's so-called bluecoats, were raw as newly sworn recruits. Of the five Kentuckians hired by the major at Limestone, Nathan Breed and the two Telows had fought the Shawnee; and Cam Downing and I were no drier behind the ears than Jacob's bluecoats. All told then, five of the thirteen armed men descending the Lick had at some time fired on an enemy. Of course, if Nathan Breed failed to locate the Shawnee in any number, my tally had no significance whatsoever. On the other hand, if Breed did encounter the Shawnee in force and pointed for the Ohio, the courage of not just the bluecoats, but *every* member of the column would be sorely tested in the ensuing redstick assault.

I tramped the last mile to Eagle Creek in full darkness, pondering, as the doubting lad will, every possible calamity that might befall us before we sighted Limestone on the morrow. And I shamelessly admit my greatest fear in the end wasn't of being killed and losing out on the fifty dollars gold and hundred free acres due me from General Brandon, but whether Fell Cooper could somehow postpone meeting his maker long enough to kiss his first girl, hopefully a pretty one.

About some things, Shawnee or no Shawnee, a young man could be downright unrelenting.

2

With darkness came the beginning of night winds that tugged at coat collar and hat brim. The raw bursts hinted it would grow colder by the hour. Loose clouds scurried from the southeast, dimming the light of the newly risen moon. Such conditions drew the keen weather eye, for they often presaged winds that circled from southeast to northeast, and yielded snow from the latter point on the compass at dawn or shortly thereafter.

High ground rose abruptly to our front and shoved the Lick eastward in a final sweeping bend before it merged with the larger Eagle Creek. Over the years the Lick had carved a pocket at the base of that deflecting ridgeline with the depth to partially shelter thirteen men and their exhausted animals. The major agreed with Jacob Telow's choice and we encamped there.

Cam Downing was anxious to off-load the horses and light the supper fire, but I delayed him a-purpose. Previous nights we had assembled our camp with Kentuckians and Virginians on opposite flanks of hobbled horses and mounded gear. Tonight was different. Tonight we suspected with some certainty the enemy was afield. Perhaps the major wouldn't want the horses stripped bare in case an unplanned departure proved necessary. And even one fire seemed too many till we heard from Nathan Breed.

The moonlight was sufficient for Major Fowler, from astride his gelding, to spy Cam and me standing idle. He touched his mount with his spurs and rode before us, servant Jaimie Crown glued to the gelding's heels. The major dismounted, the Virginians collecting within earshot behind him and Jaimie. "You'll yet become a fair soldier, Mister Cooper. Your hesitation is well founded. Unload only the heaviest gear and our food stock. Tie your horses in a single row, saddled, with loosened cinches. We'll forgo picket ropes and hobbles."

The major wheeled and addressed the listening bluecoats. "We'll have our customary two fires, spaced well apart," he stated, extracting his gold-cased watch from a coat pocket. "The fires will burn for two hours and two hours only, time for you to fill bellies and warm yourselves. We'll then wait at the ready for Mister Breed. Mister Crown will assist Mister Cooper watering and feeding the horses. Mister Downing and Mister Reem will cook as before. There's firewood for the taking at the bottom of the cut bank. We need be quick after it. Mister Block, you and your men stack your muskets and follow me."

With Hump Layton posted behind us and Jacob Telow roving ahead downstream where we would march next, the major risked fires of short duration. He really had little choice. Unabated hunger, numb feet, and fingers too stiff to load a gun had hastened the demise of many winter soldiers.

Cam Downing was jubilant over not missing his supper. We had both bunked at Ned Henry's Limestone Livery three years and Cam's craving for vittles day and night astounded me still. With Cam, missing even a single sitting at the table was tantamount to starvation. He relished his assignment as cook at the Kentuckian's fire since it provided him the opportunity to eat every pan clean and drink every boiling noggin dry. It was no secret why with his every move his portly frame jiggled from unshaven jowls to belly hole.

"Unload that deer quarter first," Cam chirped. "Me an' Noah'll whack her in two whilst the wood's gathered. Ain't nothin' but roasted meat gonna satisfy my innards. Noah here's empty as I be, don't you know."

Noah Reem seldom spurned his fair portion at mealtime. But where Cam ran to fat, Noah ran to bone and sinew on a frame narrow and slender. At ten and six he was the youngest of the Virginians. Being related to General Brandon by marriage, he wore his blue greatcoat, metal cartridge box, gray woolen breeches, and canvas gaiters with great pride. The lean cheeks beneath his cockaded hat hardly bore enough whiskers to challenge the dullest of razors. Cooking was the most boring of chores for young Noah, camp duty falling to him because of his youth. But not desiring to imperil his chances for more exciting assignments with the general in the future, he toiled willingly each night with Cam Downing, gleaning, with his endless questions, every speck of knowledge he could from their joint endeavor.

I lifted the hide-wrapped deer quarter from the saddle-trees and Cam carted the bundle clear of the horses. He and Noah knelt in the snow, unwrapped the hide cover, and began their meat splitting. I eased cinches and off-loaded four of the eight pack animals, gaining with the final un-loading two leather piggins for water fetching.

Jaimie Crown, slender as Noah Reem and gray-bearded with cow eyes, tied the major's gelding to a length of drift-wood and quietly accepted the piggins when I passed them. For Jaimie, anything exceeding "yes, sir" and "no, sir" was a flowery speech. He was past fifty and had faithfully served General Brandon and Major Fowler throughout the eastern Redcoat war, attending their daily needs and wants. After long years as an unarmed orderly, he had taken up the musket without protest for the major's Ohio expedition.

Upstream a short ways, we scraped snow aside and brushed bare an expanse of ice. Jaimie held my rifle while

I knocked open an ice hole with the polled edge of my hatchet. Without our exchanging words, he filled the piggins and lugged them back to the horses. He would make round trips with the piggins till he watered all the animals. He had never said so, and might deny it if asked, but Jaimie Crown had a fondness for four-legged beasts deep as my own.

Packhorsemen crossing the country bordering the Ohio always noted the location of canebrakes. Cane harvested with a hatchet had fed countless hungry animals in weather both fair and foul. Its tall stalks grew in bold clusters along creek banks almost without fail, and the Indian Lick was no exception.

It was a middling hike upstream to the nearest canebrake. Once there, I didn't commence the harvest right off. Suddenly alone and away from camp, with neither Hump Layton nor Askell in sight yet, I had me a healthy gander roundabout. Nothing stirred except the wind. I carefully stood my long rifle close by in the fringe of the cane and went to work with my hatchet.

That rifle leaning against the cane, an old piece scratched and dinged from stock to muzzle, was my most prized possession. Originally crafted by Cyrus Devlin of Pennsylvania's Bedford County, boss man Ned Henry had owned it from the beginning; that was, till he presented it to me as a parting gift the evening before the Brandon flatboats sailed from Limestone. Ned Henry had laughed at my open-jawed mouth and pressed the rifle to my chest, urging me to accept it. Finally realizing he wasn't funning me, I latched onto the unexpected gift with both hands.

My repeated thanks caused him to look sharply away and clear his throat. He then sorted through the clutter on his desk in the harsh light of the lanthorn hanging from the beamed ceiling of his office. He came about showing a smile of his own, proudly displaying a slim block of rounded wood pierced by five evenly spaced holes. On closer look, I saw that a patched rifle ball filled each of the holes. "The bullet block belongs with the Bedford rifle," he explained. "It was Cyrus Devlin taught me to sit the block on the end of the barrel and ram the ball home neat and quick. Ol Cyrus could reload a dozen beats faster than any ranger in Bedford County."

"I've admired the block Nathan Breed totes. It's rounded like this one," I said, excitedly. "He swears you can't take time to patch a ball with each shot. It's too slow, 'specially in the thick of an Injun fight."

A somber cast beset Ned Henry's pox-scarred features. He reached upward and dropped the bullet block's neck thong over my hatless head. "You must watch out for yourself every moment, my young bucko," he warned. "Many at the docks claim the Shawnee have moved north and abandoned their hunting grounds across the river. They are fools! Come spring, the Shawnee will be on the warpath again."

His abrupt change of mood tempered my excitement. I valued Ned Henry's opinion and sought it at every opportunity. "Is General Brandon such a fool?"

He thought on that a long minute. "No, not a fool. Just a greedy soul in a godawful hurry."

"How so?" I persisted.

"I've learned he sold his Virginia holdings lock, stock, and barrel to pay his gambling losses. With what was left, he purchased a bushel of Ohio land warrants totaling seventy thousand acres. He sold the warrants to his neighbors and they're resettling with him between the Scioto and the Miami across the river. He promised every buyer he'd have their new acreage free of Shawnee and surveyed for them when they arrive this spring."

"How could he promise that?" I demanded. "General Wayne's still recruitin' an' trainin' his legion upriver at Logstown. He's bogged down there for who knows how long. An' nobody else's gonna tame them Shawnee anytime soon."

Planting both haunches on the corner of his desk, Ned Henry stroked his heavy mustache with a thumb. "Lad, you've sliced open the very heart of General Brandon's troubles. He counted on his friend Wayne to distract the Shawnee. But Wayne languishes at Logstown shy the recruits to fill his ranks while the general's Virginia buyers prepare for their westward trek anticipating upon arrival they'll find what they paid for in advance. And where's our dear general? Why, having parted with his home, he's forced to spend vast sums each month quartering his family and his wife's servants at Pittsburgh. And he can't linger at Pittsburgh doing nothing with time a-wasting. If he does, he'll exhaust his remaining wealth and his land scheme will collapse of its own accord. Suffering the gaol for bad debt and fraud isn't part and parcel to the grandiose intentions of General Hugh Rolfe Brandon; that I can attest to personally, never having met the esteemed gentleman.''

Despite the big words spicing his speech, I understood the drift of what Ned Henry said. ''So the general gambles and dispatches Major Fowler to make his Ohio survey 'thout General Wayne's skirts to hide behind,'' I reasoned, ''countin' on the Shawnee to be too occupied with their winter huntin' to find him out.''

Ned Henry chuckled and regained his feet. ''Couldn't have said it better my ownself. It's get on with it for the general or pray he can bribe the judge at his trial.''

Ned Henry was always square with me and I had to ask. ''You don't have any great concern about Cam an' me crossin' the Ohio with the major?''

''I'll not play the fool with you and claim there's no Injun danger involved. But if we won't supply the major his horses, others will. Don't forget, his survey can be completed in two weeks or less and Nathan Breed's the finest scout anywhere on the Ohio. Hump Layton'll be your spy. On top of that, Major Fowler's surveyors are armed and he's hired the Telow brothers, too. Jacob and Askell may be wild as unbroken stallions, but they're tolerable camp guards an' wouldn't back down from the devil. Hell's bells, if the odds didn't favor the major, I wouldn't've rented him my best packhorses for a thousand acres of my own.'' He gripped my shoulder. ''You and Cam are bound out to the Henry Livery for another four years. Then what's there for you? Neither of you, no more than I, can walk away from the general's gold and Ohio land of your own. If either of you decide not to improve your acreage once the Shawnee are pushed back for good, I'll buy it for twice its value. How can you lose on a proposition like that?''

Arguing with Ned Henry was akin to splitting large rocks with a small sledge: not worth the sweat for the gain. I managed a meager smile and hefted the Bedford rifle. "I guess there ain't no way we can lose, long as the Shawnee don't catch our scent."

Ned Henry escorted me to the door, pegged leg thumping the plank flooring. "Promise me one other thing. Watch out for Cam. He dwells on his stomach too often and lets his mind wander. Nonetheless, he's not mean-spirited with the stock, and he cooks better'n the whole damn bunch of you." Opening the office door, he paused, eyes peering straight into mine. "I've considerable faith in you, Fell Cooper. Young as you are, you're sharp between the ears and the top packhorseman on the Henry crew. I trust you to bring Cam and my horses safely home. Now, get your rest. You're off on what should prove a grand adventure."

Ned Henry had been sincere in everything he said that evening. The catch was his compliments were much more convincing on the Limestone side of the river: There I shared his confidence in Fell Cooper. But across the wide Ohio, it was an entirely different tale. On the Lick's frozen surface harvesting cane by moonlight, it seemed he had said those same compliments to someone else, a stranger unknown to me, and I worried I might fail a master who put gold in my palm instead of the lash on my bare back side.

I felled cane, chopped the stalks through in the middle, and stacked them in piles for easy carrying. At the finish of each pile, I looked and listened, never more than a single stride from the Bedford rifle. The wind was strengthening and slowly circling around to the northeast. Its growing chill nipped at what little feeling remained in my nose and ears. The clouds scurrying across the face of the moon had

thinned, a commonplace occurrence with the wind circling
like it was. Downstream, the glow of flames danced on the
high wall of the cut bank. It was an uplifting sight. Cam
and Noah had the supper fires burning and vittles roasting
and stewing. I licked lips dry and chapped: There wouldn't
be any extra for Cam Downing tonight.

This go-round I saw and heard Askell Telow at the same
instant he did likewise with me. I recognized him immediately. Wearing his furry bearskin hat, fashioned so his
face replaced that of the animal, he looked in the moonlight
the pointy-eared bear walking on its hind legs. Askell didn't
share my certainty when it came to recognizing what con-
fronted him. From where he stood, I was a black lump
shaped differently than the tall cane stalks beside my kneeling body, something seeming out of place and perhaps
threatening. Never a timid soul, Askell threw rifle to cheek
and drew bead on me, cocking his weapon as the barrel
came level.

Not wishing to be shot dead by mistake, I ignored my
own weapon and froze in place. It took all the nerve I had
to stay absolutely still and let a few beats of total silence
pass. Taking pains to move nothing but my mouth and jaw,
I said in the firmest, clearest voice I could muster:

"Askell, you know damn well it's a waste of powder to
kill anythin' you can't eat an' don't mean you no harm."

Breath exploded from Askell in a sighing rush. Snorting
and laughing all at once, he lowered his rifle and eased the
hammer from its cocked position. "Never came closer to
shootin' one of my own," he admitted. "You was wise not
to move an' invite a bullet, Fell."

My own sigh of thanks was just as heartfelt. I was glad
Askell couldn't see my hands shaking. "I appreciate yer
holdin' off thataway. Had it been me, I probably would've
fired and been damn sorry afterwards."

Hump Layton wasn't there, then with a whisper of noise
he was at Askell's elbow. It amazed me how a man of his
bulk got about so quietly whenever he wanted to. "Well,
if'n you two are finished confessin' yer monumental near

sins, maybe we oughta grab hold of that cane an' find out what Cam an' Noah's servin' tonight. That be, 'lessen yer gonna stand here jabberin' back an' forth till you freeze or starve to death. Me, I ain't plannin' on doin' neither.''

He handed Askell his musket, restacked four of my six piles into two large ones, gathered both in his overlong arms nifty as you please, and taken out for camp. It took some hustle for Askell and me to snatch up the balance of the cane and keep him in sight.

By the time we arrived at camp, Hump and Jaimie Crown were dividing cane amongst the ravenous horses. On sighting the cane, the animals ceased raking the snow for browse. They lipped those dried stalks like they was whiskey-soaked corn. I set aside the stalks Askell and I toted for their dawn feeding.

Hump ran a wary eye over the scrawny, loosely tied horses. "Those extra miles wore on 'em," he observed. "You know your strings. If'n they must, can they travel afore first light 'thout falterin' on us?"

"Mister Henry likes high blood and shiny coats in his ridin' stock. He breeds pack animals for lung, muscle, an' bone, an' no balkin' at what's asked of 'em. With a few hours' rest, they can flag their tails again," I assured him.

"That's heartening news," Layton conceded. "If'n Breed brings the opposite, I prefer everythin' favors our landin' at Limestone 'thout engagin' the Shawnee. I aim to build a cabin in this country afore I'm buried in it." He turned and studied Cam's fire. "Let's move along. I'll sup with you Kentuckians same as Jaimie. He an' Askell are eatin' now, an' I'd hate for that cook of yours to grab the notion we ain't hungry. He's faster'n the woods rattler with that ladle when he's stuffin' his own gullet."

Cam Downing's fare consisted of venison strips roasted on iron spikes embedded twixt the logs of the fire; johnnycake made from meal, flour, bear's oil, and water and baked in hot ashes; and white beans seasoned with deer tallow and boiled in the stewing kettle, all of which he served heaped together, thick beans on the bottom. We ate with tools and fingers, the only sounds those of swirling night wind, popping flame, and the scrape of metal spoon on battered tin plate.

Chewing and gulping accomplished, we squatted on our heels with arms extended and soaked in the glorious warmth of the flames. I wasn't alone pinching nose and ears, the pain proof neither was frozen beyond recovery.

The hollow knock of wood against wood heralded the approach of Noah Reem. His final supper chore was the dispensing of the major's daily rum ration, duty drawn by Noah since the smallest swig sickened him something awful. The rap of gill cup on the stopper of the wooden rum horn was the call to form in line for the drinking down. Not a man refused. The lightning scald of the fiery liquor watered my eyes and shivered me from tongue to heel. We each bolted our gill and hastily reclaimed our places around the dying fire.

Cam Downing wedged johnnycake into his mouth and talked around it, a feat at which he was quite skillful. "How much longer, Noah?"

"Major says we douse the fires in forty minutes. He granted us an extra half hour."

"Breed's been on his scout five hours now. Maybe the major's thinkin' the Shawnee ain't out after all," Cam ventured.

Askell Telow's fur-crowned head shook. "I wouldn't wager spit on that was I the major," he said. "Nathan's part redstick, an' any dog can scratch his own fleas. Nathan's wrong about as often as the creek don't rise after rain."

"Well, no matter what he finds, I don't recollect agreein' to fight no damn Injuns for my piddlin' piece of land, free or not," Cam protested, drinking water from an iron canteen.

"Maybe you didn't," Hump Layton offered. "But the Shawnee don't harbor any liking for white surveyors or those who tend their horses . . . or do their cookin' for 'em.

Long as they're free to paint their faces, there ain't no cheap land north of the Ohio.''

With his belly full, Cam Downing could be downright bold, blissfully treading paths shunned by wiser and more cautious folk. ''You surely ain't poor as dock rats liken Fell an' me, Captain Layton. How come yer chancin' yer scalp with the major an' the general?''

Cam's complete disregard for camp manners was so blatant and unexpected not a soul looked anywhere but at the big spy. Prying into the private affairs of a man who had never before graced the Kentucky supper fire was trespass of the highest order. And the person suffering the affront had every right to seek redress as he deemed appropriate: That was the way of it twixt hunters the length of the Allegheny frontier.

Cam took no notice of the sudden silence surrounding him. Having intended no insult, he grinned openly and waited for an answer to his question. The rest of us tensed for the forthcoming eruption. Hump Layton's temper was legion wherever men struck steel with flint.

Flaring anger tightened the corners of Hump Layton's hazel eyes. But just as quickly he caught himself. He glanced briefly at his huge paws and cracked his knuckles. When his gaze rose to meet Cam's, his accompanying smile was friendly and forgiving. I mean to tell you, my respect for the general's spy grew a bunch then and there. Nobody would ever convince me there was anything small about Hump Layton: A truly big man overlooked the inadvertent mistakes of those he could whip out of hand.

''You're on the mark, Downing,'' he conceded. ''My purse ain't bare. But back across the mountains, land that ain't too tuckered out to grow other'n weeds is pitiful scarce. An' disputed claims to yer rich Kentucky bluegrass outnumber the acres for sale south of the river. So, this ol' soldier's chancin' his scalp to grab some fresh Ohio ground he can prove up on afore he disappoints his sole offspring.''

Layton's frank honesty quieted us as had Cam's poor manners. All of us, that was, except Cam. ''How old's yer son?'' he continued. His fascination with the huge Virginian exceeded mine.

Layton never hesitated. ''Mike's not my son. She's my daughter.''

Askell Telow managed to smother much of his snorting laugh. What escaped his lips drew everyone's attention. Embarrassed, he pulled at his red beard. ''Never heard of such a thing. A girl named Mike!'' he exclaimed. ''Damned if'n that ain't the thick end of the switch.''

Another touchy moment ensued till Hump Layton's head tilted back and his booming laugh eased the situation once and for all. If Askell's remark about his daughter's name hadn't roused the big spy's ire, it seemed nothing would, at least not this evening.

''I'll tell her what you said,'' Layton promised. ''Mike will likely chuck a rock at me, but she's the most fun when she's madder'n the baited rooster.''

Cam's curiosity was relentless. ''How'd she come to be called liken a man?''

Hump Layton beamed with pride. ''Ain't nothin' ordinary nor dull where my Michaela's concerned. She scorns the notion men ride while women must walk. She demands equal harness or she won't share the traces.''

''Does she win out often?''

On that subject the big spy was slow to render an opinion. The same wasn't true of Noah Reem. The gill cup thunked his rum horn as he shifted his feet. ''Most times she wins out. You can't hardly deny her whatever she asks of you,'' Noah said. ''Mike Layton's mighty familiar with the word 'yes.' ''

So much attention reddened Noah's pink cheeks. His head dipped. ''Sorry if I spoke out of turn, Captain,'' he apologized. ''I mean Mike no ill will. She may be stubborn as all get out, but she's not spoiled to the core like Miss Rebecca.''

With a new gate open before him, fearless Cam plunged ahead. ''Don't stare at yer toes, Noah. Who the hell's Miss Rebecca?''

Young Noah nudged the rum horn higher beneath his bluecoated arm, secured a nod from Hump Layton with raised brows, then said, "She's the general's daughter, his only offspring. Many swear she's the most beautiful girl in Northumberland County, even more beautiful than her mother, Laina."

"Well, bygod, in for the sip, in for the keg, that's what I always say," Cam contended. "What about the major? Any females in his stable that'd set a man to droolin' in an eyewink?"

"Afraid not," Noah answered. "The major's a widower with no daughters."

Cam's face soured. His next inquiry was almost an afterthought. "The major wants Ohio land just for hisself?"

"No, his son, Brice, will join us in the spring."

Askell Telow frowned. "He too young to fight Injuns?"

Noah Reem shifted his feet. He wet his lips and glanced at Hump Layton. His hesitation wasn't lost on his listeners. For whatever reason, Noah wasn't comfortable explaining the absence of the major's son.

The cracking of Hump Layton's knuckles was loud as a drum roll. "The gout felled General Brandon at Pittsburgh," the big spy asserted, studying Askell close enough he could have counted the hairs of the younger Telow's red beard. "On his father's orders, Brice stayed behind to see after the women an' servants."

Now, I didn't know the major's son from the dark side of the moon. But I knew without a qualm to the contrary that Hump Layton was dancing with the truth. Why else was his voice underscored with a challenging tone in response to such a harmless query on Askell's part?

Askell, like me, sensed the change in Hump Layton. He leaned, hawked, and spat into the darkness. "Might be we'll all wish we was tendin' the general's door in Pittsburgh afore the night's over."

"Ain't that the gospel," Hump Layton agreed, the sharpness fading from his voice. He rocked to his feet. "The major's signalin' fires out. Come along, Askell. Nature calls, an' we need to have a final look-see upcreek. Breed should be along soon.''

The younger Telow and the spy were hardly beyond the firelight when Cam began badgering Noah. "What's the trouble with Brice Fowler? What would you write about him in yer journal? Better yet, what's already in there?''

Though he never revealed what he wrote, Noah had schooling and recorded personal entries almost every evening in a leather-bound tablet he carried in the pocket of his greatcoat. He would thaw his bottle of ink at the edge of the coals and ply his goosefeather quill with brisk strokes. The secrecy of what he wrote made the nosy Cam that much more desperate to unearth the journal's contents.

Noah laid his rum horn aside and helped Cam and me scour the dinner plates with snow. "My journal doesn't contain a solitary mention of Brice Fowler.'' He paused, deciding again whether he should speak at all of the major's son. "Brice would steal my journal from in front of my very eyes if he even suspected I'd penned anything, good or bad, concerning him . . . Either of you ever have dealings with him, be forewarned: My father would rather treat with a poisonous snake. He says Brice can lie to the Lord while holding hands with Satan himself.''

Cam shoved plates and metal spoons into his canvas haversack. "I'll not forget yer warning. But if'n I ever meet yer Brice an' he don't breathe fire, I'm gonna be sorely disappointed.'' Cam eyeballed the Virginian section of camp and saw blackness where flames spurted bare minutes ago. "Fetch the water quick, Fell. Late as it be, I'd rather not provoke the major any. His bite's worse'n his bark.''

We doused the embers and smothered them with snow for good measure. Cam left a portion of venison and beans in his kettle for Jacob Telow, who was still scouting downstream. Together with Noah and Jaimie, we arranged the repacked haversacks and pouches alongside the horses for prompt loading at dawn. The major became plumb surly if any careless oversight prevented our jumping off at first light.

Given the location of the moon, I could tell it was coming on midnight. I hunkered down out of the teeth of the wind atop a pile of gear twixt two of the sleeping horses, lower face and ears wrapped in a woolen scarf, flop-brimmed hat tugged low on my forehead, an oiled sleeping tarp drawn close about my entire frame. I missed the warmth of the Telows, who usually shared the confines of the tarp with me. What I didn't miss was their unusually rank smell. Jacob and Askell considered an occasional walk fully clothed through chin-deep water in only the warmest of weather all the washing required of woodsrunners like themselves. Consequently, by January the brothers were ripe as freshly dropped goat turds.

Despite the day's toll on body and limb, unlike the horses, I couldn't sleep. My mind kept drifting back to the talk around the supper fire. It was difficult for me to fathom Hump Layton's daughter. A female who demanded equal station in the harness with her male counterparts defied imagination. Was she pretty or decidedly unhandsome like her father? Did she dress in long skirt or men's breeches? Did she swear like a man if her wishes were thwarted?

Rebecca Brandon's purported beauty was much more pleasant to ponder. Was she fair or raven haired? Slim of ankle and round of hip and breast? Did being spoiled distract from her beauty? Noah's appreciation of her looks, if not her temperament, seemed boundless. And for his tender age, Noah was right about more things than he was wrong.

I dwelled but briefly on the unpleasant Brice Fowler. Was he as devious as Noah portrayed him, a deliberate liar out for his own gain? Had he protested the orders that left him behind in a safe haven with the Brandon women while his father sought future holdings for the both of them in the face of great danger? Though it was a tad vengeful and disrespecting, I wondered, too, how the stern, ruthlessly honest Major Fowler regarded a male heir whose courage Hump Layton felt duty bound to defend in his absence. Not well, I supposed, not well however the major judged those of his own blood.

At some point during my posing of questions that had no answers, I dozed off. I slept without dreams of strangers white or red. What rest I enjoyed proved invaluable in the hours that followed, for Jacob Telow returned after midnight with the direst of news:

The Shawnee weren't upstream coming from behind our column as we had previously believed. They were camped farther downstream, smack between us and the safety of Limestone.

3

Voices brought me awake. I struggled from the throes of deep, dreamless sleep, curious, but not frightened. What I overheard flowed from white tongues.

"Found the damned Injuns for you, Major," Jacob Telow was saying.

I frowned at that and loosened the sleeping tarp so as to come about and better my hearing. Something was awry. Nathan Breed, not Jacob Telow, should be reporting the location of the Shawnee.

Hump Layton, Major Fowler, and the Telow brothers stood in a tight cluster before my packhorses. The moonlight sifting through streaks of black cloud was bright enough I identified the rounded bulk hanging from Jacob Telow's fist: It was Cam Downing's stewing kettle. Undoubtedly swooning from hunger, Jacob clawed a wad of cold beans from the kettle. The major's sharp order stopped his hand short of his face:

"Belay that, Mister Telow! Finish your report! Where exactly are the enemy to be found? And how many did you see?"

Jacob Telow disliked authority of any stripe as much as
he disliked denying his belly. His blunt tone betrayed his
own impatience. "The redsticks are less'n a mile from here,
due south along Eagle Creek. Six of 'em they is, squattin'
round their fire, swillin' whiskey an' stuffin' themselves
full of meat," he related, hand again lifting toward his
mouth.

"You're not finished, Mister Telow," the major reminded him sternly. "How can you be certain there's only
six of the Shawnee and no more?"

An exasperated Jacob flicked wadded beans from his fingers. The flying vittles missed the kettle and splattered the
front of the major's greatcoat. " 'Cause I slow footed past
them redsticks in the dark an' scouted another mile towards
the Ohio. You got my word on it. Six is all there be. Anythin' else?" Jacob demanded.

Soiied coat or no soiled coat, Major Fowler's sole interest was the enemy barely a mile away. "Their arms, Mister
Telow?"

Jacob sighed at having to further delay his already be-
lated meal, but he wasn't careless with his answer. "Seen
four . . . no, five long guns, two thick in the stock, maybe
Brown Bess muskets. They tote war clubs or hatchets,
sometimes both. I think on it, each cut at that meat with
his own knife."

"One last question, Mister Telow. Are they afoot?"

"Mostly. I seen only three horses for the bunch. Saddle
stock, they was, likely stolen from across the Ohio same as
their likker."

The major relented. "Well and good, Mister Telow. You
may eat."

Jacob scooped beans from the kettle and swallowed huge
bites, Major Fowler watching silently for some little while.
When he next spoke, he turned to Hump Layton beside
him, addressing the big spy by his old militia rank. "Captain, Mister Telow's Shawnee are unaware of our presence
and we outnumber them. But rashness is the bane of the
trained soldier. Night attacks with mostly unseasoned

troops present great risks. Holding firm till dawn is our best course of action.''

The halter now broke on the younger Telow's patience. "For chrissake, Major," Askell protested. "We can catch 'em dead drunk asleep in their blankets. It wouldn't be no chancier'n wipin' snot from yer nose.''

In prior years, if on duty with the Brandon regiment, Askell's outburst would have garnered severe punishment, possibly the flogger's whip. As it was, Asa Fowler was too long the officer to brook insubordination from a mere hunter and hired camp guard. He gathered himself and his gloved hand clasped the hilt of his sword.

And Jacob Telow was too much the brother to continue feeding his face while an unarmed Askell was taken to task for stating what Jacob himself would have said had his mouth not been full. Jacob's fist opened, the bean kettle landed with a thud on the trampled snow at his feet, and the rifle barrel previously resting loosely against his chest was in the space of a quick spit aimed at Asa Fowler, the rasp of the hammer dogging home grating on my ears above the rustle of night wind.

The major, fully aware Jacob harbored no qualms about killing anyone threatening Askell, stayed the drawing of his sword. His gathered stance, though, relaxed not an inch, and his clasped hand remained on the hilt of his sheathed blade. Asa Fowler faced death with no sign of fear. He would relinquish command with his final breath.

It was a touchy standoff that might have sparked a senseless bloodletting twixt Kentuckians and Virginians had not an arresting contention issued from the shadows a step beyond our range of sight:

"Jacob, my friend, nothin' would please the Shawnee more than was you to pull that trigger.''

"An' why would they give a damn, Breed?" Jacob cried, eyes never leaving the major.

Nathan Breed floated from the shadows, his own rifle slanted casually across a shoulder. "The redsticks liken the odds in their favor, the greater the better. An' there's already more of them up the Lick than us'ens 'thout you whittlin' down our numbers any. If'n it's an Injun fight you Telows crave, you're gonna be arse-deep in black-painted heathen right soon.''

Breed's sobering assessment dampened Jacob's anger and the older Telow slowly lowered the muzzle of his rifle. ''Sometimes I'm a mite hasty where Askell's concerned. But I bygod won't never be accused of helpin' the Shawnee cause,'' he pledged with an exaggerated nod of the head.

Major Fowler offered no excuse for his actions. Neither did he apologize. With a forceful ''Your report, Mister Breed,'' he was once again in charge of all about him.

In the gleaming wash of the half moon, the advancing Breed was an eerie, imposing sight. His winter garb made him a near match for the tall, stalking wolf. An entire pelt of that animal, ghostly gray in color, covered his head and shoulders. He peered out from behind the pelt's empty eye sockets and his lower face, plucked free of every single hair Injun fashion, jutted forth in place of the wolf's bottom jaw. Bronze cheeks marked at the center with daubs of red and yellow paint, and earlobes cut and wrapped with strung beads, provided further evidence of Breed's mixed blood. According to the most reliable account of his birthing, our scout was at least one-quarter Mingo.

Without salute or bow, Breed slid the wolf mask back on his head, exposing the whole of his bronze features, and launched into his report. ''I stumbled on to so many Shawnee they struck four fires for the night, an' unfortunately, they know where we are.''

''How so, Mister Breed?''

''Those three whose tracks we crossed earlier fell out one at a time as they withdrew,'' the scout said. He patted his waist belt. ''I put the sneak on the first two an' taken their hair. I missed the third somehow. He gained their camp.''

Every listener leaned forward. Four fires was a passel of Shawnee, probably twice our number. And they were aware they outnumbered us. The major figured the same. ''How soon, Mister Breed? How soon before they overtake us?''

''They'll move at the first peek of daylight. An' havin' no horses or baggage with 'em, they'll cover six miles each hour in the worst of weather,'' the scout judged.

Major Fowler hitched his sword higher on his hip. ''They'll be at our rear two hours past dawn, with us well short of Limestone,'' he said. ''Then there's our other dilemma. You heard Mister Telow tell of the heathen presence downstream.''

''I did,'' the scout confirmed.

''Is there any other path of escape available to us? Any route by which we can avoid the enemy parties, both large and small?''

Breed's response was brutally honest. ''No, sir, they's not. The ridges on our flanks, both east and west, are too steep for fast travel 'lessen we abandon the horses an' gear. An' even was we to do so, up high, stretched out single file, we'd be prime pickin' for the Shawnee. They's no choice for us but straight down Eagle Creek to Logan's Gap. We fetch the Ohio's near bank 'thout bein' bloodied too badly, we're an even toss of the bones to reach home alive.''

''Then we'll wait for first light, take the smaller party of heathen by surprise, and proceed directly to the river,'' the major concluded.

''We delay too long, sir,'' Hump Layton ventured, ''we won't be no surprise for 'em.''

''And why's that, Captain?''

The big spy pulled his woven cap tighter on his massive head. ''It's gettin' colder by the hour, an' that wet snow we traipsed over today's gonna freeze hard as iron. After it does, every footfall of ours will sound yards ahead of us. One of them Shawnee's bound to hear us an' wake the others.''

''Won't they flee a well-armed, superior force?''

''Maybe, maybe not,'' Breed stuck in. ''I don't believe Jacob's heathen know of the big party behind us. But lettin' just six Shawnee prowl our flanks ain't wise. They slow our pace any at all, we've no hope of skirtin' a fight with the big bunch upstream.''

"You're suggesting what, Mister Breed?''

"The Shawnee ain't by chance overnightin' in Morgan Ramsey's old lean-to, are they?'' the scout asked the older Telow.

"They surely be!'' the Injun-hating Jacob fairly shouted.

Breed studied the night sky. "These clouds don't thicken, the moon'll shine another two hours, time for us to catch the six of 'em abed while the snow's still not crusted over.''

The scout's proposal tendered Major Fowler a new bone to gnaw on. Always thorough in his deliberations, our commander sniffed the meat before baring his teeth. "How is the enemy camp situated?''

"They're asleep in an open glade on the west bank of the creek, right below a narrow run. You an' your Virginians can fire a volley into the lean-to from the trees on the higher ground this side of the run. Us Kentuckians will flank the lean-to out on the creek ice, an' down any of 'em that jumps outen their blankets after your volley. No warnin' of any kind, mind you. With the redsticks, the dog that bites first and deepest wins the field.''

The major tugged at his glove tops in turn, his smile rare as the double-tailed mule. "Your tactics are commendable, Mister Breed, commendable and insightful. Any objections, Captain?''

"None, sir,'' Hump Layton boomed, knuckling his forehead.

"Then see to Mister Block and the other of our troops,'' Fowler ordered. His searching gaze spotted me amongst the horses. "Rouse your Mister Downing and prepare the animals, Mister Cooper. We'll lead them forward far as Mister Breed allows. They'll not spook at the noise of musket fire, will they?''

"No, sir, short of an explosion under their hindquarters, Henry horses don't scare none.''

"I'll hold you to that, Mister Cooper. We'll decamp in

ten minutes. Ten minutes and not a second later.''

Ned Henry forever insisted Cam Downing slept the sleep of the dead, the result of an overstuffed belly slow to empty. It required two raps on the shins with my rifle barrel to stop his snoring, and a third to open his eyes. Grousing and cursing, he wrestled free of his tarp, falling twice. His knees finally locked and steadied his legs.

Cam rubbed at his eyes with the heels of his hands. The rubbing ceased suddenly as he realized where he was. He glanced wildly behind him. ''We ain't been attacked, have we?'' he inquired, voice quaking with fright.

''Be quiet and hear me out!'' I snapped.

Cam was some older than me, but he knew I'd not tolerate any silly shenanigans from him. He listened with rapt attention and I explained what had transpired while he snored merrily away. When I finished, he pursed his beefy lips and, voice now trembling with excitement, said, ''Damn fine thing it'll be, us killin' the red bastards in their blankets 'thout sufferin' no harm our ownselves.''

We went about our work with speed and dispatch, Cam talking up his courage at every tug of the cinches. I didn't share his enthusiasm—or that of the Telows—for the task awaiting us downstream. I'd no fuss with slaying our enemies, no matter how we killed them. It was just that the Lord blessed me with a fine and faultless memory and I was recalling Ned Henry's haunting observation over the supper fire two winters ago. ''The cornered Shawnee's no less treacherous than the wounded catamount. 'Lest you're almighty cautious, he'll rip off a hunk of you at his dying gasp,'' the boss man had warned, banging the plank floor with his pegged leg, ''or worse yet, take you to the grave with him.''

Stout words those . . . and true.

4

Deepest Night, January 24

After the narrow Indian Lick, Eagle Creek rivaled the width
of eastern post roads allowing coaches to pass without their
hubs touching. We descended that frozen, moonlit highway
in Major Fowler's proscribed line of march: wolf-masked
Breed and bearskinned Telows in the lead; our commander,
Hump Layton, and the Virginia bluecoats filling the middle;
and Cam and me bringing up the rear with Jaimie Crown
and the horses. Only the muffled scrunch of loose snow
yielding to the press of foot and hoof betrayed our passage.

The silence was neither accidental nor an act of provi-
dence. Every man had checked and rechecked his person
at the outset to insure hatchet, cartridge box, powder horn,
metal bayonet, and knife handle, the most common offend-
ers, were properly spaced about his waist so as not to clunk
upon each other. Every man followed in the footprints of
those before him, precluding any unwarranted stumbling as
well as the night march's greatest calamity, an outright fall.
And not a man hardly even grunted, the major's stark reminder that a single careless noise might prove ruinous
having sealed our lips like an unseen, unfelt hand.

Our first halt came at the halfway point of the mile separating us from the enemy camp. We left Jaimie Crown there with the horses, the major trading his pistol for Jaimie's musket. Shed of the animals, Cam and I followed the major around the Virginians to the head of the column. The bluecoats watched our every stride, their beardless faces pale and drawn beneath cockaded hats. Fearful, they looked, fearful and worried. Or maybe I just thought that since a knot of uncertainty was festering in my own chest.

Breed acknowledged our joining him with a simple nod and led off down the creek, anxious no doubt at the prospect of losing the moon to clouds before we were in position for the attack. His concern was genuine, for the weather was worsening. The constant night wind gathered itself and blew in raw, chill gusts out of the northeast against our left shoulders. If nothing else favored the Shawnee, we would be approaching them from the north, upwind, a tactical disadvantage the major had surely weighed and discounted given our desperate desire to escape the country.

Our second halt came eighty yards from our eventual destination. Nathan Breed's keen eye spotted the slight opening in the treetops lining the west bank, which revealed the presence of the narrow run beyond which rested Morgan Ramsey's lean-to filled with slumbering redsticks. The scout stepped aside and motioned rearward toward the bluecoats, his moonlit shadow waving back at him from the snowy surface of the creek. His signal returned, Breed reversed himself, and we were under way again.

Fifty yards from the run, Breed waggled his rifle above his head without turning about or slowing our pace and the Virginians angled for the creek bank on our right. I glanced that direction a tad later and couldn't help but chuckle silently at massive Hump Layton and the five smaller men in his wake. The big spy was every bit the old bull guiding those of lesser experience into battle.

Breed kept us Kentuckians well left of the creek's centerline, his walk slouching more with each careful stride.

As we drew closer to flanking the run, every man had at least one eye searching where the enemy was to be found. Sycamores and beeches crowded the run's north bank, their moonlit trunks tall sentinels of white and gray guarding the clutter of black forest farther up the narrow waterway. I heard Cam's surprised gasp. Glimmers of bright red winked and flickered at the edge of the treeless glade on the run's south bank. With each additional step we took, it was more and more apparent the Shawnee had not completely extinguished their cooking fire, a break for us of unparalleled proportion. The surviving embers, glowing and pulsating, provided just enough brightness to pinpoint the exact location of the lean-to's slanting roof and its bark underside from our position some thirty-plus yards away. I almost whistled aloud. As well as we could see from the ice of the creek, it must have seemed to Hump's bluecoats in the sycamores and beeches on the run's elevated north bank that they were staring down into the very beds of our blanket-warmed enemies.

Everything, every last detail, had unfolded in accordance with Breed's strategy. Other than the hindering darkness, both our contingents were deployed to best advantage for an ambuscade. We had the enemy in our sights at short range. He was unaware we stalked him. We needed only to slip lock covers from Kentucky rifle and bluecoat musket—charged, balled, and primed prior to our departure from the Indian Lick—and the killing could commence. Nothing, it appeared, could prevent us from successfully dispatching the enemy, as Cam had said, ". . . 'thout sufferin' no harm to our ownselves." Nothing, that was, except the fickle whims of fate, which, as we have all learned through many a bitter travail, wax sour as well as sweet. Ned Henry, my friend, knew of what he spoke.

At the circling twist of Breed's arm we Kentuckians wheeled right and knelt as he did on left knee. We made no move as yet to remove the covers from our rifle locks. There would be time for that after the bluecoat volley.

Scudding cloud dimmed the moon a hair. Tree branches

caught and tossed by the gusting wind clacked together on the creek bank behind us. Far off to the west, the howl of a wolf floated from the ridgeline. We were holding our breath to the man. In such near quiet, the bluecoat musket volley was a succession of ear-splitting, fire-spouting booms coming so atop one another they equaled the loudest clap of thunder, echoing over and over in the creek bottom at their finish. Amidst the echoes, we heard Breed's solemn ''Free your locks an' stand, gentlemen!''

We pocketed the cowhide covers and sprang upright, feet spread, weight balanced, rifles slanted across our chests, eyes fixed on the would-be target. The echoes died and Hump Layton's brusque instructions for the bluecoats to reload their pieces wafted to us, each word distinct as the bellow of a cow.

Two lean shapes struggled upward within the lean-to, their shadows dancing on the ember-lit rear wall. Perhaps the two redsticks fought encumbering blankets. Perhaps they were already badly wounded. Neither possibility was of any consequence. The Shawnee weren't known for surrendering themselves, and we professed no interest in the taking of prisoners. We raised and leveled our rifles without needing orders to do so. ''Cock your pieces and bead the target, gentlemen,'' Breed said calmly. The scout sounded as casually carefree as he did when calling for another rum flip at Monet's, his favorite Limestone roadhouse.

''Fire!'' commanded Breed.

Our volley was as fairly executed as that of the bluecoats. Lances of flame leaped from our barrels. Both redstick shapes within the lean-to jerked backwards, toppling like ship masts severed at the base by cannonballs. The reports of our rifles echoed and reechoed and a haze of powder smoke rank to the nose and smarting on the eye drifted downwind.

Calm and steady as ever, Breed yelled over the ringing in our ears. ''Reload, gentlemen, reload! We ain't certain they's dead meat yet!''

Tearing my eyes from the fallen enemy, I butted my rifle

in the snow, poured powder from my horn into a cupped palm, and hurriedly dumped the charge in the muzzle, not concerned about the few grains that missed the opening. Powder charge in place, I centered one of the patched balls of my bullet block over the muzzle and, holding bullet block and barrel end with left hand, slid the ramrod from its thimbles and drove the ball home. I was freeing the ramrod when a bluecoat shouted, "Watch out! They're still alive!"

Curiosity overwhelmed Breed's training. My hand froze and my head lifted. Shadow parted and rejoined under the lean-to. A long black finger poked past the slanted roof. My heart skipped an entire beat. Lord forbid, a musket barrel! . . . and it was aimed straight at the trees hiding the Virginians. The musket boomed and almost at the same instant another bluecoat voice, rampant with shock and dismay, screamed:

"The major's hit! The major's hit!"

Sorry for Major Fowler, but shamelessly heartened it wasn't Hump or Noah Reem wounded, I forced my head down, yanked the ramrod clear of the barrel, stashed that wooden shaft in my left boot for temporary keeping, and leveled the Bedford before my waist. Tugging the hammer to half cock exposed the pan. I reamed the touch hole with the metal pick strung to the strap of my shot pouch, and using the charge cup hanging below the pick, measured powder from my horn and primed the pan. All the while, though I didn't dare look, I damn well heard what was happening about me.

The Virginians, despite the disruption and horror of the major being shot, managed a ragged volley, just three of their six weapons getting off a round. In the lull that followed, the ever persistent Breed, his own reloading completed, pushed us to finish also. "Seek the target, gentlemen, seek the target," he exhorted.

I closed the frizzen, set the hammer at full cock, and sought movement across the ice, ready for Breed's next order.

Had we finally killed all the enemy for certain?

The answer came with frightful suddenness. There was no warning poke of long black barrel as had occurred with the bluecoats. Burning powder flared low to the ground in front of the lean-to. In the hair's breadth that preceded the roar of the musket, a shaft of fiery red shot forth, pointed squarely at our position. By the time us Kentuckians realized we were being fired upon, it was too late for anything more than the widening of an eye in alarm, if that.

I was so anticipating the jarring thud of the bullet that would snuff out my lights forever, I initially ignored the soft *plop* at my elbow. It was the wet gurgle of the grievously struck animal immediately thereafter that seized my attention. The gut-wrenching visage awaiting my turned head stunned me to the core. Cam Downing was still on his feet, rifle clutched rigidly astraddle his belly, staring across the creek with eyes gone cold and empty. Blood welled freely from a gaping hole extending from his right jawbone to his lower throat. The musket ball had gouged through the side of his neck, ravaging beard, skin, underlying flesh, and a portion of his windpipe. The wet gurgle repeated itself, air escaping failed lungs, then his every muscle went slack in unison and Cam collapsed into the snow beside me.

Shawnee threat totally forgotten, I hovered over his lifeless body, fighting back tears. I should have cried then and there for Cam Downing. Orphaned young and bound to masters quick with scalding tongue and stiff-handled whip like my ownself, he deserved the full measure of a friend's sorrow. But that wasn't to be, for no matter how crazily circumstances changed course and distracted other men, Nathan Breed's mind never wavered from the dangers confronting himself and those in his company.

"Chin up, Cooper! Get your chin up, Cooper! I ain't buryin' anybody else I can help it."

He waited for my head to raise.

"Gentlemen, ain't but one red bastard shootin' at us. He's hidin' amongst his own dead to reload. We're gonna

charge an' flush him into the open or kill him where
he lays. Hold your fire till we see him good. Make ready
now . . . Charge!''

We bolted across the ice of the creek, Breed and the
Telows enjoying smoother going in their moccasins than
me in my heavy jackboots. Our forward rush and the gusting wind sawed my hat brim back and forth. The rapidly
freezing snow crackled underfoot. In a few lunging bounds,
I was so excited my heart pounded in my ears and my eyes
watered.

Where was the red bastard?

Why didn't he flee for his heathen life?

The answer this time was as frightfully sudden and
nearly as tragic. That familiar shaft of fiery red blossomed
to our forefront. I couldn't help cringing inside, but kept
my feet pounding away. Jacob Telow grunted, slowed, and
went crashing headfirst into my path, his red-bearded cheek
skidding on the hardening snow.

''Don't stop! Don't stop!'' Breed shouted.

I bent at the knee, leaped the sprawling Jacob, landed
awkwardly, caught myself, and ran on. A dozen scant yards
from the creek bank, Breed yelled, ''There he be, left corner of the lean-to. Kneel an' fire, boys, kneel an' fire!''

The scout and Askell dropped to one knee in front of me
to my left. Their rifle barrels rose and steadied, a pause
ensued while they drew bead, then they pulled trigger close
enough together the two shots sounded almost as one. For
the most fleeting of moments a shadowy blur halted at the
corner of the lean-to. When the still form moved again,
Breed cried, ''Missed goddamnit! Fire, Cooper fire!''

I had the heathen cleanly in my sights. But the insane
luck of the devil rode that Shawnee's shoulders high and
handsome. In the blink of an eye, deep cloud black as midnight shrouded the moon, and my target, like a thrown blanket, leaving me to shoot by guess and feel. I held firm best
I could and squeezed evenly on the trigger.

It wasn't necessary to see I'd missed. The *thwack* of
flying ball meeting dry wood, louder than my rasping

breath and the wind, confirmed I'd overshot the target. The clouds before the moon thinned again and muskets roared in the trees yonder to our right as the fleeing redstick negotiated the open ground behind the lean-to. Cursing from the bluecoat quarter told us they'd been no more successful than we Kentuckians in our vain attempt to bring down the most defiant and resolute of enemies.

Breed advanced slowly on the enemy camp. "Hold your fire, Virginians! It's me, Nathan Breed!" he called. Hump Layton emerged from the beeches and sycamores and joined the scout short of the lean-to's slanted roof. Askell went past me in a hurry and knelt beside his brother. Jacob sat on his haunches, rifle cradled in his lap. His right hand was buried in his left armpit and his chin lolled against his chest.

I rested on my knees, reloading the Bedford while Breed and the big spy decided what was next for us. I overheard enough to learn the major was alive, but suffering much from a wound low on his right side. By my count then, we'd wiped out five Shawnee and let one escape unscathed. On our part, Cam Downing lay stone dead and the major and Jacob Telow were hurt badly enough they would both require considerable tending and assistance when we traveled farther down creek. Including Jaimie Crown back with the horses, the Brandon party now totaled but ten effectives. For all our effort and toil, we'd paid dearly for the upcoming opportunity to hopefully outrun Breed's larger Shawnee party, yet to enter the fray.

I hated the very thought, but Limestone suddenly seemed as far off as the cloud-blanketed moon.

5

Breed and Hump Layton talked only a few minutes. Their decisions made, the big spy called for the bluecoats to fetch the major and for Askell and me to do likewise with Jacob Telow. While we were about our appointed tasks, Breed and the big spy stripped bark slabs from the lean-to's roof and piled them on the remaining coals of the Shawnee fire. The big spy was away and gone up creek after Jaimie Crown and the horses by the time Askell and I laid an awake and moaning Jacob beside their fast growing blaze.

On the fire's opposite side, the unconscious major's clean-shaven features were limestone white and tightened with pain in the harsh light. A wide circle of blood stained his tailored greatcoat over the whole expanse of his right hip. Block and Welker, the two surveyors, removed the major's sword, unbuttoned his coat, and slid his linen shirt high for the inspecting eye of Noah Reem, the veteran of two years' reading with a Northumberland surgeon. His own features white as the major's, young Noah's report to the waiting Breed was devoid of hope. "The bullet's in too deep for extraction. We'd practically disembowel him digging it loose. From what Dr. Christiansen taught me, he probably can't last a full day," Noah judged, doubling the major's linen shirt over the opening of the wound.

Jacob Telow's injury was no less severe. The musket ball had snipped through his heavy bearskin coat and buckskin frock none the worse for the passage and entered his body at the curve of the left rib cage, shattering at least two ribs and tearing a fist-sized oval of flesh from his back side upon its exit. Though he lacked training with any surgeon, trail-wise Askell uncovered the wound and packed the exit hole with handfuls of buzzard down from the bottom of his possible sack, then bound the shattered ribs with a wide swatch of deerskin sliced from the hem of his own hunting shirt. "Ball's not still in you, Jacob. You got enough gumption, you'll live long enough for somethin' else to kill yuh off."

Breed piled more wood on the fire. "Crowd round an' warm yourselves, lads. We've a long cold march awaitin' us. If'n yuh ain't noticed, the wind's damp on the nose now an' it'll be snowin' not much past first light. But mayhap that'll work agin' the other heathen still out an' about." He eyed the surveying crew and young Noah. "Captain Layton'll return shortly with Jaimie and the major's gelding. Till then, yuh gentlemen hang close about. Mister Cooper an' I'll hunt up the ridin' stock Jacob claimed the Shawnee had in tow. At my heels, if'n you please, Mister Cooper."

The scout led into the trees west of the lean-to. He walked with rifle barrel pointed straight upward alongside his jaw, elbows close to his body. I matched his manner, for he slipped through the dense growth at the fringe of the glade with but the softest brush of parted branch on hide cloth. Past the outermost shine of the fire, the forest blackened rapidly, akin to entering a cave. Not wanting to spook the horses before Breed spied them, I clung to his heels and planted my thick-soled jackboots often as I could where he'd already broken through the crusted snow.

The scout followed the most direct course available to the edge of a small clearing not sixty paces from the lean-to. He halted and held forth an extended arm so I wouldn't ram into him in the dark. He spoke in a whisper. "Shawnee've known forever Morgan Ramsey an' me sheltered horses here on winter hunts. They's rock walls north an' west of the clearin' with a spring at the bottom of 'em, it ain't froze over." He slid the wolf mask away from his face. "You go ahead of me. You got a whoppin' horse smell to yuh. They smell wolf, they'll get nervy on us right off."

A half step into the clearing I stilled and had an earnest look all around. I first sensed, then saw the neck and back lines of the two horses standing with their necks craned in my direction. The third horse reported by Jacob Telow was missing. I began talking gently, wanting my voice to reach the two watching me before any further sound of my approach. "Easy, boys, easy. Papa's gonna take yuh home. Easy, boys, easy."

With the wind blowing from behind me, both mounts had a solid whiff of my scent. My smelling like white folk and horse instead of Injun bear grease and wood smoke allayed their initial fear and suspicion, and given the horse's penchant for studying an approaching man's head, my flop-brimmed hat was more familiar than tufted scalplocks spiked with feathers. A friendly nicker and blowing of lips informed me I was dealing with animals stolen from Kentucky, and I soon had a grip on their rope hackamores.

I whistled softly and Breed came forward. "You knows yer horses, Fell Cooper. There bein' only these two, I'm bettin' our fleein' Shawnee made off on the other. Wouldn't a-been no help to him to try an' scatter these two in woods thick as this. They wouldn't a-gone two rods, an' he likely believed he was too shy of time anyways. Can you tell if'n they's fit to travel?"

I ran a hand over their flanks, shoulders, legs, and hocks and found no hampering injuries or swellings. The ice frozen high on their legs and in their manes and tails indicated they'd swum the Ohio recently, probably just yesterday. "They're solid. Mite tuckered, but solid," I pronounced.

"Damn lucky for us'ns," Breed said. "We've got enough ridin' stock now to cart the major an' Jacob an' yer friend, Cam. I figured yuh wouldn't want his body left behind for the Shawnee scalpin' knife. Let's shuck for camp. I'll lead the big bay if'n it suits yuh."

The news Breed intended to see the dead Cam across the Ohio delighted me. I hadn't as yet decided how I would tell Ned Henry I'd failed to watch out for my fellow packhorseman as he'd requested. Perhaps he'd be more understanding if I at least brought the body of his favorite cook home for burial. Perhaps he would. Redeeming yourself with a boss man as strict and demanding as Ned Henry was never an easy set of stairs to climb.

At the fire, the bluecoats, back sides aimed windward, were still warming themselves. They stared into the lean-to with undivided attention. Closer on, Breed and I discovered the cause of their fascination. Askell Telow, knife dripping with blood, was lifting the scalp of every single Shawnee. None of the Virginians had seen any prior action in the ongoing tussle with Ohio's Shawnee, Miami, and Wyandot, and more than one appeared disgusted and disapproving of Askell's prize taking.

"Lookeehere, Breed," the elated Askell beckoned, ripping loose the topknot of the slain enemy sprawled at the nearest corner of the lean-to. "This here heathen's face-first in the snow clear out from under the roof, an' he's been hit three times, oncet in the head. Any of the balls would've killed him instanter. How do you explain that?"

The scout passed me the lead rope of the recovered bay horse. "Our fleeing redstick was clever, clever as any I've ever drawn bead on. We couldn't miss at that range, Askell," Breed surmised. "Hell's bells, we wasn't thirty feet away with the moon shinin' strong. He shielded hisself with that one, dead though he be, till we wasted our shots. Then the light petered out on Fell an' he made his break for the woods."

I was thankful Breed's recounting included no further mention of my errant shot. I wasn't as certain as he that the vanishing light totally excused my having completely missed both the Shawnee and his lifeless shield. Breed and Askell wouldn't have been quaking with excitement, and they would have fired on a slowed, outgoing breath. They would have touched ball to some portion of the target, however small. And so would I, by damned, in the future.

Askell swished his freshly taken scalp in the snow to scour it free of blood. He rose, wiped his knife blade on his thigh, and slipped his final trophy behind his sash belt. "Somethin' else you should see," he said, bending and reaching into the jumble of blankets twixt two of the red-stick dead. "Ever laid eye on such as this?"

The younger Telow presented for Breed's viewing a Shawnee war club. The club's maple handle, worn smooth by sweat and the rub of flesh, was two feet in length. Its top end flared into a carved bear's head whose jaws clamped a rounded ball. The ball's curved edge sported a wedge-shaped iron blade the size of my thumb. Brass beads, carefully arranged in precise rows, studded the handle beneath the bear's head. A tassel of woven hair looped through a hole in the handle's lower end. Wielded properly, the club's easy heft and striking power made it an ideal weapon for close-quarter killing.

Nathan Breed fisted the club's polished handle and swept the carved bear's head to within inches of his bronze face. The scout's throaty chuckle of amusement surprised everyone. He stepped past Askell, and turning bodies whenever and wherever necessary, took a careful gander at the scalped remains of each expired Shawnee. Ganders completed, he knelt beside the prone figure of Jacob Telow. "Guess what, my friend," he said, laughing. "Yer oldest red enemy be the one that blowed that awesome hole in yuh. Ain't that the tip of the catamount's tail?"

Wounded Jacob could only moan in response. Askell, puzzled as the rest of us, spoke for his brother. "What you poundin' yer jaw about, Nathan?"

The lanky Breed rose, peered upcreek over the shorter bluecoats across the fire from him, then slowly nodded in their direction. ''Yer captain ain't in sight just yet with Jaimie, so there's time enough for me to spin a yarn yuh best hear an' remember. I want you should know who it was shot Jacob here. Mayhap he's flagged his clout for now, but he'll be back, bringin' that other party of red buggers with him. An' we ain't ready for 'em, they'll drag us through the pits of hell till there ain't enough meat left on our bones to feed their dogs.''

Breed hesitated, then started anew once he confirmed all eyes, including mine and Askell's, looked nowhere but at him. ''Back in '84, Jacob came out from Jersey, bound for Kentucky with his new bride. He was to claim acreage for his kin—his paw, maw, an' a loft full-a sproutin' brothers liken Askell here. He bought passage at Fort Pitt on a flat-boat with four families an' their brats, large an' small. Everythin' went well till a cow lost her skull an' threatened to gore the children. They beached their boat on the big island north of Wheeling an' went ashore for the night, givin' themselves time to settle the cow or off-load an' shoot her for the meat. It was a crisp spring evenin', peaceful as a deacon's hearth, an' after vittles, Jacob tromped into the bushes to answer the call of nature. Bein' in somewhat of a rush to get on with things, he didn't bother takin' along his rifle or belt weapons.''

The handle of the war club smacked Breed's open palm. ''That's when the heathen struck. They came from everywhere at once, screechin' an' howlin' an' burnin' powder. The whole affair lasted lessen a quarter minute. It was finished afore Jacob could button his breeches. Unarmed liken he was, he'd no druthers but listen while the redsticks killed an' butchered his bride along with every man, woman, an' child. An' Jacob, he lost any hope of hidin' till they was gone when the heathen spotted the sleeve of his bearskin coat stickin' from the bushes where he'd throwed it so as not to have it interfere with his squattin'. He shucked his boots off an' lit out on the dead run for the water, leavin' his coat for the Injuns. Bein' a strong swimmer, he gained the Ohio bank ahead of his pursuers an' the balls zingin' about him. He got into the woods only to find his breeches an' leggins, soaked through an' through, was slowin' him somethin' awful. He stopped long enough to strip bare below the waist, then lit out again, the screeches of the Shawnee louder'n ever in his ears.''

Breed helped himself to a deep breath. ''Afore long, Jacob commenced to tire, runnin' all that way on a full belly, clothes or no clothes. Hopin' to slow the pursuit, he went plumb up the front wall of a steep ridge that blocked his path, grabbin' toeholds and handholds anywhere they was to be found. For a spell, he seemed to be regainin' the ground he'd lost undressin'. Then the worst he could imagine happened. He heard Shawnee lingo ahead of him on top of the ridge: The heathen, bygod, had him surrounded.

''Lads, Jacob here's down an' hurtin' now, but he's not bent to call it quits afore he's spilled his last drop a-blood. He scrounged about that fast fallin' night, an' lo and behold, short of the ridgeline, he discovered a ledge twice the width of his shoulders. Even when the ledge went nowhere both left an' right, he refused to knuckle under, for at its eastern corner was a rock cave sizable enough to hide him. He backed into that narrow hole, hunkered down, an' sat out the night, shiverin' an' shakin' with cold each miserable hour.

''At dawn, he made ready. He didn't doubt the enemy had by then pinpointed where he be. There was nowhere else to hide on that steep wall. But I'm tellin' yuh, Jacob Telow never lost his nerve. His bride had sawed off every lick of his hair days afore to rid him of head lice. He shed his frock shirt, denyin' the Shawnee yet another means of layin' holt of him. He cast about at his feet in the growin' light an' fessed up two rocks that fit his hands. Then he waited, buck nakid, listenin' for the first watery gabble of the enemy . . . It wasn't long in comin'. Them heathen might be heathen, but they weren't fools. They laid about the front of his cave an' began shoutin' what Jacob determined was Shawnee taunts an' threats. He decided he wasn't gonna linger in there nakid with a rock in each hand till they stuck a musket barrel in the openin' an' killed him off 'thout poppin' any sweat a-tall on themselves. He worked up a body full of hot red anger over the loss of his bride an' charged forth with a scream that stifled every Shawnee tongue. First thing he spied was a solitary Injun, armed with hatchet an' knife, blockin' the ledge. Jacob cocked his arm to fling one of his rocks an' two more of the tricky devils jumped him from their hidin' places above the cave entrance. They knocked him flat, facedown on that ledge, an' he was had, then an' there. His captors pinned his arms behind him an' yanked him to his feet, holdin' him steady for the bugger blockin' the path. Up an' back went that red bugger's hatchet, an' Jacob knew he was a goner for dead bygod certain.''

I feared the others had heard my noisy, gulping swallow. But not an eye strayed from the scout. The only twitch of movement amongst the Virginians was Noah Reem's fingering of the journal in his coat pocket. How he must have craved to have had quill in hand, recording Breed's every word. Askell Telow's gaping mouth hinted he was learning details of his brother's past heretofore unbeknownst even to him.

"But at the last possible second," Breed related, "that red bugger stayed his hatchet. Instead of slayin' the helpless Jacob on the spot, he suddenly cracked a huge smile, laughed crazy like, an' pointed a finger twixt Jacob's bare thighs. Lads, believe yuh me, a quarter breed, it ain't true full bloods don't never laugh nor tease nor make light of themselves or their enemies. The Shawnee can carry on so for days at a time. An' that was what spared Jacob now. You see, Jacob's bigger'n any stud stallion when it comes to his manly parts, an' his captors started cacklin' an' joshin' an' pointin' an' the next thing he knows, they've strung him to a pole, still buck nakid, an' he's on his way home with 'em, their prisoner to do with as they pleased.

"It wasn't till they fessed up to the Shawnee home village two days later that Jacob could get a notion what they had in store for him. A runner went ahead an' spread the good news, so a crowd of redsticks was waitin' when they led him into the center of the village. With one peek at him an' a few overdone gestures from his captors, every last Shawnee went to gigglin' an' pointin' at his manliness. They prodded him to the open ground beyond their huts an' cut him loose from that pole. Then the crowd parted into a gauntlet line. Jacob stared down the runway twixt that double row of his enemy an' there at the far end stood the Injun who'd spared him the first go-round. He had donned Jacob's bearskin coat, and behind him, other redsticks heaped wood on a big fire beside a pole buried in the ground. He was to run the gauntlet, warriors, women, an' heathen offspring poundin' away with clubs, sticks, an' whatever else they could lay hand on; afterwards, they'd torture an' burn him for his bother.

"I believe most every man would've thought hisself finished then an' there. But not Jacob Telow. He lit out at the gallop, a smile plastered on his lips, an' no matter how often or hard they struck him, he kept his feet under him. A few yards from the end of his dash, he spied mixed in with those beatin' at him, a tall, beautiful Shawnee gal watchin' while she nursed her newborn child. How he thought of it he's never said. But Jacob bulled his way over to her, snatched that sucklin' red baby from her breast, an' afore anyone could stop him, he threw that young'un, blanket an' all, into the fire they was stokin' for him. What followed was exactly what Jacob expected: It was like hell itself parted at the seams. Every heathen rushed forward to rescue that baby, an' in the confusion, Jacob fought through 'em the other way an' bolted for his life. The outraged Shawnee got their wits about 'em soon enough and fired a ball or two at him, but Jacob fled into the woods 'thout any cripplin' injuries. For three days he outwitted an army of angry redsticks, hidin' in laurel thickets an' thorn bushes, eatin' raw frogs an' whatever else he could catch barehanded. He finally reached the Ohio agin. The next evening he hailed a passin' flatboat, an' if'n he hadn't suffered enough already, his own kind was so scared it was an Injun trick they forced him to swim out to their boat afore they allowed him to come aboard.''

Wild and seemingly impossible as Breed's story sounded, I doubted not a word, for though the scout was of mixed blood, Ned Henry insisted he was whiter than his palest Kentucky neighbor. A peek at the bluecoats confirmed they, too, believed Breed's yarn. They stared at the wounded Jacob with a newly marshaled respect that bordered on total awe.

"Look at me, Virginians," Breed commanded, voice urgent. "There's more you need hear an' time's short. That redstick who spared Jacob on the ledge an' paraded at the torture fire in his bearskin coat, that redstick an' the father of the sucklin' babe Jacob snatched up be one an' the same Injun. An' from the day his son was burned to death, that redstick took the name Bear Hunter. He wears garlands of fur made from Jacob's coat about his neck. He carved this here war club as a constant reminder of his vow he'd slay his stallion of an enemy with the red hair an' yellow eyes. An' its our sorry arse, misbegotten luck we chanced upon him tonight. Lads, there ain't no fiercer warrior among the Ohio redsticks. No Injun's more wedded to the fight. Ponder on it. With nothin' at all in his favor, he killed one of us outright, put a ball in both Jacob an' the major, an' got clean away. An' he didn't run off just to save his own skin. He run off so's he can have at us agin later on.''

The scout nodded at the nearby woods. "You can damn well accept it as gospel; he's out there in the trees right now, watchin' an' waitin'. Come daybreak, them Shawnee trackin' us from upcreek will run into him. Then Bear Hunter's gonna lead them hard after us with less mercy in his heart than ol' Satan hisself.''

The handle of the war club smacked Breed's palm. "Lads, I don't aim to scare the bejesus outen you. But when a man's in for a mighty mean mornin', he best understand what's facin' him. We can't outrun the Shawnee all the way to Limestone, wounded or no wounded. It's too late for that. Our only hope's to be prepared for anythin', anytime. No matter what, you got to keep yer nerve liken Jacob done, stay in line, an' obey Captain Layton's orders.''

The scout's arm extended sideways and the spiked ball of the war club pointed at the Shawnee dead littering the floor of the lean-to. ''Mind what's left of them full bloods. Don't never forget what you see there. Cause if'n any single one of you shows yellow an' runs, Bear Hunter'll be waitin with the scalpin knife an' yuh'll end yer days same as these heathen did—a cold pile of bones with yer hair missin! An', lads,'' Breed continued, pointing now at each of us with the war club, ''even an Injun dog deserves better'n that after his last breath, don't he now?''

The scout knew how to hold your attention from beginning to end, he did. Me and the bluecoats could only shudder and rapidly nod our heads in full agreement. So persuasive was Breed, not a soul circling that fire questioned the meanness of a day yet to dawn.

6

Just after the dull smear of first light stained the eastern ridgeline, the sound of hooves punching through crusted snow carried to us on the stiff northeast wind. Jaimie Crown rode the major's gelding from the lessening gloom, followed by Hump Layton and the Henry horses. I counted empty saddletrees on six of the eight pack animals. The big spy had off-loaded the surveyor's transom, poles, and chains, the bluecoat tents, sundry tools, and the major's folding camp desk. He had kept what he deemed vital to our upcoming march: the final ration of vittles, including the rum horn, and rolls of canvas tarp.

The surveyors and chainmen muttered amongst themselves, disgruntled with the loss of their equipment. Me, I was happy we wouldn't go hungry and the big spy hadn't turned loose my horses: I didn't need anybody steepening the stairs to the good graces of Ned Henry.

Though he had certainly been forewarned, Jaimie Crown's cow eyes showed grave concern when he spotted the wounded major. He halted the gelding and lifted a leg to dismount. A brusque command from behind the gelding promptly dropped him back into the saddle, the rough edge in Hump Layton's voice silencing the grumbling of the surveyors and chainmen.

Every head twisted in the direction of the big spy. Aware we were watching him, Layton freed the strap tying the rum horn in place and, toting the liquor cask in one large paw and his musket in the other, tramped to where Noah Reem knelt beside the major. "They's up to it, pour a swig into Asa an' Jacob. Don't tarry, lad," he urged. "The enemy's on the move by now."

The big spy cradled his musket in his arms and faced the rest of us, the steely cast of his coarsely bearded features matching the gruffness we'd heard in his voice. His hazel eyes bored into ours. If Nathan Breed had put the fear of the Shawnee in us, I sensed Hump Layton was about to add to that the fear of the Lord, and more.

"We're taken out jack quick," he announced, "an' I'll give the orders till the major's on his feet again. I'll brook no dillydallyin or fool questions. Understand me, I'll promise bluecoat . . . an' Kentuckian . . . but one thing: Any of you fail the major, you best pray I ain't still alive. I'll shoot the first slackard in his tracks even if'n it costs me my last ball."

His meaning was unmistakable, sharp and blunt as the blow of a fist on the jaw. He expected no response and not a peep of protest was forthcoming. Hell's bells, huge as he was and the unnerving way he was glaring at us, the Shawnee suddenly seemed the lesser threat. The redsticks at their worst couldn't be any more difficult or dangerous to treat with than a displeased Hump Layton (or so he made us believe that winter dawn on the west bank of Eagle Creek).

Those unblinking hazel eyes swept from right to left, taking stock of all present and the Injun horses recovered by Breed and me. His orders came in a rush. "Listen close! We've no time for litters. The wounded are gonna ride home."

Eyebrows lifted, for the major had yet to stir, but the big spy ignored our astonishment, and we dared not speak.

"Block an' Welker," he snapped, summoning the two surveyors, "get the major up in front of Jaimie. Moon an' Williams, soon as Askell's seated on the bay Cooper an' Breed brung in, you chainmen do the same with Jacob."

Once the wounded were bundled in tarps and lifted aboard their mounts, Layton passed Askell his rifle and Jaimie his musket. "Hold yer barrels across their chests," he instructed. "Thataway, you won't let either of 'em slide off. If'n you wear out, yell an' we'll trade a spell."

Then it was our turn. "It's six miles to Logan's Gap, an' after we reach the Ohio, another six miles to Limestone. There'll be no stoppin' afore we gain the river. Block an' Welker, you know the creek bottom ahead from our survey, so the point's yourn. Askell an' Jacob will follow on the bay, then Jaimie an' the major. Next'll be Noah, along with Moon an' Williams. Whatever happens, you bluecoats stick with the wounded. Cooper'll be right at yer heels with the packhorses. Breed an' me, we'll fetch our dead packhorseman an' cover the rear. Now, check yer weapons an' line out."

While the column formed in place as ordered, the big spy and Breed led the second Shawnee mount, a steady roan mare, across the frozen creek to Cam's body. They wrapped an old trade blanket from within the lean-to about him, draped him chest down over the mare's back, and bound his hands and feet together under her belly. Collecting the dead was a grisly, disheartening task anytime, grimmer still at the start of a gray morning heavy with cloud and smelling of snow.

Layton gripped the mare's hackamore and waved us forward. We descended the shallow bank onto the ice and proceeded downstream, in the process marching past Cam's blanket-shrouded body. Nothing, I can attest, hastens the stride of the soldier fleeing the enemy like the sight of his own lost in battle.

Within the hour, Eagle Creek flowed between twin shoulders of high ground. Beyond that point, the waterway clung to the base of the eastern ridgeline. The creek bottom here

ran flat to the west, then angled upward to a level bench
that continued the same direction three-quarters of a mile
before encountering the opposite wall of what was an en-
closed valley. It was at the head, or northern end, of the
valley that Major Fowler had decided the future Brandon
Station was to be built, and during our survey, we had
girdled scores of tall oaks on the western elevation to pro-
vide pickets for the palisades and logs with which to build
the blockhouses. South of the station site, on the floor of
the bench, we had done likewise with acres of sycamore,
elm, and black cherry, the first step in clearing spaces for
outlying cabins and fields of corn and flax, and possibly
tobacco, if General Brandon held sway at the outset.

Four miles below the station site, the eastern ridgeline
merged with the forested heights bordering the Ohio's north
bank, walling off the southern end of the valley. Its flow
blocked, Eagle Creek bent westward, departed the valley
through a break in the heights to the southwest, and mated
with the wide Ohio yet another mile downstream. Our immediate destination was the most direct route to the river—
Logan's Gap, a narrow upland notch separating Puff Ridge
and Cedar Hill at the southeastern corner of the valley. And
our arrival there couldn't come any too soon.

As if we hadn't troubles enough, beyond the station site
the storm that had been brewing since the previous evening
finally struck. The already overcast morning darkened and
the wind flashed teeth razor-sharp. Freezing gusts laden
with icy specks of snow streamed from behind us, the
creek's treed banks funneling the norther's fury hard about
our ears. Shoulders hunched and back sides braced, we
slogged onward, gun barrels plugged against dampness. Not
for a heartbeat did anyone dare tender the thought foul
weather might discourage the Shawnee, not after hearing
Breed's Bear Hunter story.

Without planning so, we drifted toward the east bank,
seeking whatever lee the ridgeline above us could offer. A
slab of rock jutting from the creek's frozen surface shied
Buck sideways. With his unexpected tug on the rein I dis-

covered my lead hand, despite its protecting mitten, was an ice-covered lump of numb flesh. It was awkward as all get out, but without dropping the Bedford, I pried the rein free with my other hand and beat feeling into my fingers on my thigh. A check of nose and toes spawned a flurry of rubbing and stomping.

Though the biting wind and numbing cold held my attention, I couldn't help but notice the large bulk now walking next to me. Hump Layton's chuckle was a brief scrap of noise. He leaned closer. "Curious, ain't it," he said, "how you take to duckin' the wind all the while an' forget to keep yer end parts warm."

I nodded wholeheartedly as the big spy peered along the column from beneath ice-crusted brows. The Virginians marched with their tricorn heads lowered, seeing only what lay before them. Jaimie Crown clung to the wounded major with both arms, his shoulders and the gelding's rump barely visible on the far side of the bluecoats so thick was the snowfall.

"How many of yer animals can be rode?" queried Layton, voice raised above the roar of the wind.

"Two," I answered, teeth chattering. "Buck here, and Sweet Lou, the first horse in Cam's string."

"Figured as much," the big spy responded. "We'll switch those two with the geldin' an' the Injun bay once we're through Logan's Gap an' commence our final trek for Limestone."

He glanced my way. Miserable cold and shivering or not, I took some pride in the fact I could look him in the eye better than most, what with his topping my six feet by a mere four inches. I just wished I could shun the cold as easily as he and his buffalo namesake.

"Don't lag any," Layton ordered. "I'm countin' on yer animals to shield the bluecoats an' the major if'n the Shawnee jump us from the rear."

At my "Yes, sir," he clapped my shoulder and fell away. In a half dozen steps, the snow swallowed him whole same as the whale done ol' Jonah. I clucked at Buck and quickened my pace, Hump Layton's reminder the enemy was unquestionably on the prowl pumping new vigor into feet that seemed to have shed considerable weight of a sudden.

The eastern ridgeline melded with the heights blocking us from the Ohio and the creek bent westward, signaling our arrival at the foot of Logan's Gap. The Gap was anything but a true break in the heights. The departed Cam Downing, forever dwelling on the ladies or lack thereof, had likened the shallow notch to the arse cheeks of a plump female were she lying on her stomach. It required a steep climb from the small of her back, he'd claimed, to reach the flat of her tailbone, after which came an even steeper descent twixt her opposing buttocks to reach the bank of the river.

Cam's devilish wit provoked no new laughter on my part, for I understood what we risked by shortcutting through the Gap—the lives of Jacob and the major. The climb up and down would jostle them something fierce, further aggravating their injuries. The column would save four miles of travel; the wounded might perish. To spare the many, Hump Layton chanced the few, a weighty decision I was glad wouldn't torment my soul should the morning prove it wrong.

We abandoned Eagle Creek and wound upward on the northern slope of the heights. The path, a rain-gouged slash fraught with sharp rocks, fallen limbs, and loose courses of gravel in the best of weather, was doubly treacherous beneath ten inches of old and new snow. We lunged and scrambled and clawed past stands of tulip tree and sugar maple that gradually yielded to ash forest and clusters of green cedar. Higher still, brown leaves rustled on towering white oaks.

At the summit, both men and horses were gasping and heaving for breath. But orders were orders, particularly those of Hump Layton, and without hesitating we tackled the opposing slope. Down we plunged, treading heel first for balance, but still slipping and sliding every other step. I was at a near run staying free of Buck's thrashing hooves.

With the heights now shunting the wind over our heads and the snow thinning at last, the air cleared and there, looming below us, was the black water of the Ohio. The column lurched to a halt at the bottom of the slope. We stood spraddle legged where we stopped, recovering breath and strength. Then, at Noah Reem's bidding, the bluecoats swarmed around Jaimie and Askell and eased the major and Jacob from their exhausted mounts.

Noah and his helpers had for the moment forgotten the Shawnee threat. Our captain had not. Hump Layton shoved past me, rum horn wedged beneath his off arm. "Fall in, bluecoats," he bawled. "The Injuns ain't partial to our wounded for chrissake."

Heads swiveled, legs churned, gaitered shoes sent snow flying in their wake. The next thing I saw was six sober-eyed musket bearers ranked before the big spy in a single, close-ordered row, weapons properly shouldered, back-bones ramrod stiff.

Layton grounded the butt of his own long gun and glared at his charges. "It gladdens my heart the lot of you at least showed enough brains durin' the snow to plug yer barrels an' keep yer locks dry. Attention! Poise yer piece! Remove barrel plug! Pocket yer plug! Remove lock cover! Pocket yer cover! Shoulder arms! Now, at the word, to the right about . . . face!"

The ranked bluecoats seized cartridge boxes with the right hand and pivoted as one, describing a half circle.

"Now, gentlemen, watch for the enemy. Mister Reem an' Mister Moon, dispense the ration to one an' all," the spy commanded. "We've time for a half gill, a palm of parched corn an' two strips of jerk each, no more, no less."

Noah carting the rum horn and Sam Moon a sizable leather pouch Layton extracted from the hairy fold of his buffalo coat, the two Virginians went amongst us. Every man ate and drank except Jacob Telow and the major, nei-ther of whom had the wherewithal to swallow. The rum was welcomingly wet and fiery, the parched corn, mixed with crumbled sugar, sweet as the kiss of a maiden the likes of Rebecca Brandon, a savory thought that added spice to the liquor's bite. Fanciful notions aside, always dreading the ache of denied innards, I chewed the corn and sugar till my jaw cramped and squirreled the jerk in a pocket for later.

While Noah and Moon were issuing the ration, Hump Layton seized those few minutes for a parley with Nathan Breed, who was alongside Buck and me, replacing the flint in the hammer jaws of his rifle. "You still believe it a fool's errand to dispatch a rider on ahead?"

The scout nodded. "It ain't likely there'll be huntin' parties on the prowl with all the new snow, an' the ferrymen don't linger on this bank neither in the winter months. They love the home hearth an' rightfully fear the Shawnee. That means any rider must draw opposite the town, make hisself known, an' wait for the ferry to row across. Then once he's in Limestone, he must locate Kenton an' his boys or a host of others anxious to tangle with the redsticks, recross the river with 'em, an' guide 'em to meet us. Bear Hunter'll be on us like mud on a dry stick long afore that."

"Where you reckon the Shawnee are now?" Layton asked.

"Somewhere twixt here an' the ferry landing, closer this direction than the other. With the storm, Bear Hunter'd forgo overtakin' us in the Gap. He'd slant east over the ridgeline an' pick a promisin' place for pouncin' on us."

"Have you hunted these bottoms?"

"Much as anyone."

"Can you point out the prime sites for an ambush?"

"I will, but I allow they outnumber my toes an' fingers. The river heaps whole trees along the bank like broom straws whenever she runs high. There's also thickets of willow, cattail, an' brush big as islands that would hide twice the Shawnee trailin' our bums. An' that don't shorten yer wick none, you can't hardly make any headway a-tall 'thout followin' the most open path, pretty much tellin' those full bloods where we'll be damn near ever step."

The huge spy didn't flinch. Nor did he sigh in exasper-

ation hearing Breed's bleak picture of the miles we'd yet
to travel. He pondered silently, then said, "We can't let the
heathen surprise us, an' we don't dare string out. We'll
march in tight formation, always in sight of each other. Our
sole hope is to fire in volleys an' keep from fightin' 'em at
close quarters, bayonet against hatchet an' knife. We do
that, maybe we can forge through to the ferry."

"What then?" Breed inquired.

"Need be, we'll burn the landing an' snag the eye of
your fellow Kentuckians. They spot smoke an' white men
signalin' afore their very noses, they oughta band together
an' come a-rowin' in anything they can float."

Breed grinned, creasing the paint centering his cheeks.
"They'll sweep the taverns clean. Ever milksop that can't
visit the privy 'thout warm bodies at both elbows will join
in. They'll use their tankards for oars, I swear."

The scout's wry musing set me chuckling. Not so with
Captain Layton. His mood didn't lend itself to humor of
any bent. "I'll smile with you then, Breed, no sooner. The
point's yourn from here out. Cooper, bring yer ridin' stock
forward at the hurry if'n you please."

I separated Buck and Sweet Lou from the rest of the
Henry horses and led them around the bluecoats standing
watch. Despite traversing considerable rugged country, both
animals, having traveled unburdened since dawn, were ea-
ger to be under way. An unusually glum Askell Telow accepted without question my choice of the deep-chested
Sweet Lou as his brother's remount.

"He'll carry double, no doubt," Askell judged. "If'n
these be Jacob's endin' hours, I'll not trust his care to
strangers."

From the older Telow's appearance, Askell's fears for
him weren't misplaced. Jacob lay sprawled atop a canvas
tarp. A fistful of frock shirt lodged in the flap of his bearskin garment glistened with freshly shed blood. Fever mot-
tled his cheekbones and forehead, the splotches red as his
beard. His chest movement was so slight, without the fever's coloring, I would've guessed him ready for the shovel

and the preacher's prayer. Though I'd never enjoyed the love of a brother, Askell's saddened spirits gave truth to another of Ned Henry's fervent beliefs: When kin suffered grievous harm, a man needn't bleed his ownself to hurt something awful.

At the remounting, exhausted Jaimie Crown could barely lift his foot into the iron stirrup of the saddle I switched from the gelding. Nonetheless, he spurned Layton's suggestion he should be relieved of such tiresome duty, and twixt the three of us—the spy, Breed, and me—we heaved the dead weight of the major before him on Buck. It wasn't a bit easier positioning the equally unconscious Jacob Telow astride Sweet Lou in Askell's embrace. Given the blood they'd lost, the cold, and the rough passage awaiting them, a farthing seemed too great to wager either officer or camp guard would last much longer.

I hustled the riderless mounts to the rear. Captain Layton then presented the bluecoats with their marching orders. To gain their ear, he scooped up the empty rum horn and whapped its wooden bottom with his musket barrel, the hollow thump matching the beat of a drum. His sharply rendered "To the right about . . . face!" again brought him and the Virginians eyeball to eyeball.

"Gentlemen, don't believe what ain't true. It don't change anythin' we're halfway to Limestone. The Shawnee won't quit the field. They'll be hidin' somewhere along the river waitin' to ambush us. An' when they do, they'll try to overrun us so we can't bring our muskets to bear. But if'n you don't panic, an' hold yer places, we can whip 'em. Ignore their howlin' an' yellin' an' listen only for me. Do exactly what I call out. After the first volley, we tap load . . . Remember, don't panic. Do exactly what I call out. After the first volley, we tap load . . . Attention! Fix Bayonets!" The bluecoats slid their bayonets from belt scabbards and twisted the sockets of the slender blades over the studs welded to the end of their musket barrels. "Now, you young pups," Layton growled, "left face, on the common step, to the front . . . march!"

I was fast respecting the big spy as our captain. His terse observations and instructions never confounded or confused. In a few boldly spoken words, he made us keenly aware of what was most likely to confront us as well as precisely how he wanted us to respond. And we knew from his previous promise back on Eagle Creek concerning slackards how he would react if we failed him.

Still, every marching bluecoat had to share my nagging doubt: Even with the indomitable Hump Layton to lead us and prod us into the best possible defense, did we truly have any chance whatsoever against an experienced, resolute enemy twice our number?

It was a fight-or-die question about to be answered in blood.

7

At the outset the Ohio's north bank was a flood-scoured shelf bounded on either side by the heavily wooded incline of Puff Ridge and the dark sweep of the river. Expecting no attack from the steep slope with its hindering forest, Breed moved briskly, with little hint of caution. His pace slowed of necessity when Puff Ridge surrendered to Flaugher Ridge, for the river bottom grew wider with each quarter mile and looming now in our path were the heaped deadfalls and islands of brush, cattail, and willow the scout had portrayed in his parley with Captain Layton.

Clinging to the riverbank angled the column away from the towering ridgeline and exposed us once more to the full force of the wind. An hour shy of noon, short of Big Three Mile Creek, the snow resumed, swirling round men and horses in ragged flurries. Captain Layton, marching twixt me and the Virginians, cursed the bluecoats years his junior for bowing their heads at such trifling discomforts; after which, in an outburst that would have blushed the cheeks of his own strong-willed daughter, the big spy defamed the Lord unmercifully for deserting his loyal flock in dire circumstances: Seems the Almighty at least owed us decent weather if He deigned to intercede in a more helpful manner on our behalf.

No matter how raw the elements this late morning, there was no resorting to barrel plugs and lock covers, not with the Shawnee perhaps near enough to shadow our every movement. The Virginians bore their bayoneted muskets slung from shoulder straps in front of their bellies, hammer set at half cock, frizzen closed upon priming pan, right palm and fingers cupped over both pan and frizzen as a final barrier to prying wind. They needed only to cock the hammer fully and lift stock to shoulder to loose a volley.

Big Three Mile Creek flowed from the ridges to the northeast and drifted back and forth in the river bottom before dumping into the Ohio. The open span of water at the creek's mouth measured waist-deep and nudged us inland in search of a suitable ford. Thin trunks soaring above our hats framed the scant trace Breed located. The going was uneven and trying, but the dense willows at least held the brunt of the wind and flying snow off of us.

Half an hour later we arrived at our scout's choice of fords. The willows thinned, revealing a stretch of creek bed in which boulders sufficient for stepping stones littered areas of rippling current and patches of ice too thin to support the weight of man or horse. Our being three-plus miles from the warming hearths of Limestone, a dry fording was no little thing. Others in the past had survived a wet crossing, yet later lost toes and more to the ravages of freezing cold and its friend and ally, frostbite.

Breed crossed first, surefooted as the catamount on the ice-rimmed boulders in his tall moccasins. He scanned the country ahead from the far bank, then waved us onward. Askell and Jaimie rode into the water downstream of the boulders. The Virginians, fearful of slipping in their hardsoled shoes, trod carefully where Breed had stepped. Each stride from boulder to boulder was a decided challenge for short-legged Sam Moon, and Bone Williams couldn't resist funning his fellow chainman. "Damn shame, ain't it, Sam, you bein' coupled like a frog and not able to jump more than six inches even was your arse a-fire,'' Bone chided.

The ribbing occurred during a break in the wind, carried the length of the column, and should have sparked hails of laughter. But that wasn't to be, for from across the creek, Breed's blaring shout of ''Captain Layton!'' was as startling as the sudden squeeze of enemy fingers about one's throat.

My gaze flew to the far bank. The hand topping the scout's extended arm was definitely clenched in a fist. Even more momentous was the repeated circling of that upraised fist: Breed hadn't just discovered the tracks of the Shawnee, he had sighted them in the flesh.

The surprised bluecoats halted of their own accord and stared past the signaling scout. I did the same. Beyond the ford, wedges of yellow saw grass shared an expanse of treeless swamp with hummocks of snow mounded by the wind. On the far right, the Ohio was a thick black line. To our left, along the fringe of the swamp, sparsely timbered ground, festooned at the base with snarls of cattail and willow, swelled gradually and crested in a low hill bare as a newborn opossum.

I stared till my eyeballs hurt with the strain of it and saw nothing, nothing but swirling snow and what appeared empty swamp and hillside. Where were the red bastards?

Hump Layton's voice rang out, solid and unshakable. ''Stop yer gawkin' an' calm yerselves, gentlemen. Move ahead an' look only at Breed. Lead off, Mister Reem!''

Enemy or no enemy, Noah did as he was told. But the big spy's orders puzzled me. If the Shawnee lay in wait for us, why march into their very laps?

Layton came about and stuck his bearded jaw in my face. ''We run, they'll kill us off piecemeal, an' we don't dare close with 'em in the creek. They can't be nowhere except amongst the cattails an' willow yonder. Ford yer horses above the boulders an' get betwixt the hill an' the swamp. Quick now, lad, we may lose some of yer precious pack-horses, but that can't be helped.''

With no more hesitation than Noah, I tightened my grip on the gelding's reins and led him into the fast-flowing creek. The tying ropes tautened and the other animals plunged in after the gelding. The current lapped at my boot tops. The creek bottom deepened, and chill wetness dampened my woolen socks. The bluecoats heard me splash by but paid me no heed. Breed eyed me and nodded with a wink, and I knew he and the captain were reading from the same page.

A few bounds from the far bank, fear dried my mouth, and my chilled feet seemed too heavy for my legs. Plain and blunt, I was inviting fire from an Injun ambush and feared most what I would neither see nor hear—the deadly strike of an enemy ball, the same as had felled poor Cam. My courage might have deserted me altogether had not Hump Layton's bull tones, steady and undaunted as ever, rung out again from, of all places, the very bank I so dreaded reaching.

"Bear right for the swamp, Cooper! Rally to me, bluecoats, rally to me!"

Heartened by the big spy's commanding presence, I scurried up the rock-strewn bank, keeping the gelding on a short halter, and slanted into the saw grass and snow hummocks of the swamp. Over my shoulder, I saw the Injun mare toting Cam's body, the last of the horses, pop from the creek. I was across and doing what the captain wished, screening the Virginians while he hastily formed them into a skirmish line with their weapons aimed where the enemy was thought to be.

"Fall in, Cooper!" the captain roared. "Join to yer left, now!"

I shed the gelding's reins and lunged backwards. It was then the entire hillside erupted with the opening shots of the hidden Shawnee. Flame spurted from behind and within every snarl of cattail and willow. Balls whistled near my elbow and buzzed my ear. I turned at the end of the bluecoat line and snapped rifle to cheek.

Hump Layton's calm "Hold yer fire, lads, hold yer fire"

froze my finger on the trigger. ''Wait till the buggers show themselves.''

The three centermost packhorses were down and kicking. Dark shapes rose and emerged from cover along the lower tier of the hillside and the Shawnee charge commenced, their whooping war cries defying the wind. They hurriedly covered the few rods separating them from the downed horses and came on, the running wave of their attack bunching at the middle to pass twixt the terrified horses still standing. From thirty yards away, the enemy's fur-clad chests, surrounding skin of plucked head and bare arms paint blackened and striped with crimson, filled our sights. It was danger so menacing and threatening, it required all the nerve I could muster to hold my barrel steady and not stain the seat of my breeches brown, green, and yellow.

''Cock yer pieces an' pick yer target, lads,'' the captain ordered. He waited half a breath. ''Fire!''

Wind and damp to the contrary, we suffered not a single powder failure in pan or barrel. Muskets boomed. Rifles cracked. The center of the enemy advance, cramped shoulder against shoulder, fell like ripe hay before the sweep of the scythe.

Though the thunderous volley briefly deafened my ears, I heard Hump Layton immediately shout, ''Tap load! Tap load!'' at the bluecoats, for the demise of their red fellows did nothing to diminish the scalp lust of the remaining Shawnee. Those closely bordering the dead and wounded simply leaped their fallen brethren and resumed the assault. The balance of the screeching heathen split left and right, circled the stomping, neighing horses, and rushed us from both flanks.

Captain Layton bellowed the reloading commands for the bluecoat muskets. Eyeing only their work, the Virginians yanked paper cartridges from the slotted boxes on their waist belts, bit off the cartridge end containing the ball, held the ball in their mouths while priming the pan, then poured the powder left in the cartridge paper down the barrel, and spat the ball after it. A solid thump of butt on ground—the tap—and their muskets were ready for firing, the whole exercise completed in seconds.

I ignored the captain's commands and made no attempt to reload the Bedford. There wasn't time enough before the Shawnee charge reached us for me to shove a patched ball down its rifled barrel with the ramrod. I fisted my hatchet, and as I crouched low, that bladed weapon in my right hand, rifle barrel poked forward in the other, the bluecoats triggered their second volley with the Shawnee but two jumps from our skirmish line.

A flanking Shawnee, unseen and unexpected, smashed into my right shoulder, and I was suddenly falling. A painted arm smelling of woodsmoke snaked over the opposite shoulder and wrapped around my neck. I realized without knowing how, lest it was remembering tales of past battles told at the Henry supper table, that the arm not about my neck was striking for my belly, fingers gripping the handle of the knife that would gut the life from me. I thrust my rifle in front of my body. My reward was the *chunk* of a knife blade on my rifle stock. My elation was fleeting at best. The blade skidded sideways on the wooden stock and sliced into the flesh of my left hand, paining me something fierce.

The Shawnee and I hit the snow locked together, his knife trapped under my rifle. The shock of our landing loosened the painted arm encircling my neck and I sucked a draught of air into my lungs. I heaved upward, and feeling the least weight on my left hip, twisted that direction. The painted forearm slipped from my throat. Another heave and the Shawnee flopped over. I landed atop his chest. There beside his plucked head lay my hatchet. I snatched it from the snow and bashed the savage's forehead. I drew back and bashed him again. And again. And again.

I flailed away, the battle raging around me forgotten. The muscles in my arm began aching. The hatchet grew heavier with each blow. My arm slowed and I heard breathing, hoarse and desperate, and sobbing, not sobs of grief and sadness, but the deep, abiding, soul-quivering sobs of someone laboring with every ounce of his being. The fear slowly seeped out of me. My head cleared, and listening closer, I learned it was my own breathing and sobbing I overheard.

Fingers latched onto the handle of my uplifted hatchet. Alarmed, I squirmed about and found myself nose-to-nose not with the dreaded heathen, but Nathan Breed. "He's dead, Cooper," the scout pronounced. "On yer feet, now!"

Embarrassed, I lowered my hatchet and scrambled upright. A war whoop exploded at my heels. Breed shoved me aside, leaped forward, and parried the thrust of a most unusual redstick weapon, a broadsword, with his rifle barrel. The scout's tomahawk swished in a short, blurring arc and he lopped off the entire peak of the Shawnee's roached topknot. Bone, blood, and gray brains flew in a spraying mist of meaty gore that landed shockingly hot on my cheek.

"Fall back," Breed ordered. "The captain's behind us."

I looked around and discovered the surviving Virginians and Askell Telow, along with Hump Layton, ringed Buck and Sweet Lou farther into the swamp. I scurried toward them. An arrow had pierced the haunch of Sweet Lou and he was kicking wildly. The big spy calmly stretched beneath the chopping hooves and dragged forth a crawling Noah Ream, in the same motion shooting a vaulting Shawnee flush in the brisket with the musket he clasped single-handed in one huge paw. The rescued Noah, cockaded tricorn gone, dark hair matted white with snow, angrily tore at a fresh cartridge with his teeth and set about reloading. I plowed through mounded snow and saw grass and dead bodies—three, wearing familiar coats of blue—and took position beside Askell Telow.

The younger Telow scavenged a bayoneted musket from the icy slush at his feet to replace my missing rifle. "Grab hold, bucko," Askell said. "By Christ, the red devils loathe cold steel."

New Shawnee screeching sent shudders the length of me and, hand wound dripping red, I grabbed the musket from Askell. How I prayed he told the truth. There were just seven of us still in the fight—the captain, Noah, Jaimie Crown, Sam Moon, Breed, Askell, and me. The enemy, now totaling less than twice our count, gathered themselves and rushed from every quarter. Armed with a long gun I again had no time to load, I could only watch and wait.

An arrow flicked my hat brim. "Stand firm, lads," Hump Layton bawled, shouldering his own piece. "Take aim! Fire!"

Boom! Boom! Boom! Boom! Four muskets roared, belching flame and smoke. Three savages stumbled and went sprawling. It was that round of shots, when Noah, Jaimie, and Sam Moon stood solid as stone with the captain, that wrung the guts of the Shawnee dry. They no longer overmatched us with great numbers, and lurking before them at the finish of their charge was a wall of sixteen-inch bayonet blades honed to razor sharpness.

Amidst the fading reports of the musket volley, the Shawnee war whoops slackened. A heathen voice, matching the iron authority of the captain's, gobbled like the calling turkey. The enemy rush ceased. They spun about and broke for the protecting cover of the hillside.

I sank to my knees then and there and thanked the Lord aloud for deeming it fit He should intervene on our behalf after all. I neither worried nor cared if my fellow survivors scorned such sentiments or considered me foolish: A truly thankful man suffers no shame.

Violent cursing attracted my attention. Peering through Buck's legs, I saw Askell was also on his knees. He was kneeling next to his brother. I couldn't see the whole of Jacob's head, but I made out that where red hair had once covered his crown, there was now the pinked red flesh of a large, circular hole. Jacob Telow had been scalped as he lay helpless at the edge of the battle.

An anguished cry spilled from Askell's lips. I thought at first he was bemoaning the loss of his beloved brother. Then his arms lifted. I gulped in dismay. Filling his hands was a garland neckpiece fashioned from the same fur as the coats of the Telows.

We won the field that midday, but Bear Hunter had finally taken the hair of his white stallion of an enemy.

8

Balance of the Day, January 24

The heart-pounding excitement of the brutal encounter with the Shawnee ebbed, and with its fading, I could no longer ignore the throb of my wounded hand. On close inspection of the damage inflicted by the Injun knife, I learned a deep cut cleaved the flesh on the outside of my palm opposite the thumb, and the top joint of my little finger dangled from a shred of skin. There was nothing else for it, so I drew my own knife, placed the mangled finger on the stock of my borrowed musket, and sliced through that connecting shred of skin. Dangling joint removed, much as Askell had when previously binding Jacob's ball-shattered ribs, I sawed a strip of cloth from the front tail of my blanket coat and wrapped my palm, snugging together the raw edges of the cut. Maybe it hurt godawful at the tiniest movement, but twixt my thumb and remaining whole fingers I had use of my left hand.

"Cooper!"

My immediate thought was that the Shawnee were on the attack again. A glance at the hillside dispelled that notion. The heathen, for the time being it seemed, were with-

drawing, stealing away into the swirling snow like retreating wolves, employing as they went every speck of
cover and never presenting a worthwhile target.

"Cooper!"

I turned then, eyed the source of the call—Captain Layton—and answered, "Yes, sir!"

"Fetch yer horses," Layton ordered. "Breed will accompany you."

The gelding, two packhorses, and the roan mare toting
Cam Downing stood hipshot with lowered heads where I'd
abandoned them, each still roped to their slain counterparts.
Dead were the Injun bay and four pack animals. As I freed
the gelding, I could almost hear myself recounting for Ned
Henry how I'd managed to lose half his best horse string
in the span of a few minutes. Well, hell's bells, I decided,
if my yarn didn't wash with the boss man and I had to
endure a hiding from the sharpest tongue in Kentucky, I
wasn't fessing up at his office without the rifle he'd given
me. That loss I couldn't explain.

The Bedford proved an easy find. Its barrel poked from
the snow alongside a lifeless body whose painted features
bore no recognizable shape. One peek at my handiwork
with the hatchet and I was swallowing furiously to stem a
wave of bile in the back of my throat. But while the sight
of what my mindless fear had provoked sickened me, I felt
no honest sorrow for the faceless savage. Any Injun, by
damned, was the enemy first and foremost now and forever.

At another beckoning call from the captain, I swallowed
a palm of snow to rinse the sourness from my mouth, hefted
the Bedford, and with Breed, finished gathering the horses.
The gelding and surviving pack animals appeared unhurt.
The roan mare, too long burdened with Cam's remains, an
oversight I could only curse inwardly about at this late
hour, walked haltingly, favoring her left foreleg.

The first words from Captain Layton indicated what was
utmost on his mind. "Gentlemen, afternoon's upon us and
we can't linger mourning our dead. We can't cart them any
further either. We'll take the horses that ain't wounded or

bunged up an' resume our march for the ferry site. Come tomorrow, we'll secure the necessary reinforcements an' bring in our own for burial.''

Askell Telow's sentiments leaned a different direction. He lurched to his feet beside his brother, rifle held loosely before him, and said loud enough for all to hear, ''I don't believe so, Mister Hump Layton.''

Quick as the wink of the night star, there wasn't a slouching backbone amongst the lot of us. Askell's thumb poised over his rifle cock. His yellow eyes, honest to thunderation, were flame and ice at once, you couldn't tell which. His dander was on the rise, the fuse creeping near the powder. ''They took Jacob's hair,'' he stated, voice quavering. ''They ain't layin' no blade on another part of him. I'll carry him my ownself I have to.''

The younger Telow's rebellion caught Hump Layton by surprise. The stock of the captain's musket rested in the snow at his right heel. And Askell could cock and fire his rifle before the captain could draw either knife or hawk from his belt.

Standing as I was with Buck twixt the two of them and me, I watched across the horse's saddled back side. It was the major's saddle, and hanging from the cantle was a leather holster holding that officer's flintlock pistol. Having heard no pistol shots during our fight with the Shawnee, I was positive the weapon was primed and balled. Without the slightest consideration of the consequences for myself or anyone else, my hand eased upward toward the pistol.

''Don't!'' Breed hissed behind me. ''It's the captain's top to spin, not ours.''

The scout was right, of course. Askell was sufficiently riled, any move to aid the captain might see him shot instead, exactly what I didn't want to happen.

What ensued was forever remembered by those present. Hump Layton, who feared nothing that walked on two legs, raised his huge paws clear of his musket and belt weapons, signaling peaceful intentions. And when he spoke, his bull voice was astonishingly smooth and beseeching, so much so it seemed a stranger had snuck inside his buffalo hide coat without our knowing it. And that smooth and beseeching voice was also most respectful in tone, markedly different from how the defiant Askell had addressed him moments before.

"Mister Telow, I've no quarrel with yer desire to deny the enemy further pleasure with Jacob's earthly body. I've stood where yer standin, lad. With me, it was someone precious, too. Not a brother, but a wife dear and beautiful. We left Jane Mary and seven others unburied on the bank of the Buffalo Bend, an' stole away in the dark to spare the other women an' children. And—"

The big spy's speech faltered and his hazel eyes hooded over, stark testimony how severely such memories tormented him even now. "And it wasn't just for a night she laid there in the open, prey to the ravages of red men an' wild beasts, but a whole year, a whole damn year till I got back to her an' buried what little of her I could find."

Hump Layton sighed heavily and his hazel eyes opened. "The Shawnee may not have quit the field for good, and much as you loved yer brother, 'lessen we bunch together and keep a looksee every direction, we may bait them into jumpin' us agin. Lad, you can't do anythin' more for Jacob here an' now than I could for my Jane Mary, except maybe end the day dead beside him. An' I believe Jacob set enough store by you, he'd suffer wherever he be if'n you fell under the Injun knife same as him."

The big spy lowered his arms. "Askell, the horses are spent, an' you can't carry Jacob three miles an' keep up. We must get to the ferry quick as we can. With this wind and snow, it might take a while to signal someone on the far bank. The worse thing yet would be to spend part of a night with the Shawnee shootin' at our fire. We need yer rifle, lad. I don't want you left behind. You have my solemn word, we'll come back for yer brother in the mornin' no matter what else bygod happens."

There was no thwarting the will of Hump Layton. When the authority of rank didn't hold sway or he couldn't command by threatening you with a thrashing, he had the raw gut courage to reveal the most private of his past affairs to win you over. He was a bold leader whose brains rivaled his God-given size and strength. And I suspected, standing there in the shabby gray light of winter afternoon on a battlefield littered with the dead of friend and foe, I might live a hundred years and never meet his equal.

The wind ruffling the fur trim of his bearskin head covering, the heat leaked from Askell's yellow eyes and he did what any of those listening would have had we been wearing his moccasins: He shouldered his rifle. "You're the captain, Mister Layton, an' much as I hate to leave Jacob, I'll not ruin the Telow name by refusin' your orders. I owe my brother more'n that."

Hump Layton nodded and cradled his long gun aslant his huge chest. "I've never doubted you Telows. You trod the proper trail once you scent it. Neither the major nor I ask for more. Now, future surgeon Reem, your report if'n you please, an' be snappy with it."

Noah stepped forward, the powder residue on his upper lip and hairless chin black as beard. His report was as requested, terse and without embellishment. "Mister Block, Welker, and Williams, as well as Jacob Telow and Major Fowler are beyond our help," he gulped out.

Hump Layton's capped head sank. "I feared such," he admitted, "and am sorry to hear it. Never forget, lads, we could be any of them with a stroke less luck." He let us ponder that sobering reflection, then his saddened gaze lifted and cast about. "Any serious wounds to report?"

None were set forth by the others and I made no mention of my bandaged hand. Serious wounds were those that prevented you from fighting or marching. Though mine smarted like the bejesus, they hindered me at neither.

Hump Layton started to speak again and a squealing grunt from Buck interrupted him, followed instantly by the report of a rifle cracking at us from the tangled hillside. Buck's legs jellied and he slumped onto his knees. The shot had come from my rear, angling downward, and the collapse of the shielding horse exposed the bullet's real target—Captain Layton.

Breed, who had been alertly studying the hillside, realized what was happening same as me. "That ball was meant for you, sir. I can chase him outa there if'n you want."

"Is it Bear Hunter?" I blurted from flat on my belly in the snow.

"Could be," Breed acknowledged without looking at me. "He'd know the headless snake is easily carved for the fire. Captain?"

"Stick with the column an' maintain yer watch, Breed. Cooper, you an' Askell move low an' string together the horses that can travel. Bluecoats, gather behind Cooper's string soon as they're lined out. Move, move, move! That bastard's lingerin' up there, he's reloadin' right now!"

Strung nose to tail, the surviving horses offered but scant protection. Only the gelding and the two Breed and I'd retrieved had four good legs beneath them. Poor Buck had breathed his last propped awkwardly on his knees. The arrow lodged in Sweet Lou's haunch agonized him so, he shied at our approach and limped into the saw grass toward the creek ford. And shed of Cam, the Injun mare appeared too leg sore for any steady effort bucking the heavy snow. We tied her at the nether end of the string anyways, Askell agreeing she was too finely limbed and well wrought to perish from starvation or an attack of wolves.

Askell and I hunkered down along the hidden flank of the horses with Noah, Jaimie, and Sam Moon while the captain stripped the pouch containing our survey maps and the major's spyglass from Buck's saddle. Meantime, we tended our weapons. I spilled some powder reloading the Bedford, but with Ned Henry's bullet block aiding my injured hand, I got a ball seated with the ramrod before Captain Layton joined us.

It was an unexpected turnabout, our squatting in the scant cover of dumb beasts, shivering with cold, bone tired, and fearful as ever of an enemy we'd whipped fair and square.

What little exuberance and fleeting pride we'd experienced at being the victor evaporated with the slaying of Buck, for with that telling incident we dared presume nothing except that the Shawnee still occupied the hillside and had withdrawn to regroup, not to abandon the fight. And seasoned soldier that he was, Captain Layton responded accordingly.

"Gentlemen," he began, broad nose practically touching ours, "those who stay the final roll of the wheel will reach the ferry landin' safely with me. So be forewarned, any that fail the pace better have their prayers ready. I'll not suffer a one of you the favor of wastin' a cartridge on a laggard. Any questions?"

Lordy, how loud the wind blew in the resulting quiet. Weighed against his earlier assertion the big spy would shoot the first slackard, his present threat to forsake any of us slowing the column was an even sharper slap on the cheeks. Jaws leveled and eyeballs bugged. A quick, painless death by the strike of a flying bullet was a kinder fate than dying slowly and cruelly in the clutches of the redsticks. "No, sir" was too much of a feat when you didn't trust your voice not to squeak. Thus, we stared at the big spy and tried our best to shake our hats from our skulls.

Underlings solidly hooked, Hump Layton grinned at his catch. "I was certain you lads would choose the pan instead of the flame," he conceded, beckoning for Breed to join us.

"Am I right rememberin' I saw another stream this side of the ferry durin' our downriver trip on the flatboats?"

"You be," the scout answered. "That'd be Fishing Gut Creek two miles further along. The Gut's narrow an' shallow, probably froze over."

The big spy unhinged at the thighs and came erect. "Its yer country, Breed. I'll trust to you for the fastest and safest route across the creek an' on to the ferry dock. We'll march in the previous order, bluecoats in the van, Cooper an' the horses, me an' Askell guardin' our backtrail. Offen yer heels, Virginians, an' rank yourselves single file."

The column shaped itself as the captain desired, and at

his command, we tromped past him, matching Breed's customary brisk pace with admirable precision. The scout beelined for the Ohio's distant waters and the enemy-infested hillside receded with our every step. Nigh onto the river, long tapering snowdrifts displaced the hummocks and saw grass amidst which we'd fought our battle. We wended thisaway and thataway, Breed naturally skirting the widest and highest of the drifts. It was a grueling, breath-robbing march from the very beginning, but paralleling the ice-bound riverbank brought us over ground open enough it was virtually impossible for the Shawnee to lay the sneak on us again.

Nearing Fishing Gut Creek, the underfed and unwatered animals were laboring badly. Expelled air billowed from their nostrils in white plumes. Muscle exhausted from constant strain quivered and bunched on their shoulders. The lot of them were stumbling regularly now. It ripped at my heart when we clattered across the frozen Fishing Gut without halting to rest and water them.

The snow ceased, but the wind, ever a constant, chilling presence, grew colder as the afternoon light weakened. My toes, damp and clammy inside boots soaked through from the outside, had little feeling in them. Odd it was how the increasing cold was welcome higher on my frame where it numbed the pain of palm cut and severed joint.

A short jaunt beyond the Fishing Gut, Nathan Breed pointed at the eastern skyline and emitted a trilling whistle. An elongated gray smudge stretched far downwind beneath the low-hanging cloud cover. It was smoke from the many chimneys of Limestone.

Though perhaps only wild speculation, the prospect of a seat in front of a roaring fire with the lasses of Monet's Roadhouse serving their wondrous rum toddies provided the surge of determination our flagging spirits needed. Sam Moon, the short coupled Virginian, was suddenly extolling the friendly and generous virtues of the river village he'd derided twenty odd days ago as the ideal haven for dull louts, blasphemers, and bearers of long rifles who consid-

ered smiling a sin and killing on insult an act ordained by
the Lord Almighty solely for Kentuckians. Our yips and
shouts excited the horses, and ears pricked and twitching,
the gelding, veteran of many campaigns with the deceased
Major Fowler, thrust his head high and followed doggedly
in my tracks, tugging the rest along behind him.

The ferry landing we sought was a wooden platform
twenty feet square supported by oak pickets sunk into the
riverbank. Abutting the rear of the dock were the charred
ruins of a small cabin built to shelter ferrymen during the
day hours. The heavy timbers of the dock had to date resisted frequent redstick torchings.

No cable or permanent structure connected the landing
with Limestone across the wide channel of the Ohio. The
ferry consisted of oared bateaux the Fagan brothers and
their rag-tail cousins rowed each direction on demand. Not
being hollow twixt the ears, the Fagans favored passengers
who conducted their business heavily armed, never over-
nighted on the Ohio bank, and, in winter, when the weather
made crossings doubly difficult, operated only the Limestone end of the ferry.

Upon our arrival, the captain detailed Askell to guard
our incoming path, dispatched the bluecoats to gather wood
from the ruins for a fire downwind of the dock platform,
and with Breed, mounted the platform himself, the major's
spyglass firmly in his grasp, leaving me free to care for the
horses.

Slipping downstream, I located a slot through the ragged
drifts and ice cavities clogging the riverbank. The opening
was too narrow and treacherous for the exhausted animals,
and lacking leather or wooden vessels of any sort, I carried
water to them in my hat. It was an arduous task that went
slowly till the bluecoats had their fire started and Jaimie
Crown made his legs and tricorn available. After the watering, we worked the horses around the bluecoat fire and
situated them in the lee of the cabin's charred walls out of
most of the wind.

"Wish we had feed for them," Jaimie lamented from

alongside the roan mare's lame foreleg. He reached and patted her neck. "I hope this one recovers. She never quit on herself. Mike Layton would love her."

"Why's that?" I asked, curious despite how anxious I was to warm my frozen parts.

"She's a horse breeder. She talks of nothing else. You should see her blood bay stallion, Red Boy. They'd make a great pair, this lady and Mike's stud."

Quiet as Jaimie normally was, his statement was for him a lengthy speech, indicating he shared my fascination regarding Hump Layton's daughter. I was on the verge of asking him a host of questions, and would have, had I not wriggled my toes and felt nothing whatsoever, sign I didn't thaw them they might well be lost to the surgeon's knife. "Come along, Jaimie. I don't stick my feet to the fire, I'll have Noah loppin' dead meat offen me in the mornin'!"

Not the least bashful my woolen socks were holed fore and aft, I plopped bum foremost before the bluecoat's crackling logs, shucked my boots, and began rubbing with both hands. Old Ash Cooper had done more than lend me his last name and drive me whip-hard for seven years twice over. He'd also forgotten twice what others knew about sustaining yourself in woodlot and barnyard. From him, I'd learned to rub sensation into cold skin before subjecting my limbs to the heat of the fire. He'd never explained why he understood such things, and I'd known not to delay my chores with inquiries he always ignored. With old Ash, the popping of sweat was talk a-plenty.

Lacking vittles for the pan as well as the pan itself, the bluecoats scalded river water in tin cups from their haversacks and flavored it with crumbled chocolate from a muslin bag belonging to Sam Moon. Noah offered me a cup of the brown brew, and I delved into my coat pocket for the jerk I'd squirreled away that morning and shared with him and the others. It wasn't much, but those few measly bites of dried meat seemed a veritable feast.

Nathan Breed stepped beside Jaimie and held his hands over the flame. "Heap on the logs, me lads. Captain wants a bigger fire. They ain't noticed us from yonder yet.''

"What about tryin' a volley with our muskets?" Noah suggested.

"Useless as teats on a gelding with the wind blowin' liken it is. The sound would travel downriver where there ain't nobody to hear it," Breed responded, withdrawing his hands. "I'm off to trade places with Askell afore his vitals are too far gone. Cooper, report to the captain."

I pulled boots still wet over feet at least dry and somewhat warm and circled the fire. Hump Layton occupied the extreme outer edge of the dock, spyglass trained across the Ohio. In the waning hours of afternoon, the river was a broad expanse of black from which chunks of ice protruded like the white teeth of gigantic fish feeding from below the surface. On the far bank, beyond bulky ledges of limestone that rose at water's edge, cabins, warehouses, barns, and wagon yards huddled beneath a pall of dirty gray smoke. To the plain eye, no movement showed around the flatboats moored at the public landing or along the winding, snow-packed streets of the village.

Hump Layton lowered his spyglass with a sigh of exasperation. "Jumpin' almighty, don't you Kentuckians walk down an' spit in the river in the evenin'?"

"We mostly save that pleasure for summer when the spit don't freeze in the air an' fall short of the water."

The captain laughed for the first time since the previous evening and passed the spyglass to me. "It's yer home, not mine. Sooner or later, someone'll notice our fire. Maybe you can decipher who it is an' tell if they've enough brains to turn out the taverns."

I centered the round lens of the telescope on the public landing and scanned left, then right. A few people did walk the streets here and there. Not a soul evinced any interest in the Ohio. We might as well have been observing them from the shore of a faraway sea.

I missed the bobbing stick figure the initial sweep, but not the second. No other person in Limestone walked with that peculiar bobbing gait except Ned Henry, another peg legger. There was, howsomever, no mistaking which one moved yonder. Where Ned Henry was thick bodied, his stable roustabout, Pratt Jackson, was rail thin, and Pratt's flowing white mane and full beard of like color shone in the winnowing daylight bright as a six-candle lanthorn.

"The Lord has smiled upon us," I announced.

"Has he now?"

"Yes, sir, he has," I repeated. "Pratt Jackson's thumpin' for Clegg's Tavern smack on the waterfront for his evenin' tankard. He long hunted over most of Kentucky when he had two whole legs. He won't miss our fire," I boldly predicted.

I let out breath to steady the telescope. My chest tightened the closer Pratt drew to the limestone stoop of the tavern. His thirst being paramount, he looked neither right nor left. My heart missed a beat as he reached for the latchstring. Then his good foot was beyond the stoop. He was on the brink of making me a liar. At that moment, with his eyes seemingly averted, his chin whipped sideways, his body stiffened like the soldier drawing to attention, and he stared plumb into my glass.

Never one to doubt his eyesight, Pratt spun on his pegged leg, shoved the tavern door open wide, and the bounce of his white mane revealed he was shouting within. Two bodies, both square as they were tall and topped by high-crowned, broad-brimmed hats, shoved around Pratt and halted on his flanks. It could be none other than Cletis and Narum Fagan, for their oversized hats were intended as a show of wealth to offset the truth that their ferrying kept them but a meal shy of the alms house and starvation.

"They've spotted our fire," I fair shouted, Pratt and the Fagans dancing in my lens. I tightened my grip. A brass tube extended from the face of the Fagan at Pratt's left elbow. "They've put a glass on us, Captain. We best make all the fuss we can!"

Hump Layton swept behind me. "On yer feet, Virginians, they're aware somebody's over here. Form a line with weapons twixt the fire an' the bank!"

The bluecoats, weariness and tired limbs less of a burden in their excitement, scampered into position. "All right," the captain bawled, "off with them tricorns, and at my order, let's wave 'em liken the finest wench in Limestone's ridin' past wearin' less than a blush from ribboned hair to her ankles. Wave, lads, wave!"

Taproom patrons poured from Clegg's. They surrounded Pratt and the Fagans, overflowing the tavern stoop. Hands and arms gestured wildly. The crowd was obviously debating who had started the fire at the ferry. Pratt would be trying to convince them it could be only the Brandon survey party, but I could discern no beginning movement in our direction. "They need some proddin', Captain, an' quick."

Hump Layton showed me a fist and turned back to the waving bluecoats. In rapid succession, he ordered their tricorns replaced and their muskets raised high. The captain added a round from his own weapon to their volley.

The flash of exploding powder, clearly visible to any telescope against the dark smoke of the burning logs, stirred a new wave of discussion across the way. The Fagan with the glass, probably the overbearing Narum, lifted an arm, fingers spread for quiet. Quarter of a minute later, men sprinted toward every point of the compass.

"They're on the fly now," I said and beamed.

Hump Layton chuckled. "They figured ain't no Injuns gonna wave white men's hats and waste their powder. How long afore they reach us?"

"Won't be dark yet when they do," I answered. "Allowin' for the current, they'll likely beach down the bank a piece."

Four bateaux were launched from north of the Limestone landing. The Fagan boats, square as their owners at the corners, raked at bow and stern, and propelled by four oarsmen, held at capacity eight passengers each. Of the four bound our direction, two appeared fully manned and bristled with rifle barrels. If the situation required any of our would-be rescuers to spend the night on what many

considered a hostile shore despite the village and its inhabitants directly opposite, the Limestone boys refused to be
caught grasping the bloody half of the stick.

Hump Layton dismissed the bluecoats and waited patiently beside me. He didn't ask for the return of the telescope and I maintained a constant vigil on the progress of
the bateaux.

"Yer Ned Henry aboard anywheres?" he inquired.

The question jarred me. I hadn't thought of meeting up
with the boss man till I rapped on his office door later that
evening or at dawn tomorrow. I scanned each craft with
great care. No Ned Henry, not at least in any of the bow
sections.

"Somethin' big sailin' from Limestone Creek," the captain observed.

I tilted the telescope and the blunt bow of a Kentucky
flatboat overwhelmed the eye of the lens. The Kentucky
was confirmation Ned Henry was on the prowl. He would
be hell bent to lay hold of his prize packhorses, and since
that flatboat now out into the Ohio's current would transport the eight animals I'd departed with, Ned Henry was
expecting to recover the full complement. I groaned. I
would hop to the fiddler's choice before the sun was down.

"It might be wise to warm yer feet again while you have
the chance," Hump Layton suggested.

Totally consumed with what I would say to Ned Henry,
I agreed, relinquished the telescope, and plodded from the
dock platform. Logs settled and popped, spewing sparks
that sizzled in the melted snow ringing the fire. I slipped
in amongst the bluecoats and warmed the whole of me.
Noah and his companions attempted several times to engage me in conversation, but I'd no interest in idle chatter
and drifted over to check on the horses before I became
boorish and offended their hospitality.

Damn, how I hated owning up to failure. Never before
had I disappointed the boss man by falling short of his
expectations. He had come to trust me with the freighting
of the most expensive goods and supplies whether by pack-

saddle or wagon. He had brushed aside the objections and resentment of older, more seasoned string riders and wagoners and placed me in charge. And unlike my years bound to Ash Cooper, and before him Hiram Fell, the sweat Ned Henry extracted from my young hide earned proper pay and proper praise. It was a source of immeasurable pride that I'd never given him cause to raise his voice to me or add to the scars on my back side with whip or knotted rope. But I feared all that would change, perhaps forever, soon as he learned how poorly I'd fared following his most recent orders. I was to watch over Cam Downing. Cam was dead. I was to bring the Henry horses home none the worse for their sojourn across the Ohio. Buck, the finest of lead horses, plus five additional head of stock, were absent from the evening picket line. And if those two horrendous revelations didn't enflame the boss man's temper, every single Henry packsaddle had been discarded during our march from Eagle Creek.

I squatted before the blackened wall of the ferry cabin. My cheek lolled against the fore end of the Bedford propped twixt my knees. Damn, how I hoped Ned Henry wouldn't regret giving me his rifle.

Cheering from the bluecoats, then they went running downriver. The bateaux had started their landings. Hump Layton strode from the platform and halted at the fire. I stayed with the horses. I didn't need to seek Ned Henry. He would flush me like the trained hound after a game bird.

The wind had finally fallen off. In the burgeoning twilight, purple streaks eked through thinning clouds. A hollow boom—wood bow meeting solid crust of ice—drifted upriver. The Kentucky flatboat had landed. Shouts to make lines fast sang out. My hands were suddenly shaking, my throat raw and parched; I didn't think I could spit on a bet.

Though the swing of the wooden leg was more pronounced, the fast-moving shape that hove into view from below the fire walked with the same bobbing gait of Pratt Jackson. Ned Henry couldn't outrun many men, but he could walk at their shoulder and seldom lose ground. Few realized outside of Pratt and me that the boss man's short-ened limb had never completely healed. I knew it because I'd interrupted him late at night pouring blood from the leather sling that cupped his stump. Pain was the constant companion of Ned Henry and he bore it without complaint. He was stout as cured hickory wood and demanded as much from himself as he did those in his hire. You did business with the packhorse king of Limestone, you best reckon with him in every detail, for as Pratt warned, "The Lord will pick Ned Henry to command the guard at his second coming. Thataway, only those with an invite will be seated in the pews."

I heard the captain greet Ned Henry. After that, I was removed enough from the fire what they said was too faint for me to overhear. They conferred at length, the boss man and the big spy, Hump Layton, as evidenced by his frequent nods, doing most of the gabbing. Then, my feet cold as ever and my nerves raw as freshly cut meat, Ned Henry tromped toward the horses, the metal tip of his wooden leg spearing a purchase through ice and snow at each bobbing stride.

I sidled around the mare into the open and he thudded to a stop two paces from where I waited. With the fire behind him, his pox-scarred features were shadowy in the fading twilight and hard to read. "Well, Fell," he said, "you've had your grand adventure and, thankfully, you're not too much the worse for it."

He was looking past me at the horses, what there was of them, counting heads for sure. The fact I detected no anger in his tone didn't settle my nerves any. My mouth felt as if it were full of dry sand. Calm down, goddamnit, I chided myself, he ain't no knife-bearing Shawnee for chrissake.

"Short animals, are we?" Ned Henry queried, his tone now a tad impatient.

Desperation mounting, I worked up spit and pried my tongue loose from the roof of my mouth. "Couldn't be helped, Mister Henry," I stammered, "couldn't be helped."

Growing darkness or no, I saw the sudden scowl that knotted his brow. "Relax, you young bucko, I'll not hold you at fault for what has happened. Why would I do that?"

"Why not, sir? Cam's dead, all but two of the horses are lost, an' the packsaddles are rottin' somewhere in the snow," I managed, the words tumbling atop each other. "I've nothin' worth the sayin' to report. I've failed at every turn."

Ned Henry's hefty frame bent at the waist. "Belay that," he snarled, "before you rile me proper."

I locked my jaws fast. I'd no excuse for my failings and Ned Henry detested whiners and carpers. My sole hope was that he might yet, by some undeserved miracle, spare me the full measure of his wrath. Much as I hated the thought, mucking stables for the balance of the years I owed him appealed far more than being shown the cobbles, forced to scrabble on my own once I'd spent General Brandon's gold coins. Any borderer with a modicum of sense dreaded finding himself destitute, bedless, and hungry in the throes of the Kentucky winter.

A sigh coursed through Ned Henry. "I believe Hump Layton has conveyed an accurate account of your tryst with the savages. It was Cam's ill fortune he took that ball in a vital spot. And in losing the pack train, or the most of it, you did so in a manner so bold and daring Layton swears you prolonged the lives of those about you. That's the truth of it, is it not?"

Hope flared within me. Hump Layton and Ned Henry's spinning of the same top outshone mine a heap and then some. Maybe I wasn't poised with one boot on the cobbles waiting for the other to fall. Much of the sand beneath my tongue melted and I forced out, "Yes, sir, it be," with sufficient flourish he at least knew I was listening with both ears.

Ned Henry stroked his heavy moustache with a curled thumb. "Fell, I'm not prone to unnecessary discourses, but we need an understanding twixt us. I'll not have you fearing me. I admit I'm the devil's own sonofabitch when protecting my interests. That doesn't make me a tyrant with no feelings for others," he asserted. "Contrary to what the rumheads and lickspittles spout, I don't expect any man in my pay to sacrifice himself saving my stock, be it one head or twenty. Horses are plentiful and fairly cheap to buy; good men are neither. Frankly, I'm right pleased you're not lying back there somewheres with the glory bound. Hump Layton bragged of how you acquitted yourself in commendable fashion fighting the enemy at close quarters, and I couldn't be prouder were you tied to me by blood."

Compliments having been lean as sunshine at midnight in my twenty years, Ned Henry's high praise, particularly his mentioning of me in the same breath with family kin, flabbergasted and elated me all at once. The door opening onto that cobbled road to nowhere had just latched with Fell Cooper still welcome at the hearth. Nothing, not even the wealth of kings, could have pleased me more that evening, and my whistling sign of relief set me and Ned Henry to grinning at each other.

My sole regret was that I never did get to thank the boss man for his flattery. Call Hardy and Will Devol saw to that. Those two Henry wagoners, anxious to board the horses and complete our departure before the dimming twilight succumbed to full darkness, barged across from the bluecoat fire, curtailing any further exchange twixt us. It was probably best they did so, for the last thing I wanted was to appear ungrateful or overblown with my own importance. I had gained too much favor with my master to risk a setback by misspeaking. Old Ash Cooper, it was, preached that the wise soul respected the hand that fed him while the vain buffoon starved.

"The Fagan brothers are chompin' at the bit," Cal Hardy informed us. "They ain't fond of rowin' at night with ice in the river."

"Neither am I," Ned Henry admitted. "The both of you grab a lead rope. The gangplank been laid down?"

"Yes, sir, it has," Cal assured him.

The boss man fisted the gelding's lead rope. "Then come

along. Our business on this side of the river is finished for the winter."

"What about Cam and the other bodies?" I protested. "Hump Layton promised they'd be recovered for burial tomorrow morning?"

Will Devol parted with a stream of brown tobacco juice. "They's gonna be. That big spy and Simon Kenton agreed Simon and his rangers are stayin' behind with three of the bateaux. The Fagans ain't happy riskin' their boats, but Layton's bigger'n them and his gold's yeller," Will related, chuckling.

"That satisfy you, Fell?" asked Ned Henry.

I turned the roan mare and headed her away from the ferry cabin. "Yes, sir. Cam wasn't laid to rest properly, I couldn't sleep with the fret of it."

"Neither could I," the boss man concurred. "The ground thaws, we'll have words said over him by the preacher. I'll not have Cam meet his maker seeming he wasn't appreciated."

I thanked him on Cam's behalf and tugged on the mare's lead rope. Her first limping step didn't escape Ned Henry's close scrutiny. "That looks bad," he judged. "She's well put together, but is she worth the bother with that sprung leg?"

I patted the roan's neck, recalling Jaimie Crown's earlier comments. "She's all heart. She'll heal just fine. Nobody claims her, she'll birth some fine colts for us."

Ned Henry chuckled then. "Bygod, Fell, spoken like an experienced horse trader. You might make us both rich yet."

And with that, we slipped past Kenton and the bulk of his rangers, who now circled the bluecoat fire. Out beyond the edge of the firelight, hatted shadows black against white snow revealed where the other Kenton men were posted as sentries. The opposite direction, out on the river, pale oars flashed against black water as the bateau ferrying Layton and the Virginians fought the drag of the current. Ahead loomed the flatboat, cleated boarding plank extending from

its starboard gunwale to the bank. Emil Smith, the size of
Hump Layton above the waist but graced with a foot less
height, anchored the bow hawser while Shorty Crothers,
four inches shorter and fifty pounds lighter, did likewise
with the aft hawser. The strain of snubbing the flatboat flush
to the bank bathed their foreheads with sweat despite the
freezing air.

Cal Hardy and Will Devol adding their weight and
strength to that of Emil and Shorty, the boss man and I
loaded the horses, all of which were too whipped and weak
from hunger to be frightened of the sway and creak of the
gangplank. The mare hesitated at the hull end of the
wooden ramp, then gathered herself and jumped, striking
the deck on three hooves without further injury. In less time
than it required for Ned Henry, peg leg thrust sideways and
hopping from rung to rung on his whole limb, to scale the
ladder accessing the roof of the stern cabin and the tiller,
the animals were feeding contentedly at the cane-filled
racks hanging from the bow's flat nose. Needless to say,
many stables were less accommodating than Henry horse
boats.

The launch was a practiced feat. The boss man at the
steering oar, Cal and Will freed Emil and Shorty from the
hawsers. The two blacksmiths, heavy footed as drayage
stock, thundered across the gangplank. Rushing aft, they
scooped long poles fitted with iron hooks from guys bolted
into the cabin wall, leaned over the gunwale, and spiked
the hooks into the ice covering the bank. At the boss man's
shout the boat was secured, Cal and Will dropped the hawsers and boarded. Soon as their boots touched the deck, the
wagoners swung the boarding ramp about and tied it off.
A few grunting shoves from the pole bearers and we floated
clear of the bank. The wagoners then manned the broad-
horns at the front corners of the cabin roof to help steer us
for the Kentucky shore. The mean, wet task of warping the
tethering hawsers aboard at bow and stern fell to the blacksmiths.

"Red fire yonder a mile downstream," Cal yelled.

"That'll be Pratt and the lads from Clegg's the Fagans couldn't transport," Ned Henry said. "They'll have victuals and toddies hot and ready when we reach them. Bear to port, gentlemen, bear to port."

The will to stand upright for even one more moment deserted me like a jug emptying. I leaned my shoulders against the cabin facing and slid downward, paying the cold deck that chilled my arse cheeks through my coat no nevermind. A chilled bum was no real discomfort compared to the renewed throbbing of my wounded hand and the cramps kinking my muscles into lumps that bulged the hide of my breeches. I leaned the Bedford alongside me and kneaded my legs from hip to ankle.

I decided then and there I wanted no further involvement with General Brandon's harebrained land scheme; leastways, not till General Wayne and his legion soldiers subdued the Shawnee and their allies once and for all. Others could risk their necks winning the glory and becoming the hero. Others could chance their lifeblood trying to impress the likes of Rebecca Brandon and Michaela Layton, fabulously pretty though they must be. I was quite content to await the outcome of the war for the Ohio wilderness quartered at the Henry Yard, well fed, warmly bedded, and free of fear. So what if the nights were lonely as all get out. Give me sweat and horse apples over blood, lust, and death anytime, thank you, please.

God forbid, how ridiculous and laughable that vow would shortly prove. But then, it's the truly young man, ain't it now, who believes he can deny the unseen maiden what she is determined to possess.

FALLING
LEAF MOON

October 1793

9

"They're here! They're here!"

Pratt Jackson's peg leg, dragging the ground such was his hurry, stirred dust on the parched earth fronting the Henry smithy. "They're here, Fell! They're here!"

Without any sign I had heard him, I lifted the glowing horseshoe from the forge fire with my tongs and centered the flange of the shoe on the anvil. I looked at my work and ignored Pratt, my hammer rising and falling in measured blows as I shaped the hot iron. My deliberate indifference rankled the old roustabout to no end. His greatest pleasure was passing news unbeknownst to his audience.

"By damned, I'll find Mister Henry," Pratt threatened, jutting his white bearded face at me. "He'll pay for what I'd give a friend free!"

I dipped the horseshoe in the slack tub and rested my hammer on the anvil. His contention Ned Henry would pay for his information roused my curiosity. "All right, who's here? It must be President Washington his ownself the lather you're in."

My attention secured for his grand pronouncement, Pratt

hooked his thumbs in the waistband of his canvas overalls and gathered wind, clacking his loose-fitting wooden teeth together. Pratt mashed rather than chewed his food, a messy endeavor every meal, and the chest of his linen frock bore witness to what he'd eaten since last washing that garment (sometime in the spring if my memory was correct).

"It ain't no damn president, for chrissake. It's more important folks than that," he corrected. "The whole wharf crowd fought each other for just a peek at 'em."

He fell silent, grinning much as he dared without chancing the loss of his false teeth. I played along, letting him have his fun for sufficient moments, then cocked my brow and tapped the anvil with my hammer.

"It's the Brandon women, the general's wife an' daughter," Pratt revealed. "You've never seen the likes. Hair black as midnight, skin white as fresh cream, lips red as wild strawberries. Sweet Jesus, weren't a man there couldn't help starin' stupid as sheep too ignorant to walk in outen the rain."

Pratt paused, savoring my interest in what he had to say. Their curiosity also roused, Emil Smith and Shorty Crothers stepped from the storage shed where they were sorting bar stock. "Git on with it," Shorty urged Pratt. "What'd the local gals think of the Brandon ladies?"

"What few Limestone lasses was there didn't care squat about their beauty. They was too busy cluckin' over their velvet cloaks and silk shoes. The general's wife even wears a mask that covers her nose an' cheeks so she don't take too much sun," Pratt advised.

"Must've been pretty tame after that, oncet you stared awhile," dour Emil reckoned.

"Naw, it wasn't," Pratt shot back. "The Brandon ladies wound through the crowd an' afore they was gone from sight, the last of the four flatboats tied up, sparkin' hubbub louder'n ever."

"An' why was that?" the impatient Shorty asked.

"There was another woman on that horse boat that beat anythin' to hit the landin' afore her," Pratt answered.

The old roustabout was known to exaggerate on occasion and Emil glared down his nose at him. "How was that? She have two heads and three feet?"

"Naw, you idjit, she was different 'cause she wasn't dressed liken no woman," Pratt explained with mounting excitement. "She was wearin' half boots, breeches, a green waistcoat, an' had her hair stuffed inside a flop-brimmed hat, she did."

"Then how'd you know she weren't no man?" the disbelieving Emil demanded.

Pratt could hardly contain his excitement. His audience now hung on his every utterance, and to ensure we'd understand him clearly the first try, he extracted his loose uppers and waved a dripping wedge of carved teeth at us as he continued. "It wasn't plain straight off. It happened when she went to givin' the poor devil at the steerin' oar holy hell for somethin' he done or said. She took to standin' with her hands on her hips an' the way she bulged out the front of her shirt left no doubt she was female. I swear she couldn't't've buttoned that waistcoat round herself for all the gold in Limestone," Pratt concluded. His laugh was a gummy giggle. "Course, more'n one of them watchin' mouthed he'd part with whatever she asked for a try at buttonin' her coat for her!"

"All right, she's buxom as a milk cow," Emil allowed. "But that don't count for flies on the same cow's behind if'n she's witch ugly. Well, is she?"

"I don't believe so. I never did see her 'thout that flop-brimmed hat, but from what I saw of her when she led that blood bay stallion across the gangplank they throwed down, she don't pain nobody's eyes. She—"

"Say again about the stallion," I interrupted.

"He's a blood bay with blazed face an' white stockings. Crowd or no, he followed her onto the landin' tame as you please. Why?"

"What's this gal's name? Didn't somebody yell it out?"

"Naw, if'n they did, I didn't hear it. 'Sides, I left to come an' tell you about all the fuss. Maybe we amble over

along the road to Monet's, we can find out who she be,''
Pratt suggested.

''No need for that,'' I replied firmly, laying my hammer
atop the anvil. ''I already know her name.''

It was Pratt's turn to suffer an attack of curiosity. ''How?
You ain't never been anywheres near her,'' he countered,
hastily replacing his wooden uppers.

''I don't need meet her. There can't be two women on
the whole Ohio who would dare dress like a man and also
happen to own a blood bay stud. Cam hadn't been killed,
he would've mentioned her time and again at the supper
table. It's Hump Layton's daughter, Michaela. Everybody
calls her Mike.''

''Don't grab the halter too quick, me lad,'' Shorty threw
in. ''No matter how she dresses or what they call her, I
can't believe that rump-ugly Hump Layton sired a girl child
whose looks don't scare a soul into next week. Maybe she
don't tempt you to come runnin' for a gander at her an'
her stallion. It ain't the same with me. I'm a-goin' with
Pratt here. Maybe there won't be another like her, ever.
Ain't been one afore that I can remember, has there now?''

''I can't fault what you're saying,'' Emil acknowledged.
''Have yer wash, Fell, an' we'll trust Pratt told his story
straight an' won't disappoint us.''

Outnumbered three to one, I could hardly do other than
join them. Besides, spying from afar was free and harmless.
I angled across the dusty ground, my destination the water
trough bordering the stock pen. Peeling off my shirt, I
ducked my head into the cooling water and splashed my
arms and shoulders, the initial drops plopping on my boot
toes dark with grime.

Behind me, the shortest route to intercept Michaela Layton spawned a rambling argument among Pratt and the
blacksmiths. Their jawboning, profane and raucous, ceased
with the abruptness of a pistol shot. I stayed my washing,
puzzled that the three of them had quieted at once. Then
Pratt gasped aloud, ''Best check the main gate, tough knots,
our prey's on a hunt of her own.''

I brushed damp hair from my eyes and done as the old roustabout recommended, not bothering to reclaim my shirt from the fence rail. The real truth of Pratt's tale bearing was about to unfold for one and all.

The Henry Yard sprawled on Limestone Creek's west bank inland a quarter mile from the river cove that created a harbor and landing for Limestone itself. A wall of ten-foot-high pickets surrounded the stock pen, roofed horse stalls, wagon barn, forge shed, log crew quarters with rope beds for a dozen men, and a smaller log structure housing the boss man's office. Entry to the Yard was achieved through a double gate opposite the creek bank wide enough to admit Allegheny freight wagons.

The gates were ajar and in the opening stood a blood bay stallion. He was, as stud horses go, a magnificent specimen—lengthy and clean of limb, deep in chest and shoulder, upright in haunch, and level of back. The stallion tossed his mane and snorted, a mass of muscle, bone, and power held in check by a firm rein in a trained hand.

Astride him, riding without benefit of saddle, was a hatted individual outfitted, not surprisingly, in half boots, breeches, green waistcoat, and flop-brimmed hat. The hat revolved right and left in sweeping arcs, the rider examining all about her, appraising what might possibly confront her while still not committed to advancing beyond the gate.

Apparently satisfied the situation lent itself to her desires, Michaela Layton touched the stallion gently with her heels and he pranced forward. Pratt and the smiths waited much nearer the gate than I, so once through the opening, she reined the stud sideways, placing the three gawking Henry employees close upon her left flank. With a sunny smile, Michaela Layton then asked, "Where, gentlemen, may Fell Cooper be found?"

Pratt, totally entranced with her, recovered his senses enough to point at me with a bony finger. "That be he, mistress. Him with his chest bare and wet."

Hump Layton's daughter peered my direction, slid from the stallion in a belly-down dismount, and passed the stud's reins to the gawking Pratt. The old roustabout's description hadn't done Michaela Layton justice in one main regard. Her height, quite evident now, was astonishing. She was assuredly the tallest female I'd ever encountered. Measuring her against the lanky Pratt, she towered within four inches of my six feet, the obvious offspring of a near giant.

Like her father, Michaela walked with a light foot—each smooth step raising the merest hint of dust. If Pratt had failed to mention her unusual height, he had been square on the mark where her bust was concerned. She filled a shirt as fully as any woman ever would. And I was remiss in slighting Pratt and the smiths for their gawking. Maybe my mouth wasn't hanging open, but I was so overawed watching her approach me, I completely forgot I was half-undressed.

She stopped walking well shy of the water trough. Slim fingers rose and removed the flop brimmed hat, freeing a cascade of honey brown hair. Her skin, unlike the creamy white attributed to the Brandon women, was deeply tanned from frequent exposure to sun and wind. She seemed in no hurry whatsoever and studied me with hazel eyes as frank as those of her father.

I owed neither the Brandons nor anyone else tied to their coattails additional service, and leery of any new demand for men and horses that might entail crossing the Ohio, I waited silently while Michaela Layton examined me with the thoroughness Ned Henry reserved for breeding stock. When it came, the sunny smile was disarming as a blush, and those probing hazel eyes livened with the curling of her lips. "I'm Mike Layton, Mister Cooper, and I must admit you're everything my father told me to expect. He did not, however, warn me you greet strangers newly scrubbed and shirtless."

I probably matched a blood red sunset everywhere she spied bare hide on me. That I couldn't help. But with the deed done, I stubbornly refused to panic and give her the pleasure of seeing me scramble to cover my nakedness. I did make damn certain I didn't forget my manners: Who knew when I might run onto her huge father again. "Ladies seldom have reason to visit the Henry Yard, Mistress Layton. I sincerely hope I haven't offended you."

"You may call me Mike, and you needn't apologize. I'm not offended. Meeting you has brightened an otherwise dull afternoon," she offered with another smile. "Other men should have as much to offer."

Her boldness was as stunning as it was embarrassing. But I didn't redden as before. She was enjoying the discomfort of a total stranger caught in an awkward situation not entirely of his making, and her seeming arrogance riled my dander to the quick.

She saw me stiffening everywhere. Her mouth flattened and she lifted an open hand with the palm facing me. "I'm very sorry, Mister Cooper, if I've insulted you. I meant no harm, really. Sometimes I'm too forward for my own friends. Perhaps you'd best cover yourself, then we'll both be more comfortable while we talk of why I'm here . . . if you please?"

Her apology tempered my anger, and with an agreeing nod, I stepped backward. A rather clumsy reach behind me without turning fully about secured my shirt from the fence rail. I spared nothing worming into that linen garment. It was purely pride on my part, but I didn't want Michaela Layton to spy the ragged scars crisscrossing my back side from shoulders to waist. Once revealed, evidence of the oldest flogging inevitably prompted questions as to the sufferer's character and trustworthiness. Whether I ever saw this tall, full-blown girl again, I wouldn't have Hump Layton's daughter think poorly of me, not if I could help it.

Michaela Layton's smile returned as I thumbed home the neck button of my shirt. She glanced briefly at Pratt and his burly companions. "Your white-bearded friend probably told you I'm accompanying General Brandon's wife and daughter. We're bound for the general's new station with all we own and have need of pack animals for the carry from the river. We wish to employ you and your horses. Are you for hire?"

There it was, plain as a message written in stone, exactly what I feared she would ask. A single wrong word and I was headed across the Ohio risking my hair at the bidding of others. I was determined that greed wouldn't get the best of me again, no matter how much Michaela Layton appealed to me. And appeal she did. The beat of my heart rang in my ears harsh as a smith's hammer striking iron. Sweat dampened my palms. It was all I could manage not to pant aloud. She was the looker whom lonely men dreamed about and never met. Till now!

"Well, Mister Fell Cooper, are you for hire?" Michaela repeated, patient as ever.

I should have said no straight off. Had I done that, she might have departed prior to the arrival of a second visitor to the Henry Yard, the one who turned that autumn afternoon sour and nasty. But I was so enjoying her mere presence, I couldn't bring myself to send her away. Thunderation, talk about holing your own ship.

"Why me?" I asked, biding for time.

"Why, my father, of course. When he left Pittsburgh in May with General Brandon and the building crew, he insisted I seek you out upon our arrival. I'm here on my father's orders to hire Fell Cooper and only Fell Cooper. If that surprises you, it shouldn't. Father holds you in extremely high regard. Quite frankly, I suspect he believes you will watch over me as you do your horses."

Call it contrariness if you like, I couldn't resist asking, "That doesn't please you, mistress?"

She fiddled with the brim of her hat. "Father worries too much," Michaela claimed. "I'm not a reckless child in need of protection morning and night. My wolfhound is chained aboard the stock boat. Once we land at Eagle Creek, he will be with me every step. And my horse Red Boy can outrun anything alive."

That was true, all right, providing she traveled the post roads of Virginia where few Shawnee dared show themselves nowadays. Though I could easily have argued her stallion wasn't likely to outrun a Shawnee ball were she to encounter the redsticks, I didn't bother. She was as prideful and stubborn as I. And nothing less than an actual Injun fright would convince her how dangerous the wilds of Ohio remained outside the walls of the general's new station.

Michaela's hat flicked against her thigh, hinting her patience was at last on the wane, and I said mild as could be, "It's the wrong season for your party, I'm afraid. All our strings are off carting winter supplies south to Lexington, a mighty big undertaking."

"When will they return?" she inquired.

"Not for another week," I predicted. "An' I'm sure you won't want to wait that long. There are other trains for hire. The Fagan brothers bought animals from the boss man, Mister Henry, just a month gone. You might—"

Pratt Jackson's bellow of "Whoa there by damned!" cut me off and spun Michaela on her heels. She was, I knew, concerned something disturbed her stallion. Pratt's shout, howsomever, wasn't intended for Red Boy.

Hooves thudded near the yard gate. A black gelding bearing a rider dressed in the same color from boots to tricorn swept around the old roustabout and slid to a stop within arm's length of Michaela. She stood her ground as dust welled high as her waist.

A face sharp of nose and chin leaned from the saddle. The voice was shrill and demanding. "Have the pack animals been secured?" Whoever he was, the rider expected an answer forthwith, for without hesitating, he barked, "Well, have they or not?"

Michaela Layton's head tilted back. Slim fingers reseated her flop-brimmed hat and carefully stuffed loose hair inside its crown. In her own sweet time, she said calmly, "No, they haven't. I've only started to bargain with Mister Cooper, Brice."

Our eyes locked together over Michaela's hat like clashing bayonets. Brice Fowler's gaze was entirely hostile and his narrow forehead, high cheekbones, cold dark eyes, and beaked nose brought to mind the hungry hawk ready to savage flesh from the carcass of his fallen prey. Make no mistake, Ned Henry's constant admonition that we shouldn't judge strangers in haste went wanting then and there. It was no strain whatsoever for me to instantly dislike the son of Major Asa Fowler.

"Perhaps I should finish the haggling, Mike," Brice suggested haughtily. "We Fowlers brook no unreasonableness from packhorsemen and wagoners. It isn't necessary."

My eyes never left him. To be fair, he was a sight to behold. A red feather adorned his black tricorn. The black cravat circling his neck was fastened by a silver clasp. Pewter buttons rowed the front of his black silk shirt. The sword scabbard slanting downward from his left hip seemed familiar. It was. The Fowler family crest shone brighter from frequent rubbings. At Brice's nether end, black riding boots polished to a burnished sheen encased the legs of black whipcord breeches. His riding habit, along with the tooled saddle and silver bit chains on the gelding's bridle, cost twice what I earned in the twelve month, four times that amount if the worth of his gelding was included. He was the perfect, overdressed dandy; prepared by wealth and station to trample roughshod any Limestone bumpkins daring to cross his benighted path. Or so he thought.

The words fair leaped from my mouth. "We've no animals for hire. If we did," I continued, "they wouldn't be available for the likes of you. Best try your luck elsewhere."

The knuckles of Brice Fowler's rein hand whitened. He rose slightly in the iron stirrups of the gelding's saddle, free hand slipping across his belly toward the hilt of his sword. It was a risky, trouble-brewing thing, my challenging him that way. But I couldn't resist doing so. I had withstood the bloodcurdling charge of the Shawnee. I had, in fact, had the brown arm of the enemy wrapped around my very throat. And after surviving that brush with certain death, I wasn't about to suffer needless insult from the tongue of a pompous fop in the presence of Hump Layton's daughter, even if he was armed and I wasn't.

Michaela saw Brice's arm slipping across his silk-shirted belly. "Brice, let it go. We—"

"Step aside," Brice interrupted, gripping the hilt of his sword. "I'll show this lout his proper place."

The sheathed blade started from its scabbard and I moved accordingly. Once he had the sword free, he would pin me against the fence with the gelding and bully me as he desired, perhaps kill me. I shoved Michaela clear, seized the gelding's bridle with left hand, stretched full length, and grabbed a fistful of black silk with the other.

Caught with his sword half-drawn, Brice Fowler resisted, pushing against the stirrups, but his legs were no match for forge-hardened muscle. He flew from the saddle headforemost and sailed clean over my shoulder. He landed on his chest, limbs pointing in all directions.

Dust rose in a cloud. It garnered no sympathy from me he was down and momentarily helpless. I ignored his choking coughs, placed a foot on his spine, and slid the long blade from the scabbard now wedged beneath his body. A hefty tug and the weapon was mine.

I made a mistake then, an error in judgment that almost cost me my life. I should have snapped that heavy blade in two over a raised knee. Instead, remembering the broadsword had belonged to his father, an officer whose courage I both admired and respected, I tossed the weapon beyond Brice's sprawled body where he could recover it later.

Our dismounted and prone dandy struggled upward and steadied himself on his knees. He was still choking and showed no inclination to engage me further, so I turned to see how Michaela Layton had fared after my violent shove. She was standing again, beating dust from the sleeves of her waistcoat. Her hazel eyes sparkled and I could have sworn the faintest of grins lurked at the corners of her lush mouth, the lower lip of which I noticed was full and particularly inviting. She wasn't the least flustered or upset Brice Fowler had received his comeuppance. 'Lest I missed my guess, amused and pleased was what she was, though she wasn't likely to say it aloud.

What followed happened in a wild flurry. Michaela's eyes flared wide and her mouth sprang open. Her warning shout wasn't noise yet as I took heed and whipped around to discover my fallen opponent was no longer unarmed.

Brice Fowler was upright and advancing toward me in a calculated rush, his speed afoot quite remarkable. In his leveled right arm, the recovered broadsword gleamed in the late afternoon sunlight, its killing point aimed straight at my unprotected belly hole. The brash bastard intended nothing less than to run me through. Sudden death was at my door, fingers tugging the latchstring.

The rifle barrel shot from nowhere. With all of the lunging Ned Henry's weight behind it, the barrel's jabbing muzzle struck Brice Fowler square in the center of the chest. His forward momentum arrested instantly, the dandy's sword arched skyward and his feet departed the ground like a bird lifting into flight. This go-round the major's son landed on his backside amidst dried manure with a bone-rattling crash that cost him every ounce of breath.

Though stunned to a fare-thee-well and moaning with pain, Brice Fowler retained his grip on the broadsword. As I should have, Ned Henry gave him his complete attention. He planted a booted foot on the dandy's wrist and dented the skin of Brice's throat with his rifle barrel. "Twitch, just twitch, and I'll gladly bury you for free."

Brice Fowler's sword hand slowly relaxed and opened. Rifle muzzle never budging an inch, Ned Henry bent and retrieved the long blade. His arm extended and he presented the weapon to an alert Michaela Layton hilt first. "You can return it once he's out of my yard."

From there, the boss man took charge as always. He shifted his weight onto his pegged leg, freeing Brice Fowler's wrist. "Emil," he called, "you and Shorty help this gentleman aboard his horse. He's had a rough afternoon."

Not about to be left idle, Pratt Jackson, cheeks flush from all the excitement, sat the dandy's lost tricorn on his head and the two smiths none too gently heaved him astride the gelding. Glaring at Ned Henry, Brice Fowler fisted the reins but held the gelding in check, for the boss man's rifle still covered him, indicating the afternoon's business was not yet complete.

The boss man first addressed Michaela Layton. "Pratt told me your name, mistress. I'm Ned Henry and I assume you're seeking animals to haul your possessions overland to Brandon Station."

"We are," Michaela concurred. "Fain Knott, our boat captain, says we have need of ten animals and three packers."

With every packhorse he owned presently carrying supplies south to Lexington, a chore that had emptied our stock pen of work animals, Ned Henry's response flabbergasted me. "You'll have them, and the men, too. Has your captain decided when you will sail?"

"He did. He preferred first light tomorrow, but the general's wife insisted she and the other women rest until noon. Mister Fowler," she said, nodding toward the rumpled dandy, "oversees the general's household and agreed we would abide by her wishes. So noon it is."

"Well and fine," Ned Henry said.

I could only stare at him. The earliest any of our pack strings would return was the end of the week, four days hence. The boss man, confident and untroubled, then addressed Brice Fowler.

"I've never set much store by apologies," Ned Henry stated, lowering his rifle. "But neither I nor my help harbor grudges. Since you speak for the general's wife, if you find my offer acceptable as does Mistress Layton, I'll have the required horses and men at the public landing prior to your noon sailing."

Brice Fowler's speech betrayed none of his pain. He would, I realized, always regain his feet with the supple skill of the thrown tomcat. "At this late hour I'd prefer not to scrounge for other beasts. I accept your offer in the general's name. He will expect the full cooperation of both you and your packers, every last one of them," the recovering dandy proclaimed, hawkish gaze lingering on me an extra beat. "If you fail to see us through to the station, you will forfeit double the monies due you. You will also tender full restitution for any property damaged or lost en route."

The boss man, ignoring the dandy's growing bluster, never hesitated. "Done, Mister Fowler," he agreed calmly, stepping from the gelding's path. "We will meet you on the morrow. Good day."

The outfoxed dandy, his claws cleverly pulled, had little choice as to his next move. He kneed the gelding past Ned Henry, "I'll meet you at Monet's, Mike" trailing over his shoulder. Dried manure rained from the rear of his black shirt as the gelding sped from the Henry Yard.

Pratt Jackson, once more in possession of Red Boy's reins, broke the silence first. He spoke slowly so his wooden teeth wouldn't clack together. "Fell, don't never show that bugger your back side. He's too mean for the Lord's heaven, an' the devil wouldn't take him in for fear he'd rule the roost."

The person best acquainted with the departed dandy took no issue with Pratt's coarse observation. "That's wise counsel, Mister Cooper. Never forget it. You'll be hard-pressed to have an enemy the equal of Brice," Michaela predicted, handing the Fowler family sword to Pratt. She then mounted her stallion with a quick hop and lithe swing of her leg. Her hazel eyes settled on the boss man. "Anything further, Mister Henry?"

"No, mistress, nothing of concern to you. It will be our pleasure to serve you. Fell, bring Pratt's mare out for him. He'll guide our guest to Monet's."

Not daring to protest a direct order, I stomped round the corner of the stock pen, mad as Hades. Why the ancient Pratt? I asked myself. Why not Fell Cooper? Holy hell, had the boss man suddenly gone blind? Was he too old to fathom how I was scenting up to Michaela Layton?

Where that was beyond question just yesterday, it didn't seem so now. Hadn't Ned Henry promised the Brandon party ten animals we didn't have? And other than me, where were the other two packhorsemen to be found? He certainly wasn't counting on Pratt and the two smiths. None of that trio had worked animals bearing freight down Limestone's Front Street, let alone forest trails no wider than a rider's stirrups.

Peeved as I was, I didn't act the spurned dimwit in front of everybody. I fetched Pratt's aging brown mare, saddled and bridled, even boosted him across her sagging middle and held my tongue when he nearly sliced off my ear with the Fowler sword for my trouble.

I stood with Ned Henry and the smiths and watched Pratt lead Michaela from the yard. Having witnessed my close call, she followed the brown mare at a discreet distance.

I might have dawdled there till dark, pondering my lost opportunity. But the boss man had other things on his mind, things he considered far more paramount than my budding feelings for Michaela Layton.

Guess who won out?

10

Ned Henry was a master of taking you to task. He left so little meat on your arse by the time he wound down, it made you appreciate the single consideration he extended the target of his anger: He never did in public what could be accomplished in his office.

He dismissed the two smiths with instructions for the preparation of the evening meal in Pratt's absence, then waved me after him. The slam of his pegged leg on the parched earth was all the warning I needed. And sure enough, soon as his office door swung shut behind me, he was off and yelling.

"For chrissake, Fell, haven't I taught you better than to fight with an armed man when you have no weapon of your own! The solitary reason you're not dead is that Brice Fowler's no smarter'n you. Instead of jerking his sword free an' slammin' you into the fence with his gelding and hackin' you to pieces, he gloated long enough you unseated him. Then, by God, you squandered the advantage he gave you. Never, never turn away from an enemy 'lest he's being guarded or breathed his last! And never let an enemy regain his weapon! You wouldn't be that careless with an Injun, would you? Well, would you?''

Surprised he was letting me answer, I blurted, "No, sir. No, sir, I wouldn't.''

Ned Henry roared on. "Thank God for that! I just hope I haven't wasted a whole winter an' summer hirin' that teacher for you. It wouldn't be worth dried spit I've a top packhorseman who can read, and figure sums correctly, if'n he's buried six feet under, would it?

He had no interest in my answering that query. "Look at me when I talk to you, damn it, and pay attention to everything I say. You were out huntin' with Nathan Breed the May week the first Brandon boats came downriver on the stern of General Wayne's flotilla. Remember that?''

My nod was too slow, but I perked up nonetheless. If Ned Henry was through chewing on me personally so fast, it was the shortest span ever.

"Well, the general sent for me while they loaded drinking water and hay, and I entered into a contract with him,'' the boss man admitted, "that obligates me to haul his wife's furniture and that of the other women to his new station. That's why I agreed to Brice Fowler's terms so readily. They don't mean nothin' to nobody. I've already struck my deal with Hugh Brandon.''

Encouraged by his softening tone, I dared to open my mouth. "What about horses and packers?''

Ned Henry thumped behind his desk and opened a ledger book. He ran a finger down the page, snorted, then leaned forward on his arms, palms flat on the desktop. "Thought I'd swallowed my pearl earlier, didn't you? I haven't, my young bucko. The Fagan brothers have carped high and low how they overpaid me for the animals I sold them. The blunt fact is, they're boatmen, not packhorsemen. They're as lost on dry ground as gar fish. So, out of the kindness of my miserly heart, I'll buy them back at the same price plus the cost of a month's feed. Nothing lost, nothing gained for the Fagans, eh? But we'll have the ten animals we need, ones we can trust not to spook or fail us on the trail.''

The boss man's smile of triumph was so wide his square brown teeth shone in the light of the lanthorn sitting on the corner of the desk. I chanced reminding him that the re-purchased horses solved just half the problem confronting us. ''And the packers?''

Ned Henry pulled at his moustache, thinking. His response was carefully drawn. ''That's a bigger bear to hunt, Fell. I counted on the general's women arriving in mid-September, a month ago, with our crews here. My plan was to honor my contract with Brandon, then dispatch our strings to Lexington . . . That's spilled water now. We'll have to forge ahead with whoever's available. Pratt, Emil, and Shorty aren't experienced handling horses in rough country, but they can all pack an' tie. Once the Brandon boats land at Eagle Creek, the four of you will start loading the animals. Nathan Breed's already at the general's station, so we'll hire Askell Telow yet tonight. We'll send him ahead to alert Nathan, and Breed can bring you some experienced horsemen as well as an armed escort.''

''Armed escort? Are you worried the Shawnee might waylay us, Mister Henry?''

''I wasn't, leastways not till that Fowler popinjay delayed Fain Knott's sailing. As it is, if'n you try to move the women and their possessions all at once, you won't raise the station tomorrow till the sun's set an' gone. The armed escort will ensure the ladies proceed straight through and avoid having to camp overnight in the open. If they're skulkin' about, we don't want to give the Shawnee a crack at the women. And with the additional horse handlers, your party should be strong enough to discourage any Injun she-nanigans, too.''

I wasn't enthralled with what the boss man was proposing. Given the nightmarish memories I bore of my last so-journ across the Ohio, not even the prospect of traveling with Michaela Layton excited me much. My reluctance must have been obvious to Ned Henry. ''I'm aware you're not cravin' any fresh tussle with the Shawnee. I don't wish that for you either. But my stump's bleedin' more every day, so I can't go it my ownself. We've got a lot at stake, Fell, with the success or failure of the general's station. We won't always have such a tight grip on the hauling and wagoning leaving Limestone every direction. And besides, I'm bettin' the Injuns are frettin' too much over General Wayne's legion to concern themselves with what transpires along the river this far east."

I really had no druthers. Whether his plan had merit or not, I couldn't refuse Ned Henry. He had opened his door when I knocked hungry and penniless. And while it was true I was bound to him another four years, he was providing free the schooling I needed. I had no intention of licking someone else's spoon forever. Deep down, I believed Ned Henry wouldn't deny me that freedom at the proper time. Lord, how I had prayed on my knees that it was so.

"We've much to do," I offered.

"Don't we though," Ned Henry agreed with another wide grin. He sighed, closed his ledger book, and stood erect. "I will suffer the arrangements with the Fagans. You must locate Askell Telow without delay."

"I'll check with Pratt. He knows where every long hunter lifts his tankard."

"You miss Pratt, try Monet's. Askell will be sniffin' under the ladies' skirts on his deathbed. He'll insist on havin' his own gander at the Brandon females."

Such a gander intrigued me as much as Askell. How beautiful was Rebecca Brandon? As beautiful as Noah Reem had declared that January night months ago? More beautiful than Michaela Layton? That hardly seemed likely. But then who would have thought any offspring of Hump Layton was beautiful enough to make your chest hurt just looking at her. Hurt it had, though. And did.

I came near pawing the plank floor with my boot toes. "I best hurry, I don't want to miss Pratt."

"Be off with you then," Ned Henry ordered. "There'll

be hot vittles waiting for you on your return.''

Bloodthirsty Shawnee forgotten, I bounced through the door and jumped from the stone stoop. Ned Henry's parting words flowed after me from inside his office: ''Keep your nose smellin', lad. Women scatter many a false scent if'n they hear you pantin' after 'em.''

I chuckled and kicked dust into the air. So much for the boss man being too old . . . for anything.

11

Of the tippling houses that occupied the street corners of
Limestone, and dotted the hill road stretching south to
Washington, Kentucky, Monet's, the last stop at the edge
of Limestone on the hill road, exceeded the others in sheer
size, splendor, and reputation. The combination tavern and
inn soared to the height of a blockhouse, a full two stories.
The lower floor contained a trading post, taproom, dining
hall with stone fireplace, and quarters for the owners, Jules
and Monique Monet. The upper story housed sleeping
rooms for travelers. In the trading post, supplies, horses,
guns, powder, ball, hides, ginseng, and liquor were sold or
bartered. Such items were available at many Limestone es-
tablishments. What set Monet's apart was the hospitality of
its owners and their devotion to guests. The taproom,
hosted by buxom wenches carefully selected by Monique
Monet, served drinks hot and cold seven days a week. The
dining hall, fresh meat and further delectables the steady
fare, fed the hungry the same hours. Then there were the
sleeping rooms upstairs. The traveler could stable his horse,
enjoy a warm supper, and sleep in a crowded loft else-

where. But at Monet's, he could do the first two and for an extra two shillings enjoy the ultimate of luxuries—a rope bed in a private room with clean sheets to cover himself, sheets free of bedbugs, lice, and vermin. Overnight guests were known to remark later, out of earshot of the family preacher of course, that the mere existence of Monet's was fitting proof the Lord had no qualms with members of his flock occasionally treating their stomachs and backsides to a spot of refined comfort and excess.

Much excitement attended any visit to Monet's. With the added lure of a fresh gander at Michaela Layton or the, as yet, unseen Rebecca Brandon, I kept the Shawnee mare at a brisk trot across the Limestone road. My excitement grew the farther the mare trotted without our encountering a homeward-bound Pratt Jackson. I was a mighty happy fellow when the black bulk of the tall roadhouse loomed in the evening darkness with the old roustabout still unsighted. Circumstance had given me every excuse to prowl the stables and tour the public rooms inside.

Bright yellow squares pinpointed the windows bracing the taproom and dining hall entryways. Shapes of all sizes, shadowy in the moonlight and noisy with spirited gabbing, milled about the separate stoops. The crowd had spilled into the dooryard, signifying unusual activity even for a weeknight evening at Monet's.

The stock gate at the edge of the building was ajar. I reined the mare through the gate and wound around to the stable. The stable's wide front door was propped open and lighted on either side by hanging lanthorns. Another milling throng blocked the rear entryway to the dining hall. Something rare indeed was afoot. I stepped down from the mare, more excited than ever. Whatever it was causing the ruckus, it had to involve the Brandon women or others of their party.

Noah Peters, the Monet's yardmaster, came from the dividing runway of the stable, hand extended for my reins. "Mister Cooper, sir, are you stayin' long?"

"Don't believe so, Noah," I said, hoping it would be

otherwise. "I'm huntin' Pratt Jackson an' Askell Telow. Are they here?"

Noah grasped the mare's reins. "They is. They's amongst the hooters and gawkers somewheres." The white eyes of Noah's black face glanced at the crowd milling behind me. "My, but the general's womenfolk has stirred the pot good. Never have so many mens watched two ladies at supper."

"What are they like? The women I mean."

"They's somethin' sir. Somethin' worth the seein'. Hard to tell which is more beautiful, the mother or the daughter," Noah mused, leading the mare into the stable.

"He's not lying, Mister Cooper," a voice I recognized instantly said from within the runway. Michaela Layton stepped forward into the glow of the lanthorns. Gone were the floppy hat, waistcoat, and breeches. A low-cut blue linen dress devoid of ruffles and frills wrapped her fully figured frame. A tiny silver watch suspended on a strip of yellow ribbon tied about her neck hung twixt the beginning swell of her breasts. The curled honey brown hair piled atop her head was bound by a second length of yellow ribbon. The only flaw on her person was a splotch of purple at the base of her throat, a rather large birthmark.

The change in her appearance from the afternoon was so startling she had to hear my breath catch. I vowed with what wind I had left I wasn't leaving Monet's till I saw the mother and daughter inside. I had to learn for myself how another woman could be more stunning than Michaela Layton.

I wasn't disappointed that Michaela laughed gently and peered into the stable, for I dreaded croaking like a frog, and churned up as I was, I surely would have had I tried to speak right then. "Noah, your brushes are on the bench. I thank you and Red Boy thanks you," she called out.

Her attention swept back to me. "Would you escort me to the door, Mister Cooper? I'm hungry and you're dying to stare at Laina and her daughter. It's something every man, young or old, must do."

I offered her my arm, and before I knew it, she was tight against me and we were crossing the hardpan separating the stable and the roadhouse. The smell of her almost overwhelmed my senses. My boots were no heavier than air.

" 'Tis a finely wrought mare you ride," Michaela judged. "Has she been bred?"

Whether it was the closeness of her or her enticing warmth, the croak I dreaded didn't beset me, and, to my surprise, I wasn't hesitant or embarrassed to talk with her of mating stud and mare. "No, she hasn't been bred yet."

"Would you consider Red Boy?"

The thought sent a tingle the length of me. What would the absent Jaimie Crown say if he were with us? It was the dead major's servant who had first broached such a far-fetched idea that winter night on the Ohio's north bank. There was, howsomever, a monumental hitch to pairing Red Boy and the roan mare.

"A cover by Red Boy would be great," I conceded. "But we've nothing to offer in return."

"Maybe I'll ask nothing more than the second foal, Fell Cooper," Michaela said, squeezing my arm.

We were at the rear stoop then and a thick-waisted gent spotted Michaela beside me. He cried, "Give way, toadies, the horsewoman's comin' through."

The crowd parted, teasing and catcalling. I paused at the edge of the stoop and Michaela preceded me into the dining hall. I missed the feel of her quick as she was gone from my arm. I shoved after her. She waited just beyond the narrow entryway. She pointed toward the hall's center and, shouting above the din, inquired, "Will you partake with us?"

I looked where she pointed, and for the second time that evening I was jolted to the heels. Smack in the middle of the hall, beneath a wooden wheel chained to the ceiling and adorned with a score of flaming candles in iron holders, sat a white-clothed table. Three people were seated at the table, two of them female. The older female was garbed in an open robe gown of satin red. White lace trimmed her revealing bodice and a jeweled necklace reflected candlelight in dazzling winks. Tresses of raven black hair tumbled over pink ears. A faint smudge of rouge blushed powdered cheeks. Her blue eyes, so deeply colored they appeared obsidian, were currently locked with those of the female opposite her.

The younger female wore the same exact gown and necklace. Her hair, too, was raven black, and her eyes dark blue. Thereafter, the likeness waned. The younger female's nose and chin were more delicately formed, and her creamy cheeks, unpowdered and lacking rouge, bore a natural rose hue that tempted a man to reach and touch at the risk of a slap or worse. The daughter, Rebecca Brandon I determined, was more attractive than her mother. But, fancy clothes and jewels aside, neither female was any more stunning than Michaela Layton. Many in the hall wouldn't have agreed, for that very subject was being heatedly argued all about me by Kentuckians whose bellies sloshed with brandy and rum.

Michaela tugged at my sleeve and I was tempted to follow her till I finally noticed the third occupant at the table, the person sitting twixt the two Brandon women. The presence of Brice Fowler stuck my feet to the plank floor. The dandy sat his chair with a smug grace, the relaxed hawk hovering over his brood. With the flair of a liveried butler, he poured tea for Rebecca Brandon and her mother from a silver pot with an upright, tapered spout, filling their painted china cups without spilling a drop. From tiptoe, I saw the balance of the evening's tableware—flowered china plates and silver forks and cutlery Monique Monet brought forth only on the most auspicious of occasions.

My heart matched the unwillingness of my feet. I was, at the final tally, the Limestone bumpkin Brice Fowler despised. The fork I ate with was carved from wood, long and thick of handle, and had but two broad tines. My customary plate was a bowled trencher, also of wood, designed to hold heaping portions of single course fare. I drank from squat tin noggins broad of mouth and lacking handles of any sort. I clasped the entire vessel and drank in gulps, not sips, for if the metal didn't burn my fingertips, its contents were cool enough to drink. Much as I hated to relinquish the company of Michaela Layton, I shook my head and retreated: The wise hare didn't tempt the hawk poised on his perch.

"Tomorrow . . . before noon," I shouted as Michaela freed my sleeve. "I must gather Mister Henry's crew."

Whatever regrets I had at parting from her so abruptly were allayed by her familiar sunny smile. She flashed a closed fist with the thumb up, turned, and strode into the surrounding sea of bodies. Buckskin and broadcloth clad alike drew aside, fashioning a narrow aisle way for her. Not a man laid a finger on her, purposely or accidentally. Ribald comment, though, a tavern tradition, was deemed harmless, and her height garnered as much of that as her bosom. One coonskin-capped old codger, wrinkled, toothless, and drooling, remarked how the tall gal hadn't been birthed in a feather bed like her two companions at the table. No, sir, by God, she had the wherewithal to wear boots in lieu of silk slippers when traipsing the dung-strewn stable yard. The old codger's slurred compliment wrung nods from his wobbly companions.

Michaela seated herself at the center table and further events sparked new cheering. A beaming Monique Monet and her servant girls toted an array of silver platters and bowls from the massive fireplace. Down on the white cloth went platters of roasted beef freshly butchered that morning, steamed mussels, baked trout, and smoked venison. Bowls swam with beans, cabbage, corn, peas, and meat gravy. Arriving next were puddings, loaves of piping-hot bread, and cool mounds of churned butter. And Monique, the renowned hostess, saved the best for last—red Madeira wine in crystal goblets with stems slender as those of wildflowers. It was a supper discussed in the taverns of Limestone for years. Every bite chewed and swallowed, every sip of tea and wine, was endlessly recounted by the town's gossips. And within the fortnight, every gossip was guaranteeing his listeners that not even the former king ousted by arms had ever, ever by damned, enjoyed more sumptuous fare.

I myself heard most of the details of that infamous supper later, for the hours were sliding past on me, and Ned Henry would be wondering why the delay. And to the boss man, tardiness was the same as stealing from the company strongbox.

My search of the crowd proved fruitless, which left the vacant taproom next door where I should have gone straight off. They were there, the two of them, Pratt and Askell, sprawled bum-first on benches flanking a corner table. Jules Monet, portly, whiskers precisely trimmed, was at his usual post tending the long plank bar, his favorite friends, belaying pin and Kentucky horse pistol, reposing in plain view on a wall shelf behind him. His smile was genuine. "Monsieur Fell Cooper, welcome!"

The sounding of my name snapped Pratt's lolling head from the corner table. "Fell, me bucko. Come have a flip with us," he invited, sputtering and wheezing.

The lids of Askell Telow's yellow eyes rested at half-mast. He made no attempt to greet me aloud, and his nod of recognition, if he knew it was I, was ponderously slow, creeping frost on a winter window. I was careful with him anyways. His long rifle slanted against the wall within easy reach, and the Telows didn't take kindly to being yelled at or shaken, drunk or sober.

I seated myself next to Pratt, putting Askell across from me. "Askell, Mister Henry wants to pay you to deliver an express to Brandon Station. Are you interested?"

His response lacked speed but I understood his every word. "I am. Pratt done spent the last of my hide monies."

This Pratt vehemently denied till I shushed him. The old roustabout's resentful glare melted when he was unable to forestall a sleepy yawn. "Christ, my beard's numb," he muttered. "One more slurp an' my guts will join my tongue."

Askell's belly laugh blew rum breath far as my nose. "Wouldn't bother me yer sick, you ol' turd. I'd love to watch you lick offen the table whilst Jules covers you with his horse pistol. That'd finish the evening proper, you flip crazy blabbermouth.''

Their feistiness was heartening. They were sotted, but not so deep in the tankard they couldn't ride, or walk if necessary, to the Henry Yard.

''Gentlemen,'' I said. ''I suggest we take our leave. Ned Henry's expecting us.''

Neither of them stirred, then Pratt whacked Askell's forearm. ''On yer feet, Injun hater. Maybe we'll meet Bear Hunter on the road, an' we'll ambush him so's Fell can scalp him fast an' nasty.''

Askell, thank the stars, rose shakily without argument and hefted his rifle. ''I does the scalpin'. Some chores a body don't share. Who moved the door?''

Pratt snorted. ''It's starin' at your arse, for chrissake,'' he chirped, sidling past Askell. ''Let me open it 'fore you miss the pull rope an' hurt yerself.''

They weaved and stumbled over the empty stoop, skirted the east end of the roadhouse, and lurched toward the stable without falling. A breeze, sharply cool on bare skin, roused them somewhat. We halted beneath the now guttering lanthorns and the dutiful Noah Peters tightened cinches and led out the two mares, mine and Pratt's. Pratt patted the brown's sagging middle and said to the horseless Askell, ''Climb up after me. She'll carry two.''

Pratt got aboard and Askell, after passing me his rifle and twice missing the stirrup Pratt emptied for him, gained his seat and clamped both arms around the old roustabout. I kept Askell's rifle and we set off on the Limestone road for the Henry Yard.

All went well for a half mile, then Pratt yelled, ''I gots to stand down.''

''Why?'' I asked, halting my mare.

''My belly's gonna empty an' I'm feared Askell will drop me,'' Pratt pleaded.

A cursing Askell slid backward and dismounted over the brown's ample rump. Darkened cabins lined the roadway.

A few dogs barked, then stilled. "Not too many years gone, they'd rush out here an' tear us to pieces," Askell lamented. "Hounds ain't what they once was 'thout the Shawnee lurkin' about."

Pratt, the drunk sickness upon him, leaned forward at the waist at the fringe of the road. "Hold me, you fools, damned if'n I want to drown in my own puke."

Askell grabbed a handful of frock sleeve at one shoulder and I did likewise at the other. We deliberately averted our faces. Supporting Pratt was a sorry enough task. Neither of us wanted to witness what would surely be a horrendously foul expulsion.

Pratt's chest bobbed and, with a heaving exit, bile spurted from his mouth. The exiting went on forever. Clinging to his sleeves, Askell and I waited for him to finish, still looking elsewhere.

"He feel a tad shy at your end, too?" Askell drawled.

Both our heads spun about, and sure enough, the frock we held was empty. I ducked my head to determine if the old roustabout had injured himself falling into his own vomit, and a bee buzzed within inches of my hat.

Bee?

At night?

The slam of exploding powder mirrored my silent pondering.

"What the piss?" Askell blurted, woozy enough he didn't immediately fathom what had happened.

We were separated from the mares and fully visible in the moonlight. "Down!" I ordered. "Someone's shootin' at us an' he may not be alone."

Survival utmost in his dulled thinking, Askell plunged into the dirt of the roadway, flattening the sickly Pratt with an out-thrust arm. Wishing myself smaller, I knelt on one knee and brought Askell's rifle to bear, quartering the reverse direction of the ball's flight.

Absolute silence prevailed. Not a single cabin door so much as opened a crack. Not a dog barked. Then running feet pattered lightly on dry ground, fainter with each retreating stride. I heard, but could see nothing to draw bead on. Pools of darkness, as was their wont, befriended those souls intent upon felling the innocent.

Pratt propped himself on an elbow, white beard matted with smelly globs of vomit. "You had better manners, Injun hater, mayhap fewer folks would try blowin' a hole in you."

I maintained my vigil. I didn't correct him, but the old roustabout was wrong. The bullet had had my name on it. I measured six inches taller than Askell Telow. I topped the stick-thin Pratt by four inches and, more importantly, outweighted him a full sixty pounds. In the moonlight, with Askell and me frozen on either side of the heaving Pratt, the rifle bearer had been certain of his target. Had not Pratt slipped from his frock and caused me to hunker down suddenly, the ball would have caught me square twixt the shoulder blades—dead square.

"He gone, Fell?" Askell inquired.

I listened to the click and whine and hum of night critters singing from grass blade and tree bark. The cool breeze bumbled gently. The roan mare's lips fluttered, rattling her bridle chains. But nothing two legged toting a killing weapon made the slightest noise anywhere.

"Ain't nobody about now," I judged. "Let's get the horses home."

Shucking Askell's restraining arm, Pratt scrambled upright. He was a sorry sight, his shirtfront smeared with as much puke as his beard, perhaps more. And the stench was awful.

"By Christ, I'll walk," Askell announced. "A buzzard retched on Simon Dagamon a-purpose an' he smelled better'n you, you ol flip lover."

It was Askell's turn to be mistaken. He hadn't had a whiff of himself recently, and being downwind of them, it wasn't readily apparent to my nose who was the ripest at the moment.

"Gentlemen, Ned Henry awaits," I reminded none too gently.

With considerable grumbling on their part, we taken out again. Without explanation, I walked with the roan mare at left hip and Pratt's brown on my right, presenting thataway the smallest possible target. I had been careless after Pratt and Michaela Layton's warning.

Never again would that be true.

Those scary minutes back yonder had taught me an enduring lesson: The dandified hawk with gold in his claws didn't have to be at hand. He was equally dangerous while comfortably seated on his perch at Monet's.

12

Though mid-October was a rather late arrival date for movers from across the eastern mountains, the following morning Limestone's public landing, every stone inch of it, was virtually under siege. Blunt flatboats, packet ships, and tapered keelboats yielded cargo constantly—be it barreled, bundled, boxed, penned, booted, shoed, shod, or unshod. And caught in the middle, opposing the incoming tide of squealing carts, rumbling wagons, lowing cattle, baaing sheep, neighing horses, clucking chickens, honking geese, and spent movers with their yelling children in tow, were Emil, Shorty, Askell, Pratt, me, and the ten newly acquired Henry packhorses. Our destination was the four Brandon flatboats moored at the downriver end of the public landing.

We threaded through the tide of wheels and bodies at the fastest clip possible, for it was nearing the noon deadline for our arrival. The Fagan brothers had not been easy pickings for the boss man. They had haggled into the wee hours before parting with the horses and packsaddles they so regretted buying earlier. Whatever Ned Henry paid, and given the stiffness of his jaw at the dawn meal not even

Satan would have had the gall to ask, the Fagans insulted him further by delivering said animals and equipment three hours later than they promised.

As the boss man had anticipated, when we hove into sight of the Brandon boats moored at landing's end, black-clad Brice Fowler, chained timepiece dangling from his fingers, paced the cabin roof of the boat tied farthest down-river. Sharing the cabin roof with him was a rotund river man dressed in red and white striped shirt and canvas trousers. Captain Fain Knott had supped at the Henry table many an evening and, once seen, you never forgot his completely bald skull and bristling moustache, which sprouted from the very nostrils of his oft-broken nose. The captain wasn't pacing as briskly, but he would be no less impatient than Brice Fowler to cast off. Respected for his knowledge of western waters and his caution, Fain Knott shared Ned Henry's distaste for unloading freight on the Ohio's north bank in the dark of night. Others could trust to General Wayne and his legion for protection against the Injuns. Fain Knott placed his trust in daylight and a loaded musket.

Below the cabin roof bestrode by the dandy and the captain, two tall-crowned hats swarming with feathers stuck above the boat's near gunwale. The dark mask shielding the face of one of the hat wearers from the late morning sun identified the pair as the general's wife and daughter. Bonneted women black of skin, unquestionably servant girls, flanked mother and daughter. More women, these with children but no servants, pressed against the near gunwales of the second and third flatboats. Every female eye stared our direction.

Pratt, plodding beside me, wasn't so hungover from the previous evening he missed any of the attention we were attracting. "Always wanted a heap of women watchin' my every step," he revealed. "But I ain't certain I like it. Worryin' I'll stumble over my own toes an' appear the clumsy oaf makes my flesh crawl."

"They're anxious to join their menfolk is all," I allowed. "An' I'll wager my last shilling Brice Fowler had the Brandon ladies aboard plenty early so he can blame us, whenever he chooses, for delayin' everyone's departure.''

Pratt nodded. ''Could be. Either way, I ain't bettin' with that white devil.''

The fourth flatboat, the closest to us, sported a smaller cabin and the cargo box built amidships on the others was absent, thereby creating a large bay for the shipment of hooved stock. A cleated gangplank rose from the rocky ground to the boat's square bow. Inside the bow's starboard corner, a platform level with the surrounding gunwales headed another cleated gangplank descending to the deck below. Whether you were boarding or unloading, it was a neat arrangement of opposing ramps that lessened the chance of sprains and broken bones amongst the four-legged.

Halfway up the fore gangplank, I spotted flicking ears and Red Boy's blazed forehead, then a flop-brimmed hat matching my own. The bay stallion was in a separate enclosure fronting the crew cabin. Michaela Layton was in the private pen also, plying the stud's crimson coat with currying brushes. Brice Fowler's unsaddled black gelding was hitched to an iron ring bolted to the starboard hull forward of the stallion's pen. The remainder of the open bay was empty.

Our loading of the pack animals fetched a chorus of cheers from the female onlookers. Michaela Layton simply leaned on the railing of Red Boy's pen and smiled. Soon as we led the final packhorse onto the inboard ramp, Fain Knott's rolling bellow to ''Cast off!'' carried above the hollow stomping of iron shoes on wooden planking.

The steersman of our boat repeated the command instantly. Emil and Shorty helped untie the mooring hawsers and swing the dock ramp aboard. The smiths then stood aside while the Brandon crew shoved the flatboat clear of the dock with long poles. These same fellows then manned the broad sweeps atop the cabin roof.

Once Askell and I had the packhorses tethered in rows to ropes stretching across the deck from port to starboard gunwale, the Henry men made places for themselves, their long guns, and their personal truck in the bow. All except Pratt and me, that was. The old roustabout spied the thin wisp of smoke trailing from the chimney of the crew cabin. Always in pursuit of hot vittles (only Cam Downing had proven hungrier each hour), Pratt sauntered around the stallion's pen and entered the cabin without calling out or knocking. Brave are the empty-bellied.

Much as I wanted to loll about and admire Michaela, my packhorse chores couldn't wait. I went from animal to animal, checking cinches and halters, and lengthening tethers. I borrowed cured hay from the supply wedged beneath the inboard gangplank and fed them. They ate like the Fagans had starved them.

Chores finished, I recovered my Bedford rifle, shot pouch, and haversack, and Michaela having disappeared for the moment, I joined the Henry men. Askell, Emil, and Shorty were seated where hull met deck, chewing jerked meat, content as cows resting in a shaded pasture. An afternoon free of the heat and sweat of the forge fire was an absolute luxury for the two smiths, and from their cheery red cheeks, I suspected the iron canteen they passed twixt themselves and Askell contained some drink with more wallop than springwater.

"Wouldn't get too settled was I you," Askell said.

"Why's that?"

"That Layton gal's beckoning from the cabin roof, an' she ain't interested in any of us'ens."

Michaela's voice welled behind me. "Mister Cooper, will you join me?"

I leaned my Bedford against the hull. She was atop the cabin sure enough, long legs dangling above the stallion's pen. " Come along, Mister Cooper, we need to talk."

"Well, go along, you young pup," Askell urged. "She fills them breeches mighty fine an' she can't bite deeper'n a big dog."

Askell was right. There wasn't any polite way to decline Michaela's invitation without appearing rude and ill-

mannered. It wasn't her fault I was half-afraid she would
find me boorish. I skirted Red Boy in his pen and scaled
the ladder on the front wall of the crew cabin, wondering
as I did where the wolfhound she mentioned earlier might
be. Till Askell mouthed the word "dog" I had forgotten
her claim at the Henry Yard she owned a tame wolf that
guarded her every step.

She patted the roof beside her hip and I plopped down
next to her. Lord but she was a fetching creature. It had
grown warmer as the day unfolded and the slightest skein
of sweat glistened on the tan curve of her jaw. Her waistcoat was unbuttoned and the linen shirt she wore beneath
it clung to the rounded swell of her breasts. Before she
caught me staring, I hastily looked front and back and observed, "Don't believe I've seen your wolfhound anywheres."

"He's tied behind the cabin. Captain Knott was concerned Hump might spook your horses," she related.

"Hump?"

Michaela smiled. "Well, it seemed the proper thing to
name him. Hump is half-wolf and half-mastiff and built just
like Father—head and chest so huge the rest of him seems
small but isn't."

Trying my damnedest to keep my gaze where it belonged, and delighted at the same time she was willing to
do most of the talking, I inquired, "Is Hump a mean
enough watchdog?"

"Father has him trained to guard upon command. Otherwise, he's quite happy sleeping somewhere in a corner.
He's smart enough to attack without barking if you sic him
on someone. It's not something you do often. He nearly
chewed an intruder's arm off before he was a year old."

"Then I best be sure I don't exceed my bounds when
Hump's unchained, huh?" I suggested.

She caught my teasing tone and laughed lightly. Sunlight
made her hazel eyes gleam like gold. "Thank God, I was
beginning to worry you were the same as the other men
I've encountered for what's been forever."

"How's that?" I asked, genuinely confused.

"I'm tired of hearing how I'm tall as a tree and have busts bigger than melons," she said in return. "You may be gentleman enough I can enjoy your company."

She suddenly seemed near tears. I waited for her to speak, unsure how to proceed. Jumping tree frogs, I had never so much as kissed a woman, and understanding what they expected of me was tantamount to boiling rocks without wood for the fire and water for the kettle.

She gathered herself with a sigh. "Your mare has much to offer."

Glad to be on footing solid and familiar, I told her the story of how I had acquired the Shawnee roan, including the announcements Ned Henry and I had published in the *Kentucky Gazette* of her recovery that had gone unanswered, and established me as her new owner. It pleased me my voice never quavered the whole while. "It's the kind of luck a poor packhorseman never expects to fall his way," I concluded.

"It won't happen right off, but we'll pair Red Boy with her," Michaela promised. "My dream is to breed the finest of horses and race them. Nothing is more rewarding or exciting."

"Does your father agree with that?"

"No, he thinks I'll starve and die a broken woman. But he won't interfere. He'll not chase me off and be left to cook for himself once he builds his new cabin."

I couldn't help what I said next. "He could always take another wife."

"No, not Father. He's only ever loved my mother. She was killed years ago, and he may consort with other females beyond his stoop, but none are brought across it to his bed."

She fell silent, perhaps pondering her own words. That was fine with me. I was satisfied just spending part of an uneventful afternoon at her side. True peace and quiet were not common to the Henry Yard.

We had been under way an hour and the Brandon boats

were drawing upon Big Three Mile Creek, the site of our winter skirmish with the Shawnee. Dry weather had lowered the Ohio and wide strips of brown mud lined both banks. Bulky white clouds floated high overhead, inching eastward. A warm breeze, that would cool come evening, blew the same direction, stirring the river's blue waters. We were due a break in the weather, and high clouds and a constant breeze usually foretold such an event. It could rain by tomorrow evening. For now, the weather posed no threat to our overland travel to Brandon Station, leaving only bank mud and any lurking Shawnee to be dealt with.

Michaela lifted an arm and pointed to the autumn forest bordering the river. "What grand colors. Rebecca and I love the yellows, the browns, and that brilliant splash of red here and there. Her mother paints. Rebecca tried taking up the brush, but she's not very good."

My tongue was moving before I could stop it. "Never had time for such tomfoolery my ownself. The leaves change, I know tree nuts are ready for the gather."

If my blunt contention annoyed her, Michaela gave no outward sign. "I believe I would see to my belly also. The colors are there every year."

That small crisis behind me, I asked what seemed a safe question, one that wouldn't offend her. "You miss your home in Virginia?"

"Yes and no. It was hard to keep from crying when we started out. I lived most of my life in our cabin on the Brandon estate. But our place was very small and Father wanted more for me. He couldn't refuse the general's offer. And I didn't argue with him. We had no room for a stable and pasture of our own and I was tired of being beholden to Rebecca for boarding Red Boy. Father wasn't certain and neither was I what would become of me if something happened to him, and it didn't ease his mind any knowing I might have to seek mercy from the Brandons . . . or marry simply to eat."

I understood her fear of an uncertain future, which only made her more attractive. What she had revealed about herself whetted my curiosity. "How did you acquire Red Boy?"

She laughed. "Father won him in a game of whist with the general, then refused to sell him back at any price. He did finally agree to stand Red Boy at stud whenever the general desired. When the general came out in May, he brought his last two blooded mares with him, knowing I would bring Red Boy with me. The general even planned a stable inside his new station to protect his mares and Red Boy at night."

I didn't say it, but if I were counting on Red Boy to replenish my riding stable as the general was, hardly anything was too much regarding the stallion's safety. Without the proper stud, bloodlines weakened quickly.

Michaela fell silent, lost in her own thoughts once more. Chin tilted so she could gaze past her drooping hat brim, she surveyed her beloved autumn colors. While her attention was elsewhere, my eyes were of course fixed on her. It fascinated me I could find nothing about her to dislike.

The flatboats cleared the mouth of Big Three Mile Creek and bore slowly to port as the Ohio bent southwestward. Ahead, Logan's Gap notched the wooded crests of Cedar Hill and Puff Ridge. Beyond the Gap, another three miles downriver, awaited our destination—Eagle Creek.

Round the southwest bend, the blare of a hunting horn drifted on the breeze. The flatboats, one after the other, tacked sharply to starboard. Low water gave teeth to hazards that passed beneath vessels without incident other times, and Captain Knott was giving the recently exposed sandbar along the south bank a wide berth.

"What's your judgment of the Brandon ladies?"

Michaela's question surprised me but I wasn't prone to a quick answer. "What do you mean?"

"You know exactly what I mean. You had ample opportunity to decide which is prettiest. Well, which is it, mother or daughter?"

I sensed quicksand directly before me and sought the middle of the road. "Never seen skin so white and snowy,

hair so black, or eyes so dark yet still blue. Any man would
be proud to have either grace his arm on any occasion.
Their beauty is as rare as those Greek goddesses Ned Henry
swears by.''

Michaela's lips pursed and she jumped to her feet.
''You're just like all the other rough-tongued louts who
followed them about like hounds after a bitch in heat. Show
any of you a powdered face and a coy look, and you're
spellbound forever. I'm going below, thank you, Mister Fell
Cooper!''

I sat stunned, taken aback by her outburst. She clamored
down the ladder to the deck and slammed the cabin door
behind her. I could only scratch my head and wonder.
There wasn't any doubt about the size of this girl's temper:
Mad was damned mad.

I had to be nowhere in a hurry, and feeling warm and
lazy in the afternoon sun, I leaned back on my elbows and
remembered precisely what I had said about the general's
wife and daughter. I determined every word was the truth.
So why Michaela's anger?

Now, maybe I was inexperienced with women, but I
wasn't a stranger to wounded pride. In trying to avoid in-
sulting either of her female acquaintances, I had been un-
stinting in my praise of the Brandon ladies. Never had I
mentioned Michaela in the same breath with them. I had
thus led her to mistakenly believe that I, like many at Monet's, saw real beauty in the Brandon women, and none in
Hump Layton's offspring. I couldn't have snubbed her
more thoroughly had I planned it in advance.

The safest course in the future was the most obvious:
Never speak of one woman in the presence of another even
if either held a pistol on you. I shook my head in resig-
nation. The straightforward chores of the packhorseman had
never been more inviting. My pack animals were stubborn
and temperamental, but they didn't talk back and, more
often than not, a slap of rein or whip settled most misun-
derstandings. Would that my days would be so ordinary.

Three blasts of Fain Knott's horn sounded. The steersman behind me snapped to attention. "That's the signal to prepare to land," he called out.

I came to my feet atop the cabin roof. We were past the steep slope of Cedar Hill, and the mouth of Eagle Creek was a yawning opening in the trees of the north bank. Manning the steering oar of the lead boat, Fain Knott angled that craft across the mouth of the creek and it struck hard aground where the mud lining the riverbank was the narrowest. His crew scrambled ashore to secure mooring hawsers to tree trunk and stump while Knott waved for the following boats to make land farther down the Ohio.

As the bow of the horse boat came about and pointed for the bank, I stomped on the cabin roof. "Move your feet, Pratt. There's work waiting for you."

The old roustabout had no difficulty hearing me. He thumped from the cabin toting a metal bucket in one hand. Holding the bucket away from his body, he hopped up the ladder rungs on his good leg.

"What've you got there?" I inquired.

"Hot coals. Mistress Layton ordered me to pitch 'em in the river."

The chore was a task common to wooden ships with hearths. A wise sailor never forgot the faintest spark, particularly on an untended vessel, could ignite a raging fire in a flash amongst dry timbers. "Then you best get on with it," I urged.

Pratt nodded and turned toward the stern. He hadn't taken the first step when the horse boat's bow struck a shelf of rock brought near the surface by low water. The shock of the collision caught Pratt with his weight on his peg leg and toppled him backwards. Fearful he would dump the coals and then fall upon them, the old roustabout flung the hearth bucket far as he could.

The flung bucket arced through the air, raining coals down into Red Boy's pen. An animal squeal of pain equaling that of any human grated my teeth together. Burned and frightened, the stallion wasn't about to linger near the source of his pain. Hooves rapped the deck, and with a bunching of haunch muscle, Red Boy soared upward. He cleared the starboard gunwale by mere inches, an unlikely, impossible feat for any horse given such confining quarters.

My eyes widened again as next over the boat's side went a streak of brown fur big as most men. Long, thin legs curled to his chest, Michaela's wolf dog cleared the gunwale with ease. I ran to the edge of the cabin roof. The stallion, upright and unscathed, was fast stepping through shallow water toward the trees of the north bank. The wolfhound loped after him without barking.

A panting Michaela appeared in the near end of Red Boy's vacant pen. She hooked her arms over the gunwale, framed fingers around her mouth, and called after her fleeing pets. "Whoa, Red Boy, whoa! . . . Here, Hump, here!"

There was nothing anybody could do to stop the two runaways. The Brandon crews, busy mooring the other boats, were too far away to offer any help. Slinging a rope halter over her shoulder, an undaunted Michaela straddled the gunwale, then slid down the outside of the hull slick as a descending squirrel.

I didn't bother yelling after her. Red Boy was her most prized possession and nothing I could say would influence her in the least. The stallion would tire quickly bucking the thick growth of the river bottom. And besides, it was still full daylight and the wolfhound would watch out for the both of them. They wouldn't be gone more than a few minutes at the most. Or so I thought.

Emil and Shorty swung the outbound gangplank into place before the bow. Askell was already tying the pack animals together for the unloading. I retrieved my Bedford, along with my trail gear, and went to help him.

The outbound gangplank had settled in the river twenty yards from the bank, and the horses, unsure of their footing, wouldn't be hurried. I guided the first two onto solid ground and looked about. Michaela wasn't yet in sight, upstream or down.

I commenced to worry once the packhorses were ashore and she still hadn't appeared. "Askell, split the string twixt the three boats. I'll see what's become of the girl and her stud.''

Askell's grin was all knowing. ''I'll make your excuses for you,'' he said with a sly wink.

I started my search where Red Boy had disappeared beyond the bank. Past clumps of trampled saw grass, I located a swatch of disturbed underbrush. I pushed through, and closely set sycamore and beech surrounded me within a few strides. Head lowered, I picked my path carefully, constantly seeking the stallion's trail.

The drought-parched earth was hard as flint and yielded little sign of the stallion's passage. I surged ahead, following the most open route twixt the tall tree butts. The forest floor rose sharply and a slash in the loam where a shod hoof had slipped revealed I was headed the right direction.

The ground leveled and I hastened my pace. Best I could reckon, I was traveling northwest, away from the mouth of Eagle Creek as well as the Ohio. It wasn't likely anybody followed me, for Brice Fowler and Captain Knott might not yet be aware Michaela and Red Boy were missing.

My worry mounted with my every stride. Where the hell was that fool girl and her horse? Didn't that damn wolfhound ever bark? If anything happened to his daughter because I had let her chase after the stallion by herself, how would I explain such stupidity to Hump Layton?

I couldn't, I decided.

Sunlight slanted through a break in the trees. One glance into that small clearing and I scurried for cover behind the nearest tall trunk. I didn't need a confirming look at what I had seen. The feathered arrow buried in the neck of Michaela's dead wolfhound told all:

The Shawnee were out.

13

Stifling the urge to act quickly, I knelt on one knee behind the wide butt of that gray beech. Michaela and Red Boy would have to wait. To help them, I first had to protect my own scalp.

An inch at a time, I discarded my flop-brimmed hat, as Nathan Breed had taught me on our spring hunts, and for a quarter hour moved nothing but my head and eyes. Like Breed, I wasn't breaking cover till I was certain the Shawnee weren't hiding nearby to ambush whatever soul chanced along after the slain wolfhound. Nobody baited a trap better than the redsticks.

The constant breeze fluttered dying leaves on the surrounding trees and stirred hair on the dead Hump's shoulder. There was nothing else to be heard or seen. I was extra cautious anyway. Sticking to Breed's schooling, I did something other than what an enemy lying in wait expected of me. Rifle poised with thumb on the cock, I stepped backwards two lengthy strides, angled off to my right where the thickest cover was available, and circled wide of the clearing.

My evasion drew neither arrow nor ball, but still leery, I treed in a stand of black walnut and studied the clearing from its opposite side. Nary a redstick showed, and eyes sweeping left and right, I resumed my pursuit of Michaela and Red Boy.

There was no hesitation on my part about doing so. Michaela had been close enough behind Red Boy she couldn't have missed spotting the dead Hump, which meant she knew the Shawnee were also tracking the stud horse. If my guess were correct—and Michaela had never yet acted like she was hollow twixt the ears—she was trailing both red enemy and red stallion at a safe distance, hoping help would be forthcoming from the male members of the Brandon party at the river. It was a terribly risky undertaking for an armed man, God forbid an unarmed woman. I could only hurry fast as I dared, and pray I caught up with her before the Shawnee discovered they were being tracked themselves.

Best I could tell, I was still traveling northwest. A quarter mile from the clearing, I came upon a dry wash wide as both my arms could reach. With the afternoon sun on the wane, forest shadows had lengthened and darkened, making sign harder to locate and read. I fell to my knees and studied the stony bottom of the wash. It took some repeated looking before I spied faint scratches on the brown rocks that told me Red Boy had stepped into the dry waterway, then turned upstream. Fifty steps farther along, broken branches on brush bordering the bank heartened me greatly. The branches had been snapped a-purpose and bent double.

"Good girl," I muttered. " Help me a little an' mayhap I can come up to you before dark."

The wash, originating on the flank of a ridge, had a crest high enough I caught a momentary glimpse of the shimmering surface of the Ohio in the distance. I was convinced after that steep climb that the Shawnee were leading Red Boy. How they had gotten a rope on him, I couldn't fathom. But no runaway animal, despite being thoroughly frightened, would run himself to death. Neither would he take to high ground of his own accord.

I gulped air and got my feet moving, ever alert for Michaela's leavings. When the brush bordering the wash had petered out, she had stacked stones in small piles. On the flank of the ridge, where stones and brush were often scarce, she had blazed an X on tree butts every so often with what, I presumed, was a sharp rock borne with her from the dry streambed. Cleverness wasn't lacking where this girl was concerned.

The country thereabouts was unknown to me except for Breed's past remarks at the Henry hearth. I did know the lofty path I traveled would eventually join a much larger prominence, Howard Ridge, beyond which flowed Red Oak Creek. I forced greater speed from tiring legs. If I didn't find Michaela before dark, she was in for a long, chilly night without fire, vittles, or water; a camp I wouldn't wish upon my ownself.

When the Shawnee abandoned the ridgeline, Michaela carved a downward pointing arrow on the bole of an oak to mark the spot. It was a steep descent made rougher by numerous deadfalls. I regretted the slackening of my pace, but I couldn't risk a twisted ankle, and loud noises echoed forever in those wooded hollows.

At the bottom of the slope, I found myself in another dry wash. The light was fading rapidly now, and I cursed the minutes it took me to locate Michaela's latest pile of stones. The pile was smaller than the earlier ones, indicating she was tiring, and perhaps feeling she was needlessly wasting her remaining strength. I checked the priming in the pan of the Bedford while there was still light enough and set off again. If I didn't come up on her within the next half hour, Michaela was condemned to spending a black night hungry and shivering from cold.

The wash snaked back and forth in the hollow. I stuck to its winding bed, always on the lookout for a fresh pile of rock or some new sign from Michaela. It was almost dark when the watercourse turned abruptly toward the southwest and passed beneath the exposed roots of a gigantic sycamore. Disdaining the high bank opposite the sycamore, I crouched and slipped sideways into the biggest space twixt the hanging roots.

Sudden movement at my left shoulder caught my eye. Whatever slashed at me from the shadows was long and round and threatening. Had I been looking elsewhere and not had that tiny warning, I would have breathed my last the next instant. As it was, I ducked just enough to spare my skull a killing blow and the slashing length of wood merely ripped my flop-brimmed hat from my head.

A loud grunt followed, after which the wooden club withdrew as its wielder prepared for the next blow. Fear gripped my vitals. I couldn't lift my arms to shield myself or bring my rifle to bear. Wildly desperate, I let my legs go slack. The club slashed once more, fanning my hair, but again missing my skull.

I landed on my knees, curled into a ball, and rolled backwards, freeing myself from the tangling roots. I came to my feet, the Bedford fully cocked and aimed at my attacker. My finger was tightening on the trigger as her panting exclamation reached my ears:

"Don't shoot me, Fell Cooper," Michaela implored. "How was I to know it was you?"

I was mad enough to grab her and beat her arse with that damn club. I loosened my grip on the trigger and lowered the Bedford. "You thought I was an Injun?"

"Yes," she admitted. "The Shawnee I trailed wears a hat like yours. And being unarmed I wasn't taking any chances."

My temper cooled. I couldn't fault her for defending herself, and it wasn't lost on me she hadn't yelled out when she saw the Bedford draw bead on her. Her refusal to panic had spared her life without revealing our presence to the enemy. That kind of courage I admired.

"How many Shawnee did you see an' where are they?"

"Just the one, and I'm sure he's within shouting distance . . . or he was before I stopped to rest and you came along. I was afraid he'd spotted me and circled behind me. What are we to do?'' Michaela asked, passing me my rumpled hat.

"Late as it is, an' seein' how I ain't skillful at sneakin' up on Injuns in the dark, we better retreat back a piece and find some place out of the wind to spend the night. We can't risk a fire, but I've got jerk and water an' a blanket in my haversack. In the mornin', we'll point for the river an' rejoin the others.''

"What about Red Boy?'' Michaela demanded without raising her voice.

"Hell, woman, you've already lost your wolfhound. An' Injuns don't hardly ever scout or raid by themselves. We ain't careful, we'll be dead as your Hump, jack quick. No horse's worth that.''

"I'm not returning without him,'' Michaela declared forcefully. "I'll camp with you. But in the morning, you can fetch help if you're afraid of a solitary Shawnee armed only with a bow and a pouch of arrows. I'm tracking Red Boy again.''

The wind had a chilling edge now, and it wouldn't gain anything at the moment to remind her it had taken but one arrow to kill her Hump before he either sighted or scented the enemy. "We can talk about tomorrow later. Follow me.''

After a few strides, I glanced over my shoulder and she was right on my heels. In the black of early night with the moon not yet shining, I had to feel ahead each step with a boot toe retracing the course of the stone-bottomed wash. My destination was a sizable cut carved in the bank by high water during some past runoff. The hollow of the cut faced the east, the opposite direction of the wind, and was large enough to shelter the both of us. That was, if Michaela was willing to share a blanket with me.

We traversed that black half mile without speaking. Moonlight sifted through drifting cloud as I halted in front of the cut bank. "We'll hole up here,'' I announced.

Voicing no objection, Michaela ducked her head and sidled into the hollow opening. Once her eyes grew accustomed to the sudden darkness, I heard rocks clunk together as she fashioned a seat for herself. I slipped the straps of my haversack and shot pouch over my head and joined her, delighted her rough-built bench accommodated the both of us.

The dirt of the bank was cold against my leaning back side. I untied the flap of my haversack and pulled forth my tightly rolled blanket and a leather sack filled with jerked meat. "It don't match the fare at Monet's, but its better'n sleepin' on an empty belly," I said, handing her a wrinkled strip of the smoked venison.

Michaela sniffed the venison, then popped the meat into her mouth. "God, it's just divine," she managed twixt chews. "I'm truly starved."

I dug my wooden canteen from the bottom of the haversack. "We'll need to go easy. We're mighty shy on water. Been hotter this afternoon, we'd be sufferin' something awful by now."

Michaela nodded and drank in small sips. She was no stranger to short rations. I wondered if her friend Rebecca Brandon could say the same. But then, not knowing the young lady personally, maybe I was judging the general's daughter unfairly.

Swallowing her last piece of meat, Michaela wiped her mouth with her fingers. "Someone should reach us by morning, shouldn't they? Brice must realize we ran into trouble."

I wanted to extend her the reassurance she sought. I couldn't. I wasn't counting on Brice Fowler for anything. He was in charge at the river, and taking into account how much he wanted me dead, it wasn't beyond him to forgo a rescue party. He could claim he didn't dare endanger the other women by weakening his forces till he knew how many Shawnee might be on the prowl, and not even Hump Layton, were his offspring to perish with me, could fault Fowler for his caution.

If we could count on anybody for help, it was Askell

Telow. He wasn't subject to Brice Fowler's orders. He had been hired by Ned Henry to deliver an express to Nathan Breed at the general's station, and when he did, he would report our absence. Even then, the earliest Breed, and Hump Layton himself, could start hunting our trail was daylight tomorrow, leaving Michaela and me on our own for several hours after the sun rose in the morning.

My silence told Michaela much of what I didn't care to share aloud. "Well, since you don't have any faith in the Brandon crew, never fear, my father will track us down once he hears I'm missing," Michaela insisted, "and it won't take him long either."

"That I have no cause to doubt. Let's just make sure we're alive when he gets here," I responded.

Michaela sighed and stood. "I need a few minutes alone and I'm not going without a weapon. May I borrow your knife."

I slid my blade from its scabbard at my belt and offered it handle-first. She stepped from the overhang and disappeared into the feeble moonlight. She wisely sought a place to tend herself farther upstream.

I went the opposite direction and looked and listened. No flicker of fire showed downstream. I could hear nothing except the blowing wind and the patter of falling leaves. It wouldn't be a disappointment if the Shawnee had spurned a night camp and continued northwesterly with the stallion, not to me anyways. A fleeing enemy was the safest of enemies, leastways he was providing I could convince Michaela to travel east instead of west at dawn.

Upon my arrival, she was already ensconced in the opening of the cut bank, my unrolled blanket spread across her legs. I propped the Bedford in the corner at the end of the rock bench and plopped beside her. I then asked a question that intrigued me greatly. "How are we to sleep with just one blanket for the both of us?"

"Turn away from me and settle yourself," she ordered.

Soon as I did so, she snuggled up to me, covered us with the blanket, and laid her head on my back side. Her breath tickled the nape of my neck and I flinched. She simply squirmed closer.

It made no difference I was wearing two separate frocks and she a waistcoat and linen shirt, the sudden press of her breasts against my shoulder blades set my blood racing. Never had I experienced such an incredible, yielding softness. Sweat dotted my brow and my chest began to ache.

"You don't stink like most men," Michaela confirmed. "Could that be because you wash in the creek every day as the Shawnee do?"

Damn you, Pratt, I cursed inwardly, what else did you spill your guts about in the cabin of the horse boat?

My anger died quick as it was born with Michaela's final revelation of the evening, a statement that knotted my tongue for the duration of our initial night together:

"I saw your scars at the Henry Yard," she whispered, fingering the healed ridges through my shirt. "If you haven't yet killed whoever whipped you, tomorrow wouldn't be too late."

And I was expecting to win an argument about the worth of a horse with this same woman in the morning?

Restless and fretful, I wedged the lock of the Bedford twixt my thighs to keep my priming dry, clasped the barrel of the rifle with both arms, and hardly slept a wink.

Michaela Layton, molded to the reverse side of me, never stirred.

14

First Light till Afternoon, October 16

I awakened shortly after first light, shivering from the chill. I forced an ëye open. My blanket and the lady I had shared it with were gone. I worried not, for wherever Michaela was, the lack of any fuss upon her departure told me she had left of her own accord, and she again carried my knife.

I pried the Bedford from twixt my thighs, twisted into a sitting position, and before anything else, confirmed the firing pan still held a full charge of dry powder. That vital chore completed, I allowed myself a strip of jerk and a sip of water.

While I waited for Michaela to show, I gave some serious thought to how I might talk her out of chasing after Red Boy—if that were possible. She was of a mind a single Shawnee could be overcome without undue fuss. In so thinking, she overlooked the greater danger—the likelihood our horse thief would soon rendezvous with others of his ilk. As I had tried to warn her, Injuns seldom hunted or raided alone. They preferred the advantage of numbers same as we whites did.

There was also the chance we would lose the trail to lack

of sign or a break in the weather that would wipe out the stallion's tracks altogether. The morning light was gray and dim, indicating the clouds of yesterday had lingered and thickened. Ground fog curled amidst tree trunks bordering the bed of the wash, and the air, stirred by a light breeze, was dank and cold. Dry weather was on the wane, and I had no desire to endure a thorough soaking far afield where lighting a fire might get a man scalped. Fever from foul weather had killed nearly as many backwoodsers as the Shawnee.

Course, as I should have known, Michaela wasn't inclined to waste time arguing with me about the Injun danger or the changing weather. Blanket neatly folded under one arm, she soft-footed from the fog, getting within a few yards of me before I became aware of her presence. "Lucky for you I'm friendly, isn't it?"

She roused your ire in a finger snap you weren't careful. Her hazel eyes sparkled with anticipation. She was as fresh as if she had spent the night in a feather bed at Monet's. And before I could open my mouth, she told me what was in store for the both of us:

"Mister Cooper, I'm going after Red Boy. You can join me or you can explain to my father how you abandoned me in the wilderness. Which will it be?"

"Now, wait a bygod minute here, girl," I protested. "That ain't fair and you know it."

"Fair has nothing to do with it," Michaela countered. "There's only one Shawnee involved and I'm not letting him steal my future. Red Boy's not just any horse, he's my future. Can't you understand that?"

Rising to my feet, I beat dust from my leggins and the bottom of my breeches. Michaela's cheeks colored and her teeth bit her lower lip. Though she was hoping otherwise, she was plainly gathering herself to march off on her own.

It didn't take much deliberation on my part to reckon I couldn't allow that. The danger of assuming anything where the Shawnee were concerned and the possibility bad weather might beset us paled beside the simple truth that I was a man and she was a woman. Whatever happened, I was responsible for her and would be held in judgment not just by her father, but every borderer the entire length of the Ohio.

Besides, I consoled myself, you can't tie her up and carry her across Howard Ridge to Brandon Station, not with her kicking and scratching like a catamount all the while; and judging from the raw determination on her face, kick and scratch she would. Anger her enough trying to manhandle her, and a fellow might even lose an eye in the fracas.

I thumped the ground with the butt of the Bedford. "All right, we'll trek after your damn horse," I conceded, "but first we need to have an understanding."

"Such as?" she retorted.

I raised a conciliatory hand. "Now, don't get feisty with me. Just bear in mind that Injun's that's leadin' Red Boy won't part with him willingly. So get it in your pretty head straight off, I'm not about to give him the opportunity to kill you or me. I'm gonna lay the sneak in him an' shoot him dead. The last thing I want is for him to end up with either of our scalps hangin' from his belt. If'n we can't catch him by surprise or if'n any other redsticks join him, we back away and make for the general's station. Agreed?"

Michaela pondered that briefly, then nodded, stuffed the blanket into the pouch of my haversack, and looped the carrying strap over her shoulder. "You're in charge. How do we find Red Boy?"

"The fog's lifting, so we'll follow the wash and search for their night camp. That don't fill our bucket, we'll head west to Red Oak Creek and scour the near bank. Our Shawnee and Red Boy can't any more go the morning without water than we can. That suit you?"

At her quick nod, I taken out along the stony bottom of the dry streambed. Beyond the dangling roots of the sycamore, the banks of the wash pressed inward and ran taller than my head, a situation both good and bad. The steep banks made it difficult for the Shawnee and Red Boy to climb from the streambed without leaving sign for us. But with no cover available except at the top of the banks, we were perfect targets for an ambush from the brush and trees lining the narrow waterway. Our only protection was the wispy fog and the dimness of the morning, neither of which would stop an arrow for you.

It was a nervous couple of miles before the wash leveled and widened and its banks lowered. The black mass of what had to be Howard Ridge, the highest point of land thereabouts, loomed in the thinning fog to the north. The brush gradually thinned on both flanks, presenting a different problem. Since the Shawnee could now depart the streambed virtually at his whim, every yard of bank had to be brought under close scrutiny. Risky as it was, I stationed Michaela on the south bank, the direction I figured the Shawnee was least likely to turn, and canvassed the opposite bank my ownself.

Michaela went about her task without complaint, but I suspected she, too, was fast succumbing to disappointment and frustration. In three miles we hadn't spotted the first skinned rock, the first scored patch of earth, the first disturbed leaf, or any other sign Red Boy and his captor were traveling the wash. The short and blunt of it was, they could be anywhere.

Her thinking matching mine, Michaela seated herself on a boulder and said in a lowered voice, "Mister Cooper, we're wasting our breath for naught."

Sighing, she removed her hat and ran fingers through her honey brown hair. Watching her, my heart missed an entire beat, then another. It scared me how she could without warning unsettle me so. Lord, I pleaded, save me from making a fool out of myself till I get her home to her father.

"How far is it to your Red Oak Creek?"

Her thinking was again in harness with mine. Our last hope rested on the slim chance the need of water had drawn the Shawnee to the nearest source and there he or Red Boy had left tracks that would put us on their trail. "The creek's yonder, can't be more than a mile, two at the most," I informed her.

Michaela donned her hat, rose from the boulder, and hitched the strap of the haversack higher on her shoulder. "After you, Mister Cooper. Your canteen's empty and I haven't been this thirsty in months."

It came to pass that we heard the splash of falling water in less than a mile, and around a northerly swing, the wash joined Red Oak Creek where the current spilled over flat shelves of rock. Thirsty or not, I motioned for Michaela to stay behind me and veered into the woods before we gained the confluence of wash and creek. As Breed was prone to say repeatedly, "Be forever leery, lad; it's a habit that keeps a man mated to his vital parts."

From well back in the trees, I studied the straight-flowing creek upstream and down. What I saw was gray rock and green water surrounded near and far by dark trunks bearing brown and yellow leaves. Nowhere could I find what I sought—that first glimpse of red skin or red hair.

Michaela hid her disappointment well. "Am I to die of thirst?"

"No," I said, extending my hand. "Pass me that canteen."

She fisted the canteen and stood instead. "I'll fetch the water; you stand guard for the both of us."

I didn't argue with her. She wanted to be doing something while she got used to the idea her Red Boy was undoubtedly gone for good. And, to tell the truth, I was beginning to believe it my ownself. Our Shawnee thief was probably three ridges over and traveling fast for his village with his four-legged booty. Nevertheless, I eased to the edge of the trees masking us from the creek, rifle poised at the ready. Count the pegs any way you liked, horse or no horse, we were still a full day's march from the safety of the general's station.

Michaela did more than just fill the canteen. She knelt beside the creek, removed her hat, and splashed water on her face and neck. Even in the dull light of the overcast morning, her honey brown hair, cropped shorter than that of the other women I had observed about Limestone, had a burnished sheen to it. It was difficult not to stare at her.

She rose with the lithe grace I had come to expect at her every movement and stoppered the canteen. My mind was already racing ahead as to the shortest route to Brandon Station when Michaela stiffened like a bird dog on point.

I wasted not a moment. "Duck low an' run to me," I ordered.

She ignored my command and took two strides upstream. By her excited beckoning, I realized the morning had suddenly gone awry. Her following words were the confirmation I didn't need to hear: "We've found them, Mister Cooper, we've found them!"

Imprint of iron shoe firm and sharply defined, the hoof mark at water's edge was perfect in every detail. It was a few hours old at most. And as excited as Michaela was, there would be no giving up the chase. She recognized a fresh track quick as Nathan Breed.

"They crossed here after dawn this morning and can't be so far ahead we can't catch them!" Michaela exclaimed. "Don't you agree?"

One thing about Michaela, tall as she was, I didn't have to bend at the waist hardly at all to talk to her. The drawback was you couldn't hide much from her. She could damn near look a man tall as me straight in the eye, and I was fast becoming aware she learned as much from watching you as she did listening. I was never able to decide at which she was better—reading my face, the tone of my voice, or what came from my mouth.

"We'll take up the trail. But first off, let me cross over, find more sign, an' make certain no redstick's waitin' out of sight yonder," I proposed. "Won't take but a few minutes, then I'll signal you to join me."

Her studied look made it apparent she was debating whether she should trust me. She was remembering my earlier reluctance to even bother searching for Red Boy. What if I found additional tracks but claimed there were none? How was she to know? I was fast learning another vital thing about Michaela Layton: You didn't tell her anything you later hoped she would forget.

I will admit, whatever threat might lurk across the creek, her "Don't be long" gave me a warm feeling. It was impossible not to want to please her.

Michaela, at my bidding, stepped into the trees again. I forded the creek at the highest of the tiered shelves of stone, affording myself the clearest possible view of the far bank all the while. No arrow zipped out to meet me, and my heart calmed as I searched at water's edge for tracks. They were there—a thin white scrape on the gray rock where Red Boy had emerged from the water, and half a horseshoe print in the damp earth filling a shallow depression closer to the solid ground of the bank. The Shawnee was growing careless. Perhaps with the passage of so many hours, he believed white pursuit was unlikely. It was his misfortune—and perhaps my own before everything was said and done—that he had unknowingly stolen Michaela Layton's future.

At my signal, she crossed the creek in double-time steps. The shoulder strap of the haversack riding her hip tugged her waistcoat fully open, exposing a wide expanse of white linen shirt. In her hurry, she seemed unaware how wildly her breasts bounced within that tight garment at each footfall. I wasn't. My mouth went dry and my throat took to throbbing. I turned about and fell to one knee facing away from her, hiding my blush and the sizable embarrassment she fostered on another part of me.

She halted behind me, head lowered near my shoulder. I felt her breath on my ear and blushed worse than ever. "Anything wrong?" she asked.

"No, nothing!" I blurted without looking around. "Follow me! We've got a heap of country to cover in a hurry!"

I heard Michaela huff at my harshness, but when I sneaked a quick peek to the rear, she was plumb in my wake. I didn't let her see but the back side of me for the next mile. The woman, I swear, could numb a man's brain just rushing to meet up with him. She worked your imagination half to death every waking hour you spent with her. She could make you careless and get you killed was what she could do. Damned if she couldn't!

The Shawnee continued westward along the bottom of a treed ravine, and the black prominence of Howard Ridge faded away behind us. With little stone underfoot now, we located sufficient hoof marks on ground blown clear of fallen leaves to successfully track Red Boy. We stayed on the move, disdaining rest and sipping water as we went. We had to be gaining on our redstick thief.

I had to think of something besides Michaela's body, so I dwelled on what was in store for us at the head of the ravine. We were climbing steadily and approaching a high vantage where we might obtain a glimpse of those we pursued. 'Lest we could fix the position of thief and stallion, our chances of ever intercepting them amounted to a fanciful dream. Other than our deaths, it would accomplish nothing to trail the Shawnee clean to the outskirts of his far-off village.

I didn't relate that to Michaela, for her renewed enthusiasm knew no bounds. ''We'll spy Red Boy soon, Mister Cooper. I just know it!''

And we did. We spied Red Boy. We also spied our Shawnee thief. Trouble was, we spied more than that . . . much more.

Enough to get us both killed twice over.

15

Close-set trees, stringy vine, and moss-covered boulders clogged the head of the ravine. Gouges torn in the soft loam revealed the incline had been a real challenge for Red Boy. We followed his tracks, Michaela close enough behind me she could maintain a tight grip on my rope belt.

Years of rain had carved a notch in the crest of the high ground, and Red Boy's hoof prints led straight to it. I heard Michaela's puzzled grunt as I pried her hand free of my belt and, shunning the easy path, angled into a cluster of mossy boulders that seemingly anchored a stand of young oaks. Well short of the upper fringe of the oaks, I removed my hat, dropped to my knees, and crawled forward till I could scan the country beyond the head of the ravine. Without any urging, Michaela, also hatless, wormed her way alongside me.

The crest fell away sharply, affording a wide-ranging view of what lay west of our position. A sea of brown and yellow leaves blanketed the bottoms to our left and right and the ascending hills of the opposing skyline. Directly below us was an open meadow in which marsh grass grew stout and thick. I inched ahead for a closer look. Marsh grass grew where springwater kept the soil moist, and fresh water attracted travelers like dung did flies. Equally important, Injuns favored such sites for their comings together.

"We're wasting precious minutes, Mister Cooper," an impatient Michaela said.

"Stay still and keep quiet, damn it. That heathen's got any sense he'll graze your stallion before he turns mean as all get out."

Michaela fell silent and I went on watching. I didn't often have the feelings of pending danger others swore by, but I was reluctant to climb down the slope and expose us to whoever might be occupying the spring.

Michaela was starting to squirm again when I spotted a sliver of crimson amongst the tree butts rimming the meadow. I squeezed her elbow to gain her attention as a Shawnee warrior led Red Boy onto the marsh grass. The warrior wore a hide shirt, clout, leggins, and tall beaded moccasins. Except for his feathered topknot, every hair including his brows had been plucked from his painted head. Silver bands circled his upper arms and hoops of the same metal dangled from his nostrils and earlobes. A sheathed knife and a knobbed war club stuck from his waist sash. In his left fist he carried a long rifle shorn of any bright or fancy furniture. The rifle's plain wooden stock had the polished gleam to it my Bedford did, the dull sheen of constant handling.

From two hundred feet up the slope, the Shawnee's red facial stripes and black-painted skull put a catch in Michaela's breath. ". . . That's him . . . We've found him."

"No," I whispered in return, "that's not the same Injun. He's not wearin' the hat you saw earlier, an' he's totin' a rifle not a bow."

"Then where's the other one?"

"Stay alert an' you'll soon know. Don't move a lick. That heathen spots us, we'll have company faster'n you can wriggle your nose."

The Shawnee unwound the leather rope tied to Red

Boy's halter and the stallion lowered his head and lipped at the marsh grass. Other than the patches of scorched hair on his haunch singed by Pratt's flying coals, the stud appeared none the worse for his captivity.

Michaela tensed as a second Shawnee entered the meadow. He, too, was hatless and, except for his blue cloth trade shirt, was dressed and armed exactly as his counterpart grazing Red Boy. The two heathen chatted briefly, enjoyed a hearty laugh, then the newcomer retraced his steps into the trees.

Michaela tapped my shoulder. At my frown, she pointed above the departing Shawnee. I had to look awfully close, but eventually discerned the wisp of breeze-shredded smoke hovering in the treetops. The heathen were cooking up an afternoon repast, from which Breed would surmise they were abandoning the fast of the warpath. If nothing else of note marked their foray along the Ohio, they had Red Boy to brag about across their fire.

Michaela's original Shawnee finally made his appearance. There was no mistaking him. A flop-brimmed hat shapeless as those worn by Michaela and me covered his painted skull. Tufted shafts of arrows borne in a back-side pouch poked above his left shoulder. A lengthy hunting bow, string to the front, straddled his right arm and shoulder. A spiked war club and large bladed war axe rested behind his wide leather belt. No metal bands circled his arms, but a silver gorget, big as my palm and strung from a leather thong tied about his heavy neck, overlaid the large black dot painted on his bare chest. The absence of a long rifle on his person made Michaela's horse thief no less formidable an enemy.

The horse thief set forth what sounded like boldly rendered commands and the Shawnee in charge of Red Boy responded instantly. He fished a metal pin from inside the front of his hide shirt, drove the pin into the ground with his hatchet, and picketed the stallion in the center of the meadow. The two Injuns, underling and war chief, then sauntered into the trees the direction of their fire.

"Now's our chance," Michaela whispered in my ear.

"Chance for what?"

"We can climb down and lead Red Boy off while they're busy feeding themselves. We don't try now, I've lost him forever," she insisted, voice rising.

I slid backward, tugging her after me. She came willingly, not yet understanding what I intended. But once we were below the crest of the ravine and I continued to draw away, let me tell you, she dug her heels in good and deep.

"Where are we going?" she demanded.

"Brandon Station, that's where," I countered.

"I'm not leaving Red Boy, by damned. I told you that. I've no future without him. I'll go after him alone if I have to!"

Anger had her eyes bright with those familiar gold flecks. Her quivering lower lip, the full one, told a different story. If possible, she was on the verge of lashing out at me and crying at the same time, and I feared that once she started doing either, she wouldn't stop till she exhausted herself. Damn but she did love that horse.

I grabbed Michaela by the arm and forced her against a conveniently placed tree trunk. I had never before deliberately laid a hand on her and my sudden roughness stunned her. Her eyes widened and her mouth popped open, and I took full advantage of the situation while it lasted.

"Listen to me, girl, no stud horse, not even Red Boy, is worth your lifeblood. You can always get another horse, but nobody can start you breathing again after you're dead and gone. We can't see it from up here, but those Shawnee are camped where they can watch Red Boy from their fire. And think about this," I said, my nose almost touching hers, "there may be more of the red devils about than we've seen so far. So whether you bygod like or not, we're not goin' anywhere near them or your damned Red Boy. I have to, I'll tie you hand and foot and carry you home to your father over my shoulder. You understand me?"

Her eyes were blazing hot now and she bit down hard on that quivering lower lip. She held it in—how I don't know, but she did. She didn't speak aloud. She simply lowered her head and nodded over and over.

I freed her arm and stepped away. "Ain't no point hangin' close to them redsticks a second longer. Follow me!"

I wasted no time mouthing useless sentiments over her having lost her prize possession. I doubted she was interested in hearing more, right then, from one Fell Cooper, and she would cry enough for the both of us. He wasn't mine, but I surely hated the loss of such a fine animal to heathen who had a sorry reputation, deserved or not, as to how they cared for their riding and breeding stock. Morgan Ramsey it was always claimed the Injun fed his dog first, 'cause that beast was a right handy blanket when the snow commenced to fly.

I never once looked back. I had no qualms about Michaela changing her mind on me. And if she wanted to shed a raft of tears that was private business.

With Brandon Station a day and a half march to the east, there was no avoiding another overnight stay in the open. Where we would camp tonight was vital. The afternoon was little warmer than when we had awakened at first light and it would be cold enough tonight we might see the ground white with frost come the next dawn. So 'lest we wanted to risk a fire, it was locate another hole in a creek bank or build some kind of shelter. No matter where we camped, we wouldn't sleep empty of belly. Enough jerk remained for a scanty meal.

I marched back down the bottom of the ravine, my strides purposely long and hurried. Early on I thought I heard a few muffled sobs behind me. Then all was quiet except for the occasional scrape of boot leather on tree root or the crunch of leaves underfoot. She grieved well, Michaela Layton did.

At Red Oak Creek we halted to fill the canteen and I had my first glimpse of her face. Her eyes were dry by then, but their redness at the corners and the wet splotches on the sleeves of her waistcoat told me she had indeed cried plenty.

Michaela gave me an embarrassed smile and said, "I apologize for my silliness. I'll not have you think I'm so selfish and unfeeling I'd get you killed over a mere horse."

"Apology accepted," I responded. "Now let's talk about what's ahead of us. It's too far around to return the way we came. So we'll travel upcreek till we pass the flank of Howard Ridge, then swing east through Porter Hollow. My guess is right, that should be the shortest route to Eagle Creek and the general's station."

"We can't raise the station before dark, can we?"

"No, afraid not. But before dark, we need to put as many miles as we can twixt us and them Shawnee. Have another drink and we'll taken out. Since the brush is thinner, we'll stick to this side of the creek for a while."

Trekking beyond the western flank of Howard Ridge consumed most of the day's remaining light. And as luck would have it, when it was time to cross the Red Oak and bear east, the stream had widened and ran deeper than my boots were tall. I called a halt, leaned the Bedford against a tree butt, and taking a seat next to the rifle, began removing my boots. Michaela started to do likewise.

"No cause for that. If'n anybody sleeps with cold feet tonight, it'll be me. You can ride across on my back."

Michaela paused with one boot half-off. "You certain you want to carry me? I'm no Rebecca Brandon."

Her slighting of herself set poorly with me. "You don't seem all that big to me. And I don't want you sickly when we meet your paw."

She watched patiently while I stuffed my woolen socks with their missing toes into my boots and tied the boots together with a thong from my shot pouch. If Michaela noticed the raggedness of my socks, she made no comment. Some darning was in order when I got home to Limestone.

I draped the thong around my neck so the boots hung in front of my chest, hefted the Bedford, and squatted in a crouch. "Climb aboard, mistress. Your chariot awaits."

She laughed lightly and settled on my back side, wrapping both arms about my neck. I took the full weight of her when I straightened. "Still sure you want to go through with this?"

"Never you worry, I ain't dropped a woman yet," I answered and walked into the creek.

The water was cold as ice on my bare shins. Mud, slimy and slippery, squished twixt my toes. I moved ahead with careful, probing steps. Once I was accustomed to the weight of her, Michaela seemed less of a burden. And hell's bells, she wasn't inclined to anything rash that might unseat her.

It was a sharp stone that done me in. I felt it in the mud too late to change my stride. Pain shot up my leg and I stumbled, tipping Michaela sideways. My knee buckled beneath me. I lurched forward to regain my balance and with that sudden jerking Michaela lost her grip on my neck.

She was doomed to a dunking 'lest I threw the Bedford into the water and grabbed her with both arms. I never ever told her I could have averted the indignities she was to suffer that early evening as a result of her fall into Red Oak Creek. It was just that I feared a wet, gummed-up rifle more than I did an angry, thoroughly soaked female.

She went into the thigh-deep water slick as a knife cutting through warm butter. The splash of her landing rose no higher than my waist. It was a full dunking. Every inch of her disappeared. The only part of her left above water was her hat, which floated quite nicely if I do say so my ownself.

Being courteous by nature, I plucked her hat from the water and had it waiting at the end of an outstretched arm when she surfaced. She came up sputtering and cursing, turning the air blue with choice swear words many men wouldn't deign to utter. Lordy, foul words aside, with her shirt plastered to her breasts, what a looker she was even sopping wet.

I was in for it and there was no escape. "God damn you, Cooper, you're a blight on the day for any honest woman. I lose my Hump and Red Boy, then you dump me in the water for good measure. I could shoot you dead if I had a gun and my father wouldn't hold me at fault. Damn you! Damn you anyway!''

Whatever I might muster as an excuse wasn't going to change the course of the ensuing evening, so I stood mute, rifle held safely above the water.

Michaela snatched her hat from my outstretched hand and waded to the far bank. Her anger was unending. ''Well, Cooper, you gonna stay in there all night and let me freeze to death or build me a fire?''

I slogged to the bank and marched past her bold as brass. New curses erupted, but she wasn't about to let me out of her sight. ''Come back here, damn you. Where are you going?''

A fire was precisely what I had in mind, but much as Michaela needed to be dried out, clothes included, I had no intention of lighting up the whole creek bottom. Stuffing my socks in the overlapping front of my frock shirt, I paused long enough to shuck into my boots.

Michaela's angry glare never left me. She was shivering already.

''Hatin' me ain't gonna warm you any, girl. Gather all the wood you can carry and follow me,'' I snapped.

As I hoped, my blunt order provoked a new surge of temper that got her feet started and off she trudged, swearing every other step.

Time being of the essence, I searched for a campsite east of the creek in the fading twilight. Fifty yards from the water, I encountered the massive trunk of a fallen tulip tree. The deadfall's roots tearing loose from the ground had created a crater a dozen feet wide and three feet deep. New growth higher than my head and thick enough to hide fire shine in every direction surrounded the crater.

I hastily gathered an armload of the sticks and branches lying about. First, I had to see to Michaela. Afterwards I would slant lengths of wood against the deadfall's trunk to shelter us from wind and frost.

She came huffing along as I finished. I shoved through the new growth, deposited my armload of wood, then held the slender trunks aside to form a path for her. Her anger had by now diminished considerably, for wet clothing and a stiff breeze robbed a soul of pluck right smartly.

On my knees, backside to what little wind reached the bottom of the crater, I crumbled dry leaves into a small pile. Next I emptied the priming powder from the pan of my rifle, plugged the touch hole, and replaced the powder with a piece of charred cloth from my tinderbox. A pull of the trigger rained sparks on the charred cloth and set it to smoking. I dropped the smoking cloth gingerly atop the pile of leaves and with a few puffs of breath got them burning.

In between adding sticks and then larger branches to the growing flames, I unplugged the touch hole and charged the pan of the Bedford with fresh priming. Michaela meantime hovered over the fire, desperate for its warmth.

It was time, I decided, to move ahead.

"See how wet the blanket is," I prompted.

Shaking with shivers, she fished the blanket from the haversack and unrolled it. "It doesn't seem possible but it's only wet on one corner."

"That's good, 'cause it'll keep you decent while your clothes dry."

Michaela looked wildly about. "I'm not undressing with you here!"

"Who said I was gonna stand around gawking at you, for chrissake," I announced just as loud, levering myself to my feet with the Bedford. "Give me the blanket."

Michaela hesitated, then, at my stern look, wadded the blanket up and tossed it to me. Those hazel eyes missed nothing as I spread the blanket wide and draped the upper corners over the outermost roots of the deadfall. "Now, I'll take a gander yonder while you undress behind the blanket," I said, peeling off one of my frock shirts. "Put this on before you pull the blanket about you."

I passed her the frock shirt along with my raggedy socks. "Tie the holes in the toes shut and they should still be big enough to cover your feet. Now, don't tarry around on me. We don't have you dry and warm damn quick, you'll be down with the fever or worse 'fore I know it. You understand?''

She nodded and stepped toward the hanging blanket. ''Get along with yourself. I'm too miserable to argue anything with you.''

I made an extra noisy exit through the surrounding young trees and dallied away the better part of an hour hidden on the bank of Red Oak Creek studying the country to the west. Hard as I tried, I could not spot the light of our fire from the direction of the creek, nor could I smell smoke since our campsite was downwind. Long as we didn't go to shouting at each other, we were safe and fairly snug for the night.

The chill air and hunger pangs gnawed my patience down to nothing, and I determined my female companion had had sufficient time to disrobe and make herself presentable as possible, so back I went.

A hatted Michaela was hunched beside the fire, the blanket wrapped about her. Her breeches, waistcoat, and linen shirt hung from sticks close to the flames. She had located my tin noggin in the haversack and it was heating at the edge of the coals. The smell was mouthwatering. ''Sassafras tea,'' she informed me. ''I found the roots searching for wood.''

I positioned a small log opposite her and eased my tired rump down onto it. A slim arm reached out. ''Open your hand for me.''

She filled my cupped palm with nuts each bigger than an inch through. ''Nuts from a shellbark hickory. They're delicious.''

''You found these, too?''

''Enough to fill both my coat pockets,'' she answered.

I started shelling the nuts with my knife while Michaela laid strips of jerk on a slab of bark she had brushed clean. Together, the tea, nutmeat, and jerk made for a decent meal. It was all her doing and I congratulated her.

''You warm through yet?'' I inquired.

''At last,'' she said with a sigh, pulling the blanket tighter about her shoulders. "I can almost forgive you for dropping me. You've really been very much the gentleman. Did you learn your manners from your mother?"

"Never knew her. She died the winter of my birth."

"Then who raised you?"

Her interest seemed genuine and, as usual, I had no problem conversing openly with her. I felt at certain moments that I had known this tall, willowy girl for months instead of two short days.

"I was sent to my uncle's cabin after my father drowned the next spring," I continued. "But Uncle Ben had eleven children of his own, and at five, I was shuffled off to live with a cousin named Hiram Fell. At ten I was bound out to Ash Cooper, a blacksmith and stable owner at Fort Pitt."

Michaela poured water from the canteen and sat a fresh noggin of tea in the coals of the fire. "How did you come to be whipped?"

"Ash Cooper thought I stole from him."

"Did you?"

"No, it was his own son. But I had no proof of that. He tied me to a floor post in his stable and gave me a stroke of the lash for every missing shilling, fifty all told."

"Didn't you hate him afterwards?"

"Somethin' powerful, but the flogging couldn't be undone and few folks will feed or shelter a supposed thief. So I stayed till I served my seven years. I was owed a rifle and a gold coin, and when I had them I walked away and never looked back. I bought passage on a flatboat bound for Kentucky. I arrived in Limestone hungry and without any prospects worth mentioning. By sheer chance, I met Pratt Jackson upon landing, and when he learned I could work metal and handle horses, he saw I got to meet Ned Henry. I been at the Henry Yard ever since."

"Is your Mister Henry a fair master?"

I couldn't help chuckling. "Fair but exacting. You don't pull in the harness, he'll you show you the cobbles. Your father and Ned Henry are much alike."

It was Michaela's turn to chuckle. "Yes, from what little

I saw of Ned Henry, I would agree with that.''

We fell silent while we shared tea from the noggin. It was pleasant sitting by the fire with a mostly full belly and I didn't want the talk to end. ''You said on the river your mother died when you were very young?''

Michaela licked her lips and nodded. ''Not as young as you, fortunately. It was twelve years ago. I was ten then. My mother was a camp woman,'' Michaela admitted without any hint of shame in her tone or on her face, ''but she loved my father and always provided for me. The Shawnee overran father's militia company and Mother was killed in that first assault. Father and the other men fought them off; then, in the middle of the night Father sneaked us away. It hurt Father awfully bad he had to leave his Jane Mary in the hands of such savages. After Mama's death, Father boarded me with the Brandon family till the fighting ceased.''

I remembered Hump Layton telling last winter how his beloved wife had lain unburied for a whole year on the bank of the Buffalo Bend. If Michaela knew of that, she chose not to share it with me.

Michaela swallowed and fiddled with the front of her blanket. ''I think of Mama at some point every day. She had spirit and never gossiped or repeated hurtful things that befell her ears. She could make our supper from black bark tea and biscuits full of weevils and convince us it was a king's feast. And Mama was more God-fearing than the village women who thought her a wayward female.''

I added branches to the fire. ''Good memories are precious as gold and should never be forgotten. They can be scarce as water in a drought.''

Michaela sat staring into the fire for some long moments, then shook herself and said, ''Mister Cooper, I believe we have need of more wood, and we best be building a shelter of some sorts, had we not?''

Much as I desired to continue chatting with her, she was right. The wood we had collected previously wouldn't last the night and the dampness of the chill air definitely promised frost in the morning. I made another gather, including the longer pieces required for our shelter. Slanting the longer pieces against the trunk of the deadfall near as possible to the fire and chinking them with leaves, I fashioned a lean-to wide enough and deep enough for the two of us in short order. For bedding, I mounded leaves underneath the slanting poles. My final chore entailed a trip to the creek to refill the canteen, my absence allowing Michaela to tend to whatever nature demanded of her at that hour. I did the same with my ownself.

On my return, she had positioned the thickest logs where they could be pushed slowly into the flames to keep our fire burning till dawn. Her shirt had dried, but her waistcoat and breeches were still too damp to wear. A feel inside her half boots and she sat them before the fire again. "Leather takes forever," Michaela lamented, rising to her feet. "It seems I'll have to count on you and the blanket to keep me warm, doesn't it, Mister Cooper?"

I had been doing real well not dwelling on what, if anything, she had on under that blanket besides the frock I had loaned her. Till now, that was. The mere sight of her bare lower legs and the question of how we would fit together under the blanket with her in a state of undress sent my senses reeling.

I tore my eyes from her and got terribly busy removing the tea noggin from the coals and piling more wood on the fire. I heard her giggle. "Don't set the camp afire, Mister Cooper," she warned softly.

When I looked about, she was standing by the opening of the lean-to, her hat gone from her honey brown hair. She knelt and crawled inside. "Come along," she called. "The leaves are frightfully cold without you."

With more than one stern reminder not only who her father was, but that I would also without doubt encounter that mountain of a man on the morrow, I snatched up the Bedford and crawled in after her. She was deep in the leaves facing the entryway. "You don't mind, we'll sleep as before," Michaela suggested.

Afraid I would trip on my tongue and croak like a bull-frog, I grunted and settled with my back side to her. She wasted not an instant. Leaves rustled, the end of the blanket came sailing over my shoulder, and she pressed herself against me from neck to thigh tight as a cocklebur sticks to the hair of a woods hound. A wholesome, contented sigh and smacking of the lips later, Michaela Layton, every single square unclad inch of her, was asleep.

I spent a long, restless night wishing I had my arms wrapped about Hump Layton's daughter and not the barrel of the Bedford. But sometimes things have a way of working out in our own best interests when we least expect it, for had I been sleeping as soundly as Michaela, we would both have been taken by surprise when some unexpected guests, armed and following our trail, came calling at first light.

16

Dawn, October 17

It wasn't the snapping of a grounded branch, the splash of water at the creek, the cry of a flying bird, the scurry of the four-legged, or the carry of voices that first alerted me. In autumn, with the morning cold and crisp, and dead leaves scattered everywhere waiting to betray the movement of any creature on the prowl, it was the total absence of noise that stood a man's hackles on edge. And mine were standing tall as they could reach.

As I had twice after midnight while retrieving her clothes and stoking the fire, I slid from under the blanket and crawled from the lean-to without awakening Michaela. Was I mistaken, there was no sense rousting her from her bed.

The fire was a jumble of glowing embers. I sat on my haunches with my jaws slacked and listened for sound of any significance. The dawn light brightened and a harsh cawing commenced the direction of the creek. The cawing heightened. It was a flock of crows, and something had flushed them from their roost. In one lengthy stride I was at the front of the lean-to poking Michaela with the barrel of the Bedford. "Rise and shine, girl. We've got company and you best hop into your clothes."

She bolted upright at the waist, clutching the blanket to her breast. She freed a hand and rubbed her eyes. "Your clothes are by your feet. Get dressed quick as you can," I urged. "The Shawnee are tracking us for all I know."

I'll grant her this, Michaela could forgo acting the lady when need be. She didn't waste time trying to wrestle into her breeches in the narrow privacy of the lean-to. She scurried from the makeshift shelter like a dog with a scalded tail. "Turn the other way, Mister Cooper. I'm not the enemy."

I scooped dirt on the embers of the fire and knelt in the farthest edge of the crater. The crows had let off their cawing. No new disturbance disrupted the gray, frosty morning.

Michaela eased down beside me. The middle buttons of her breeches were undone; otherwise she was fully dressed. "Hear anything?" she whispered.

I answered with a shake of the head.

We knelt hip to hip, more convinced with each passing minute I had raised a false alarm. It was those minutes of utter silence that made the booming greeting from the sky behind us seem even louder than it actually was:

"Morning, young'uns. On the watch, are we?"

Though I thought I recognized the deep voice, I wasn't inclined to unnecessary chances with an unarmed woman at my elbow. Placing a hand twixt Michaela's shoulder blades, I shoved her over the lip of the crater, spun on my knee without rising, and aimed the Bedford rearward, dogging the hammer to full cock.

Atop the massive deadfall, Hump Layton appeared twenty feet tall. He slowly raised his musket above his capped head. "Whoa now, lad. I'm just hunting a daughter," the huge spy proclaimed with a wide smile. "I ain't meanin' to scare you into shooting me by mistake."

I felt the fool. I had convinced myself the Shawnee were approaching from the creek on the west and given no thought to the ease with which an intruder might mount the deadfall at the limb end, walk along the trunk, and attack from the opposite quarter. Cursing inwardly, I lowered the hammer of the Bedford to half cock. So much for trusting to Fell Cooper for protection of your offspring.

Michaela rushed past me. "Father, how wonderful it is you've come for me."

To my astonishment, Hump Layton departed the deadfall in a sudden leap. He landed lightly next to the buried embers of the fire and swept his daughter into a bearish hug that lifted her boots from under her. A laughing, squealing Michaela kissed the corner of his mouth.

The big spy, laughing himself, lowered Michaela to the ground and studied her from hat to boot toes. "I'm powerful grateful you're unharmed, child."

He wasn't any more grateful than I, though my gratitude stemmed from a different source. If the big spy noticed what a wrinkled mess his daughter's fire-dried clothes were or that her breeches weren't completely buttoned, he kept it to himself. Had he caught us abed with Michaela virtually naked, I suspected Hump Layton would have been more of a threat to my life than treating with the Shawnee bare-handed. The rolling of Michaela's eyes back into her head as her father extended me his hand revealed she was as relieved as I was.

The big spy's grip was no less stout than it had been the previous winter. "I'm grateful for your traipsing after her. It's not the easiest of chores."

"My pleasure, Captain," I assured him. "I'm sorry she had to lose the wolfhound, then her stallion."

"Well, it may not be quite that bleak," Hump Layton said with a sly wink.

Michaela's brows knitted together. "What are you saying, Father?" she demanded.

A trilling whistle sifted through the young growth shielding the crater, a sound from the past with which I was well acquainted. "Why don't you join Nathan Breed, daughter? I believe he's leading something that belongs to you."

Without so much as a by-your-leave, Michaela leaped from the crater and barged toward the distant creek. Hump Layton nearly bent double with tear-spilling laughter. "God, lad, she ever loves any man like she does that horse, it might be safer for him to leave the country than to try sharin' a roof with her."

"How'd you free Red Boy?" I inquired.

The big spy sobered. "That was Breed's doing. I wanted to jump them seven heathen bastards in the dark, but Nathan wouldn't hear of it. That cuss went into their bloody camp, tied stockings cut from his blanket over Red Boy's hooves, and brought him out of there 'thout so much as a snort from that animal. Only bad thing is them Shawnee are probably pissed as spurned lovers and might come screechin' an' howlin' through the creek yonder most any time. Grab what you don't want to leave behind an' we'll join Breed and Michaela."

I stored the boiling noggin and the blanket in the haversack, then nodded I was ready. I turned and looked back just before I lost sight of the lean-to. Whether or not I ever saw Michaela alone again, I would never forget my night with her in that bed of leaves. Some particular memories were worth more than gold and stayed fresh as springwater in a man's mind.

Nathan Breed wasn't wearing his wolf-pelt mask, but daubs of red and yellow paint still decorated the center of his hairless cheeks. He was garbed entirely in buckskins fringed along the sleeves and across the chest. "Good you're alive, Fell. Captain, we got a ten-minute lead on 'em—no more, no less."

"Mount up, daughter," Hump Layton ordered. "We're in for a hard, fast push to the Station. I'll not risk losing you again."

Michaela nodded, but before mounting Red Boy she ran to me, embraced me, and kissed me on the cheek. "I won't forget you or what you did for me," she murmured loud enough only for my ears.

I spotted Hump Layton's frowning face over her shoulder. "Come along, girl. There are safer places for you to thank him."

Michaela grabbed a handful of mane, bounced on her left foot, and swung aboard the stallion. Hump Layton assigned the point to Breed. He and I trotted behind Red Boy and Michaela.

During that hard, fast push through Porter Hollow, it dawned on me that where I was headed the situation might not prove much safer than what I had endured the last two days. Brice Fowler was now quartered at Brandon Station. He had already paid to have me killed once and would most assuredly try again at the first opportunity. Then there was the matter of Michaela Layton. I was, quite frankly, totally smitten with her. But one wrong advance where she was concerned and I would have the indomitable Hump Layton to deal with as an irate father, not a friend.

I had the sinking feeling that whatever transpired after I reached the general's station, I would find myself standing in the fire, not the pan.

17

Never had I traveled so many miles in so few hours. My parched tongue stuck to the roof of my mouth, and my feet, blistered from miles of walking without socks, were a source of constant agony. As a result of Hump Layton's goading and his refusal to halt for rest or sustenance, we sighted Brandon Station late that afternoon. Then, and only then, the big spy allowed us to catch our breath.

From the western ridgeline, Brandon Station was an imposing stronghold and Hump Layton was most happy to share its virtues with his daughter. "The general insisted the pickets be oak rounds at least ten inches thick. They're twelve feet high with four feet buried in the ground. Our first chore was to erect the main blockhouse at the southeast corner. The whole crew slept there while we raised the pickets, hung the gates, an' built the smaller northwest blockhouse. Every minute we weren't haulin' logs an' buildin', we were busy fellin' trees an' plantin' corn and flax."

"Where do Rebecca and her mother sleep?" Michaela asked from atop Red Boy.

"Now that they're here, the Brandons and their servants

have the main blockhouse to themselves," Hump informed her. "Brice Fowler has the cabin at the northeast corner that was intended for him an' the major. Thanks to Breed's extra sweat, you, my girl, have a cabin of your own next to the northwest blockhouse where Nathan an' me throw our blanket. Thataway, you might have to heat my vittles, but you don't have to listen to my snoring, too."

Michaela shook her head. "You were never that bad, Father. Who else sleeps inside the pickets?"

"Just the unmarried men with me an' Nathan in the blockhouse. Rest of the inside ground went to the provision shed, the forge, an' the stables. The general figures the Injuns ever beset us in any number, the walls an' the main blockhouse will hold everyone long enough for us to send to Limestone for help. That's why the other families each have their own dwellings."

Hump lifted a huge arm and pointed south of the Station where six cabins stood beyond the flax and corn plantings, each within easy reach of Eagle Creek that flowed beneath the eastern ridgeline.

"So everything has gone as planned and you've suffered no major setbacks?"

Hump scratched his straggly beard. "Onliest one was the well we dug inside the walls. The water proved foul. We solved that by cutting a gate in the east wall twixt Brice's cabin an' the Brandon blockhouse. The water gate makes the fetchin' easier an' the main gate can be kept barred at night need be."

"Sun's goin' fast, Captain," Breed observed. "Ain't too late for them Shawnee to hassle us a tad before our own stoop."

Hump Layton nodded and led us off the ridgeline. Considerable timber had been removed from the high ground for pickets and we wended our way through huge stumps in the fading daylight. The base of the ridgeline abutted the work lot on the western fringe of the Station where firewood was chopped and stacked each morning. Railed fencing bordered the southern portion of the work lot. Stark rows of stalks and vines picked clean of eared growth, beans, and gourds lined the garden plot. Though not every stump had been removed, any other growth within sixty yards of the Station's four walls tall enough to hide lurking savages had been felled, then carted off or burned in place.

As I expected, at that early evening hour, the work lot was deserted. Hump ignored the small gate in the west wall providing direct access to the forge and tromped around to the main entryway that looked south the length of the valley. Smoke wafted from the chimneys of the outlying cabins and the Brandon blockhouse, and my belly being tucked so tight to my throat it was threatening to shut off my wind, I wasn't about to be choosy: Supper at any table would suffice.

It was none other than peg-legged Pratt who spotted us from within the Station. White beard bouncing on his skinny chest, he thumped out to meet us short of the wide front gates, both of which stood fully open. Hump Layton, leading Red Boy just then, reined the stallion to a halt. A frown creased the skin of his forehead. "Who's assigned to sentry duty?" the big spy demanded.

Pratt's smile went sour and he drew to attention. "Can't blame me, by damned. Brice Fowler, it was, said there ain't no point standin' watch till after dark."

"The general know there's no sentry?"

"Can't say. I'm just repeatin' what I heard at the forge fire this mornin'. I didn't hear nothin' from young Fowler hisself."

Breed whistled softly in warning as a new voice piped in. "That's Lieutenant Fowler, thank you, Mister Jackson."

Brice Fowler was splendidly garbed in lengthy black cloak and silk scarf. His polished boots shone like glass despite the growing twilight, and the hilt of his father's broadsword slanted from the folds of his cloak. "I canceled daytime sentry duty yesterday, Captain Layton. The men were grumbling, complaining they needed more leeway to ready their families for the coming winter. Are you questioning my judgment?"

Hump Layton could have broken the neck of the major's son easy as snapping a twig in two. Maybe it was the presence of Michaela. More likely, he stayed his hand and his temper out of respect for General Brandon's authority. If Hugh Brandon had put Brice Fowler in charge in the absence of the big spy, the issue of no sentries needed to be taken up with the general, not a fellow subordinate, even if you outranked him.

News of our arrival had spread within the Station and a high-pitched squeal of delight heralded the appearance of a flushed and excited Rebecca Brandon. She rushed past the tensed Brice and the stolid Hump, paying them no attention whatsoever. "Oh, get down, Michaela, get down. It's so grand you're here to sup with us. Mother was just asking after you."

Michaela slid from Red Boy and the two women hugged each other. "Father will want to hear all about your rescue. You and Captain Layton must join us at the table."

"We will, we will, soon as Red Boy's watered and stabled. First, though, I want you to meet someone."

It was me of whom she spoke, of course, and I managed to remove my hat without dropping it. "Rebecca, this is Fell Cooper. He found me stranded in the forest and protected me till Father caught up with us early this morning."

The general's daughter bent at the waist. "My pleasure, Mister Cooper. We've been terribly worried since your Mister Telow delivered his express that Michaela was lost. You'll have to tell us what you enjoyed most about your two nights alone with my best friend."

I nearly twisted the brim from my hat. I peeked at Hump Layton out of the corner of my eye and damned if he wasn't alert as a stalking painter. And there was no escaping Rebecca Brandon's carefully thrown net. "You will accompany Michaela and her father, won't you, Mister Cooper? The general will be most anxious to hear your story also."

"He'll be there in half an hour," Hump promised gruffly. "Pratt can water an' hay Red Boy. I'll take Michaela to her cabin. Mister Cooper, Breed will show you to the northwest blockhouse. I'll trust you to be at the general's door on time.''

I mustered a thoroughly respectful "Yes, sir" and followed Breed inside the Station. Hunger aside, I was far from thrilled with spending the balance of the evening with the general and his ladies. The closest I had ever been to a proper meal was my gander at the Brandon women, Brice Fowler, and Michaela at Monet's a fortnight ago, and I had shied clear immediately for good reason. Polite talk and refined manners were a world apart from the dining of which I had partaken at the Henry Yard or Ash Cooper's table. That old reprobate had fed me in the barn or under outlying trees, keeping as much distance as possible twixt any male and his decidedly ugly female offspring, Betsy. If allowed at the Cooper family table, I was seated at the far end and not a sound was uttered till I was dismissed.

But tonight I couldn't flee, and at the blockhouse, Askell Telow, Shorty, and Emil did little to assuage my worries. Soon as Breed told them of Rebecca Brandon's invitation and Hump's promise I would honor it, the funning started. "'Member to cut your meat in little pieces, Fell," Askell led off. "Them dainty women faint dead away you stuff a whole joint in yer jaws all to once. An' don't slarp yer tea. That tells 'em you eat shoulder to shoulder with the hoggish when you're out of their sight."

"He's tellin' the straight of it, lad," Shorty confirmed gleefully. "An' don't chew with your mouth hanging open. My maw fussed at that. She said it was an unpardonable sin to oink even if'n you're famished."

Not being bound by their own counsel, Askell, Shorty, and Emil, already at supper, had no compunction about slicing hunks of venison from a cooked deer quarter, chewing with much lip smacking, and washing the venison down with frequent draughts of rum. A belch befitting a farting cow completed each labored swallow.

"Do as we tell yuh, Fell," Emil contended, "an' you'll never embarrass yerself."

"You can't imagine how helpful you've been, gentlemen,'' I acknowledged with a disbelieving shake of the head.

A laughing Breed sobered enough to tell me the wash barrel was beside the forge gate. Once outside, I doused my face with cold water and employing Nathan's razor-sharp knife, scraped the three-day-old growth from my cheeks and chin more by feel than sight. Though I ran the risk of being late at the general's door, I then removed my boots at the blockhouse hearth, warmed my toes, and smeared my blisters with bear's grease. My feet would be weeks healing.

The blockhouse crowd gave me a profane send-off. They reminded me again and again how the wiles of beautiful young women could stupefy the strongest of men and bring him to his knees choking on the very meal they so graciously placed before him on the table. They were still yelling after me across the station yard when I rapped on the door of the Brandon blockhouse.

The yelling ceased as Michaela Layton swung the door wide and greeted me with a smile. ''The table is just now ready, Mister Cooper.''

I hastily swept my hat from my head and stepped inside. The downstairs of the blockhouse nearly equaled the dining hall at Monet's. A yawning fireplace occupied much of an entire wall. The table fronting the fireplace seated a dozen people and was lighted by three brass trees each holding six candles. Instead of painted china and silver cutlery, the settings, at least on this occasion, consisted of trenchers, noggins, forks, and spoons made of pewter. Black servants, male and female, were busy placing wooden platters mounded with vittles in the center of the plank table.

''Is this your young gallant?'' asked a portly figure wearing what Michaela would later tell me was a Ramillies wig with a braided queue.

''Yes, General Brandon, meet Fell Cooper,'' Michaela said to the portly figure.

I hoped the shock I felt didn't register on my face. General Hugh Brandon wasn't what I'd expected or imagined.

He was old and fat and, judging by the broken veins of his blue eyes, overly partial to rum and other spirits. Florid, freshly shaven jowls sagged to the blue cravat that circled his beefy neck. Heavy gold braid brightened the facings of his blue frock coat and sleeveless silk vest. His tan breeches ended at the knee. White silk stockings sized for his bulky calves covered his lower legs, and his black leather shoes sported elegant gold buckles. He appeared a bloated devotee of the parlor instead of a former military commander renowned for significant achievements afield.

I was struggling to determine what to say first and was spared that ordeal by a female voice announcing, "Gentlemen, may I have your attention?" The speaker was Laina Brandon. She wore a sack gown of green silk and her unfettered black tresses fell to her shoulders. "Supper is served."

General Brandon seated himself at the head of the table. His wife and daughter filled the chairs to his left. Hump Layton, Michaela, and I, in that order, sat to the general's right. Last to be seated, in the chair flanking Rebecca, was Brice Fowler.

Monumental as my hunger had become, it was a challenge to limit both the portions I lifted from the passing platters and my enthusiasm with spoon and fork. My belly didn't suffer unduly, though, for I followed Michaela's example and she was anything but timid when it came to eating and had nothing against second helpings. With the best manners possible, I devoured smoked ham, roasted goose, and loin of beef braised with thick gravy. I found additional space for corn mixed with beans, hoe cake, apple cobbler sprinkled with brown sugar, and suet pudding laced with raisins and brandy. The bread was piping hot and the butter newly churned. I savored every morsel of the vittles and every drop of the red, dry, delicious wine that flowed unchecked into the noggins in front of us from wooden tankards borne by the servants.

As we finished feasting, a squat servant adorned in purple livery supplied each male a long-stemmed clay pipe and fired the tobacco with splinters lighted at the hearth. Michaela eased back in her chair, emitted a sigh of total bliss, and unbuttoned her waistcoat. "God, that was absolutely wonderful. I never want to be that hungry again."

Rebecca Brandon had her opening. "Was there nothing to eat at all?"

"No, we had jerk, hickory nuts, and sassafras for tea. Luckily, they held out till Father and Nathan arrived. On the trip home, we had a little meal with water that we ate without stopping."

"You were in an almighty rush, Captain Layton," the general surmised.

"Seven Shawnee had Michaela's stallion and we decided to forgo a fight with them," Hump related. "Vital thing was to get Michaela home safe and with all her hair."

Rebecca Brandon, blue-black eyes mischievous in the candlelight, had no interest in how many Injuns had been out and about. "How did you sleep without shelter, Michaela? Did you even have blankets?"

Michaela leaned forward, her elbows resting on the table. "We had only one blanket, so we had to share both nights."

Hump Layton, caught in the middle of pouring wine into his mouth, choked, then snorted into his empty noggin, aping the honk of a startled goose. His cheeks reddened just as Michaela's had on the trail with me. "You did what?"

"Captain Layton," Laina Brandon chimed in, "I'm certain Michaela was quite capable of maintaining her dignity no matter the circumstances."

Reassurance from any female other than his own flesh and blood wasn't going to satisfy the big spy. What had to be flashing through his mind was the wrinkled clothing and unbuttoned breeches in which he had found Michaela that morning. What had really happened while his daughter was alone for two nights with a stranger he barely knew? "Well, dear girl, your father's waiting for an explanation."

Michaela wasn't inclined to permit any public prying into her private affairs. Red deep as that on Hump's cheeks swelled from the collar of her linen shirt. I guessed it was the red of anger, not embarrassment, and I was right.

"There will be no explanation, Father, to you or anyone. I spent two nights under a blanket close as skin to Fell Cooper and that's all I will admit to now or ever. Beyond that, everyone at this table can believe what they like, and I for one don't give a damn. I lead my life as I see fit, not according to how others think I should, so there."

The big spy squirmed in his chair like a hooked trout. He could bully men or cajole them or shame them into doing as he asked. None of that would fly here. Michaela was too old to spank and too grown in temperament to be threatened or ordered about 'lest she was willing. It was a lesson I intended to remember.

As I was already aware, Hump Layton was a man through and through, and if you were, you had the guts to admit you were mistaken no matter the price. He didn't disappoint me. He laid his clay pipe on the table and sat his wine noggin beside it. Staring each of us in the eye, he said, "I owe my daughter an apology. She answers to no one for her actions and that includes her lout of a father. My apologies to you, General, and your wife and Rebecca, for behaving badly at your table."

The general didn't disappoint me either. "Captain, your apology is unnecessary where my family is concerned, but its sincerity is beyond question. Jerral, we will have one last serving of wine all around please."

The purple-liveried servant circled the table filling noggins. The general resumed talking after he finished. "Mister Cooper, I'm afraid we must conclude the evening talking business, much as that distresses Laina and Rebecca. I have contracted with Reynolds and Lowe of Fort Pitt for delivery of our winter stores. Without such a shipment, flour and other essentials will soon be scarce in our larder."

"What is it you want, General Brandon?" I asked.

"I will again require the services of your pack animals once the Reynolds and Lowe flatboats dock at Limestone next month. Noah Reem, whom you met on the survey last winter, will be my personal agent for this transaction. Can you and your Ned Henry meet our needs?''

I had no qualms making such a commitment on Ned Henry's behalf. The boss man had experienced lean winters in the past and disliked them with a passion. When travelers and freight didn't move, the Henry Yard suffered accordingly. And the boss man was still counting on the Brandon land venture in Ohio to prove out, further enriching the company strongbox.

''Mister Henry will have packhorses ready and awaiting your boats. He will, howsomever, insist that he take charge of how and when we move your stores.''

The general begged to differ. ''And why is that?''

''Ned Henry rightfully fears the Shawnee. He'll insist we depart Limestone at dawn or earlier so we arrive here before dusk the same day. He may also ask you to send a party to meet him same as he did this time.''

''That we can do. Your Mister Henry is correct in believing Wayne and his legion won't subdue the Ohio tribes without a fight. Until that happens, we must remain on the alert and take no unnecessary chances.''

I don't know where I found the boldness to say what I did next, but I got it out without a hitch, my gaze on Brice Fowler all the while. ''Ned Henry, sir, will be pleased you agree with him about not exposing ourselves to surprises in the dark of night. Ain't nothing worse in his opinion then being shot at when you can't locate the enemy to return his fire.''

Ned Henry never said any such thing, leastways not with me present, but I felt not the slightest twinge over telling that lie, for while the rest at the table missed the sly smile that momentarily livened Brice Fowler's stern features, I did not.

He stared at me, the hate in his hawkish, cold little eyes fierce and rampant. I was hard-pressed to smother a smile of my own. Maybe a wise man didn't bait his enemy. Then again, maybe it was better that Brice Fowler understood I was no witless horse tender too stupid to fathom someone had paid to have him killed. It might not scare him off, but he would be forced if he tried again to make sure nothing went awry and there were no witnesses. Damned if my death was going to come easy or cheap for him.

"Mister Cooper, are you listening?"

"Sorry, General, I missed what you last said."

The general was perturbed my attention had wandered, but a full belly can put even an important soul in a forgiving mood. "I was agreeing with your Ned Henry's judgment that the proper commander prefers to fight his battles when he can clearly discern his foe. Right, Captain Layton?"

The big spy muttered and jerked upright in his chair. He had been nearly asleep. "Fine with me, Hugh, fine with me!"

The general sighed, his disappointment obvious to one and all. "I do believe, Laina, our guests need to retire early. Their lengthy march has worn them to a frazzle." He rose from his chair, waited for us to do the same, then held his wine noggin before him. "A final toast, ladies and gentlemen. Welcome to Brandon Station, Michaela. Now that you've joined us, I hope you will be our guest many an evening. Your charm and conversation are always welcome at my hearth."

We drank, Michaela turning a proper pink. At the door, she hugged Rebecca Brandon and they vowed to walk together the following morning. The general's daughter then offered me her hand, and when I clasped it gingerly, she stepped forward, stood on tiptoe, and pulled my head down so she could kiss my cheek. "Thank you for not letting Mike suffer any harm. I pray my teasing didn't insult you."

My blush burned my face and tickled the blazes out of the watching Hump Layton. I ignored him. Jumping by damned, maybe I hadn't kissed a girl for real yet, but a buss on the bare cheek the same day by each of the two most beautiful women I had ever seen was definitely significant progress, and made a man instantly long for more, much more.

I drew back, mouthed a decently rendered "Good night, Miss Brandon," and plunged after the departing Hump and Michaela.

Any doubt I might have had as to whether Michaela had observed my exchange with Rebecca Brandon was dispelled at the door of the Layton cabin. With a quick hug of her shoulder, Hump forged on to the blockhouse where he slept, leaving me alone with his daughter at the stone stoop. Michaela slid close so I could make her out in the darkness. Her teeth chattered from night cold and she wrapped her arms about herself. "Store this in that handsome head of yours. Rebecca may be my best friend, but she'll not steal you away from me."

The cabin door latched behind her before I could so much as blink. Not knowing what else to do, I picked my jaw off the ground and went to bed.

18

A rough shaking brought me awake. The first opening of an eye after a hard sleep, Hump Layton's bulk seemed to fill the entire lower level of the blockhouse. "Hate to spoil your dreams, lad, but Nathan wants to parley while we're all together."

Emil and Shorty sat on the edge of their rope beds. Perched on a stool across the room, Askell Telow cleaned his rifle. Nathan Breed was at the hearth, lighting his pipe. He waited to begin the parley, allowing Pratt Jackson time to add wood to the breakfast fire, then begin kneading meal, bear's oil, and water into Johnnycakes on a roof shingle.

"Tell it plain and ugly, Nathan," Hump Layton ordered.

The scout did exactly that. "Two weeks ago the Shawnee started keepin' watch on us. I've not seen them, but they're payin' considerable attention sudden like to everythin' we're doin'."

"Those red devils got the gall to attack us strong as these walls and gates be?" Pratt queried, asking the question on every mind.

"You all remember what happened at Morgan's, don't you?"

Every head in the room bobbed up and down. No borderer would soon forget the Shawnee raid deep into eastern Kentucky the past April. Two adults had died in the raid; nineteen others, mostly women and children, had been herded into captivity, and the station's cabins and blockhouses set afire. The raid by forty Shawnee had come without warning, and the savages had escaped back across the Ohio at the Scioto River virtually unscathed.

"The Morgan settlers grew careless," Breed said. "They stopped posting sentries. The men working the fields often went unarmed. When the attack came, they couldn't mount any defense to protect themselves. We do as they did, the Shawnee will lay into us good and proper."

Breed puffed on his pipe and blew smoke at the ceiling. "If'n Brice Fowler gains the general's ear, stick with the captain here. Don't walk into the same trap as young Brice. He thinks because the Shawnee haven't bothered us yet, they won't. It'll fall to us to keep the station from being taken by surprise. The Injuns ain't got cannons or any other means of breachin' the walls except to climb over them. With plenty of powder and vittles, we can hold out for days need be."

Hump Layton then directed the talk at me. "Fell, those stores you'll pack in next month are vital. With them, the station will be well stocked into the spring. Soon as the boats arrive at Limestone, send word, an' we'll meet you at the riverbank with an escort. Take no chances on an ambush."

"That I won't," I promised.

"Now, I know your Ned Henry may not approve," the big spy continued, "but Emil, Shorty, and Pratt will remain here. If he wants them back before the end of winter, he'll have to hire replacements. Either way, tell him General Brandon will settle with him later, and to his advantage."

"And Askell?"

"Him an' Breed will help you down to the Ohio with

your packhorses today. They'd eat up our stable fodder in short order. It'll be all we can do to feed Red Boy, our other riding stock, and the draught animals through the winter.''

Breed tapped the ash from his pipe into the palm of his hand and pitched it into the fire. ''When do you want to start, Fell?''

My blistered feet were saying next week, but Ned Henry would be expecting me at the Fagan's ferry landing before dark tonight; and I doubted the boss man would accept any excuses for my being late. With Pratt not making the return trip, the boss man was already losing his cook. I didn't need for anything else, like my fiddling about hoping to get a final gander at Michaela or Rebecca Brandon, to rile him up. ''We finish eating, I'll line out my horses straightaway.''

The dawn meal consisted of Pratt's Johnnycakes, cold venison quarter, and green tea so hot it scalded the throat you weren't careful. I ate my portion quickly and returned to the rope bed where I had slept to again rub bear's grease on my blisters. Pratt thumped in front of me, dug into the folds of his frock, and pulled forth the socks I had given to Michaela two nights ago. They had been washed and dried and the holes in the toes darned.

''How did you come by them?''

Pratt grinned and clacked his wooden teeth a-purpose. ''She caught me on the way back from my early pee. She asked I bring them to you, an' tell you she wants you to call on her no later than noon. 'At your convenience' was what she said.''

I was honestly glad for the return of my mended socks. But when I began thinking on it, I wasn't really anxious to rush over to Michaela's cabin. Much as I was attracted to her, her contention she would not lose me to the general's daughter unsettled me a heap and made me leery. Having a woman the fleshly way and providing for her were entirely different propositions. With Michaela, there would be no brief tryst on a bed. Any involvement with her would be total and complete; and the blunt truth was, if a man couldn't live up to her expectations and dreams, she would never know true happiness nor would he.

Wishing things was for children and would-be kings. I had next to nothing to offer any woman. I owed Ned Henry four more years of service. The hundred acres of Ohio I had earned as part of the Brandon survey nine months ago had yet to be sited, and I lacked the monies to improve on it. Beyond that, I owned in my name only the Shawnee mare, the Bedford rifle, and twenty dollars gold. Were my prospects any dimmer, I would be standing in the middle of a darkened room.

And so, playing the headstrong, doubting fool to the hilt, I talked myself out of even a parting good-bye at Michaela's stoop. I shucked into socks and boots, waved the waiting Askell and Breed after me, stomped from the blockhouse past her closed door with nary a glance, and scurried through the front gates of the station with the speed of a frightened rabbit.

In the creek bottom east of the station where Askell had picketed the pack animals, I brooked no surliness or laziness in lining them out for our departure. If Askell and Breed wondered about my sudden haste, they kept their ponderings to themselves.

In the far reaches of the south meadow, the station gates were visible through an opening in the trees lining the creek. Why I looked back, I don't know. Danged if she wasn't there, smack in the middle of that wide opening, wearing the blue dress that had shortened my breath before the stable at Monet's.

That chance sighting of her was to stick in my craw for days.

COLD MOON

December 1793

19

Late Afternoon, December 20

I paid dearly for running out on Michaela Layton. She was on my mind constantly, and I dreamed of her nearly every night. I came to despise the cowardice I had displayed, and after a while, Ned Henry considered it a normal day when he overheard me cursing and berating myself as I toiled at the forge in place of Emil and Shorty. No woman at all, I resolved, was better than not knowing where you stood with one from whom you were separated.

My mood soured even more when the general's winter stores failed to arrive within the month as scheduled. The continuing dry weather saw the Ohio inch ever lower till passage on the river was painstakingly slow, if at all possible. The usual October autumn rains finally commenced the last week of November. The river gradually rose, but still there was no sign of Noah Reem or the Reynolds and Lowe boats in his charge.

With the rain came mud thick and gooey that turned the Henry Yard into a quagmire, and my temperament reached the bottom of the barrel. For Ned Henry, on the other hand, the mud was a blessing, for he claimed it was refreshing to hear Fell Cooper cursing something other than himself. It was probably fortunate I was the boss man's only smithy at the moment and had, however reluctantly, agreed to learn the rudiments of hearth cooking. Otherwise, I might have been set out on the cobbles after a stinging dismissal, empty of pocket and belly.

Concern for whereabouts of the flatboats heightened as the early days of December came and went. Twice Nathan Breed showed at our door at the behest of the general. The scout on both visits reinforced the necessity of transporting the delayed stores as quickly as possible to Brandon Station for the settlers' existing stock of salt, meat, flour, sugar, and other staples would soon be exhausted. The general, Breed stressed, rightfully feared that prolonged hunger during the first winter on Eagle Creek might prove ruinous to his entire venture.

The weather changed for the better 20 December. The wind howled all night and the temperature plummeted. From the loft door of the barn that morning, the stable yard was no longer a score of muddy puddles, becoming instead a sheet of frozen hardpan the color of brown sugar. The slipping and sliding necessary to gain the crew cabin and light the breakfast fire was a welcome relief from the clinging goo that had dogged us for what seemed forever.

A Henry packhorseman, Clay Kendall it was, remarked twixt bites of hoe cake and boiled salt pork that maybe dame fate would start smiling on us since the weather was as it should be. And he was square on the mark, for what should come bucking the wind and dock at Limestone that very afternoon, why none other than the overdue Reynolds and Lowe flatboats.

Noah Reem was aboard the lead craft. I arrived at the landing as he disembarked. The future surgeon was no heavier, but his once pink cheeks were ruddy, and their sparse stubble hinted that where he had been too young to shave before, he did so now at least weekly. Upon sighting me, he tightened his cloak about his narrow frame and hurried forward.

Noah and I were excited to see each other. We enjoyed a long handshake and embraced. Given the gusting wind, it was nigh on to impossible to talk out in the open. Noah spied Pratt's favorite rum stopover, Clegg's Tavern, an establishment overlooking the public landing, and I followed him there like a hound trained to heel.

The wind had swept the streets clean and Clegg's was crowded, smoky, and noisy. Noah insisted we have a table at the frosted front window. He ordered us both a hot flip, his gaze never leaving his docked flatboats.

"Watch the two buckskinned fellows on the cabin roof of the second ship, Fell," he requested. "They take their pay from Brice Fowler. They've spent the last two months waiting to join him. Neither works for food nor money, but they lack for nothing."

The two men Noah pointed out were lean, black-bearded, and armed with rifle, hawk, and pistol. "Are they brothers?" I inquired.

"Cousins, I believe," Noah responded. "Jasper and Henlon Davies, if my information is correct. Whatever you want done, fair or foul, they're always ready and willing."

I sipped from my noggin. "That doesn't surprise me. Let me tell you what Brice has been up to since I first met him in October."

And with that I told everything I knew and suspected, sparing none of the details. Noah's brown eyes never blinked. Not a single one of my accusations astonished him. "Brice is that rare person that can shake hands with the devil and pray to the Lord in the same breath," Noah concluded. "His ambition knows no bounds. He intends to have the general's daughter and his wealth for himself."

We sat quietly then, enjoying the hot flip till I asked what had been on my mind since the evening the general had announced who would shepherd his stores down the Ohio. "Why are you here, Noah? Your ambition is to study medicine, not settle the back country."

Noah lowered his head and drew a circle with his finger in a wet spot on the surface of our table. "I wouldn't admit this to another soul but you, my friend. I'm hopelessly in love with Rebecca Brandon.''

His admission wasn't all that surprising. If not for Michaela, Rebecca might have been the woman haunting my dreams. ''Why do you say hopelessly, Noah? She hasn't spurned you, has she?''

''Lord no, it's just that she's two years older than me and treats me like a younger brother. And I'm afraid she's enamored with our boy Brice.''

I felt for Noah, but I was hardly a veteran in dealing with the fair maidens. For all I knew, the woman I loved might never speak to me again after I had turned coward and left her in the lurch. If she didn't, I had no one else to blame.

Feeling sorry for Noah as well as my ownself did loosen my tongue, though, and trusting him as I did, I blurted out the whole tale of my encounters to date with Michaela Layton. I did omit the part about her having to undress and sleep nearly naked under a single blanket with me a whole night.

Noah listened with rapt attention, nodding and smiling at various acts and words I attributed to Hump Layton's daughter. ''That's the Michaela I admire and respect, stubborn and direct as ever. But you're the lucky one, Fell, don't you see?''

''What do you mean lucky? I just told you she may have washed her hands of me after the way I turned tail on her.''

Noah shook his head and pounded the table with a fist. ''No, no, never fear, she's in love with you for crying out loud. She's never revealed as much about herself to any other suitor in a year as she did to you in two days.''

I wasn't as positive as Noah that I had won Michaela's heart. Even if I had, there were other considerations he seemed to be glossing over. ''Noah, I've no prospects worthy of offering her. I'm the same as a bound servant for another four years, an' I most likely won't be any richer then than I am now.''

Noah looked me square in the eye. ''Never underestimate Michaela. She has a way of getting what she wants no matter the odds. Rebecca can change with the wind, sometimes twice in the same hour. But not Mike. I've always thought that when she made her choice, it would be that man or nobody,'' Noah asserted with a devilish grin. ''And if you're that man, and I'm certain you are, you better be ready to love her or flee Kentucky altogether. There'll be no middle ground for either of you.''

Noah let me ponder that while he drained his noggin and wriggled two fingers above his head. Barnabas Clegg, the tavern owner, hustled a new round of flip to our table. The imbibing crowd filling the taproom had grown as the afternoon ticked along. Outside, spitting snow slanted past the frosted window. Beyond Noah's boats, whitecaps flecked the dark Ohio. Winter had descended upon Limestone in one turn of the clock.

''It'll be a cold, raw sailing tomorrow,'' I predicted.

Noah, staring through the window with me, sat his noggin on the table with a thud. ''Well, lookeehere, will you, Brice's hirelings must have grown a thirst they can't deny.''

Jasper and Henlon Davies were indeed approaching the tavern. The wind tortured the tall feathers protruding from the leather bands of their flop-brimmed hats. Both cousins had donned knee-length canvas coats and bore their rifles with them. They swept inside, glanced about quickly, and sidled up to the oaken bar opposite the roaring hearth fire. After Barnabas served them, they engaged the tavern owner in some earnest conversation.

''They appear in need of information, do they not?'' Noah remarked.

''Yes, and notice the gloves behind their belts and the hoods on their coats. A man could stay out all night dressed that warmly.''

''What are you thinking?''

I swallowed flip and said, ''I believe you've seen the last of the cousins till we get to Brandon Station. That's Toby Wright answering Barnabas's yell to join them.''

''Who's Toby?''

''An old long hunter who ekes a living from guiding

settlers wherever they want to travel. His pickin's are mighty slim this time of year, an' he'd be plumb pleased to oblige the Davies.''

"Oblige them for what?" Noah asked, curiosity mounting.

"Why, ol' Toby'd be only too happy, bad weather or not, to lead them cousins straight to their source of monies—Lieutenant Brice Fowler.''

Noah nodded with an understanding wink. "You're right. They're not part of the Reynolds and Lowe crews and can do as they please. They paid their passage at Fort Pitt.''

I tapped Noah's noggin with mine. "They'll be leavin' directly. Just you wait.''

And depart the Davies did, and judging by the surprised frown of Barnabas Clegg, hurriedly enough they didn't finish the libation they had ordered and paid for. If the cousins were aware Noah and I watched their every move, they gave no sign. Perhaps they didn't give a hoot. They already knew where we could be found tomorrow.

"You'll have to be careful once we cross the river, Fell. You give him the opportunity, Brice'll sic them on you in a flash. I wouldn't ever let those two catch you alone after dark.''

"I don't intend to," I promised. "But at some point down the path, Brice and I will have a personal reckoning.''

"Wanting to be a physician and save lives, I shouldn't say this, but if you're afforded the chance, kill the bastard so he can't ruin whatever future Rebecca has. I'll do it in cold blood if need be to protect her from him. I'd hang for Rebecca, Fell, I truly would.''

"Let's pray it doesn't come to that any time soon," I said, patting his forearm.

The snow had thickened, obscuring our view of the docked flatboats. The frosted glass of the window darkened as the afternoon grew late. "Noah, you're great company, the very best. Well," I amended, "the very best, except for Michaela. But I must help prepare the pack animals if we're to sail at first light. You have no objections to that, I hope.''

"None whatsoever. Fain Knott's son, Aaron, is our pilot and he hates night landings much as his father does. We'll be ready on our end.''

"Where will you sleep? We have room for you at the Henry Yard.''

"No, thanks, I have a desk in the cabin and will want to record the day's events in my journal before I retire. And to be honest, Aaron Knott is quite a dandy cook, even better than poor Cam Downing was.''

His remembrance of the departed Cam ended our repast on a somber note. We shook hands and embraced on the tavern stoop. Noah then faded into the swirling snow toward the river and I turned south for the Henry Yard.

Whatever lay ahead for us, whether it involved a battle with the Shawnee or the cunning treachery of Brice Fowler, Noah Reem would be there, solid and unshakable, a confidant on whom I could depend to keep a sharp watch on my back side—as I would on his.

Some things a man never had cause to doubt or question.

20

December 21

We departed Limestone shortly after first light, with the two Reynolds and Lowe flatboats and a third belonging to Ned Henry on which we loaded the ten pack animals. Clay Kendall was along to handle the horse strings with me once we made our landing at Eagle Creek. The boss man himself saw us off, worry creasing his pox-scarred features. Ned Henry was concerned that Simon Kenton and his rangers were departing that same morning in the opposite direction for Lexington to partake of a celebration lasting several days. The rangers and their leader were to receive the back pay due them for federal service against the Shawnee and their allies more than a year ago. With the rangers absent, Ned Henry had honest doubts the balance of Limestone's male inhabitants could be counted on to raise sufficient reinforcements if Brandon Station suddenly professed such a need. In essence, the general and his settlers were on their own till Simon and his lads returned.

The boss man had also been concerned that we hadn't immediately sent word alerting General Brandon his stores had arrived, and requesting an escort meet us at the mouth of Eagle Creek later this morning. I had contended that the two Davies would serve just fine as messengers. If we dispatched anybody else, they couldn't reach Brandon Station any sooner than the cousins and old Toby, who were already under way. After an hour of wrangling, Ned Henry had finally relented and accepted my judgment that Brice Fowler would inform the general we had sailed without delay. The scoundrel in black would never fail to curry favor with his future father-in-law.

An inch of snow whitened the ridgelines of the river bottom. Buoyed by the November rains, the Ohio ran full bank to bank, covering the sandbars and rocks that had bared their teeth when the water was low. Heavy slate gray clouds scuttled from the west. The morning breeze was stiff enough to numb bare skin. Noah and I ignored the cold and made the voyage on the cabin roof of the horse boat, reliving as we passed the Fishing Gut and Big Three Mile Creek our bloody fight with the Shawnee and subsequent march to the Fagan ferry.

Weak sunlight broke through the heavy clouds as we sailed beyond Logan's Gap. Aaron Knott soon signaled the following flatboats we were approaching Eagle Creek. Unlike our October arrival, we landed on the creek's western bank without incident. While the boat crews secured the mooring hawsers, Clay Kendall and I swung the gangplanks into position and began unloading the pack animals.

Aaron Knott lacked his father's wide frame and hairless skull, but he had the same bristling moustaches and bull voice. He was everywhere, prodding and advising, threatening when necessary, and cargo appeared on the bank fast as Clay and I could tie and lash. All the while, we kept our rifles close at hand and one eye on the trees and brush fronting the deeper woods. Noah protested initially, then agreed to maintain a lookout from the cabin roof where he could see up the creek and down the river.

We had the saddletrees of the first horse string fully loaded, and were leading up the second, when Noah's warning shout turned every head about. He was pointing north along the creek bank. "Rider coming in," he repeated.

I snatched up the Bedford and scampered into the trees in advance of the flatboats. I crouched and waited. Hoof-shattered ice crackled at the edge of the creek. A mass of green and yellow feathers floated above the brown weeds hiding me. I eased upward and was greeted by the delicately beautiful face of Rebecca Brandon. My sudden appearance frightened her, and she sawed on the reins and halted the mare she rode.

"What do you mean, scaring me for no good reason?" she demanded. "I might have thought you a Shawnee and fallen from the saddle."

"No harm intended, Miss Rebecca,' I said, doffing my hat. "But you shouldn't be riding about alone even in the daylight. The savages have the habit of catching you when you least expect them."

My admonishment, though respectfully spoken, only deepened her anger. "You'll not tell me what I can't do— you're not my father!"

Dismissing me with a haughty toss of the chin, she reined the mare sharply around, almost unseating herself. "Good morning, Mister Cooper!"

Without so much as a backward glance, Rebecca retreated at a near gallop. Feet squashed weeds behind me. "Who was that?"

"That, friend Noah, was the woman of your dreams," I said. "I just learned your future wife has quite a temper."

"That Rebecca does," Noah admitted without hesitation. "But shouldn't we go after her? She shouldn't be riding by herself."

"I'll see what she's up to. You trot back and tell Clay to finish loading the pack animals. I shan't be gone long, I don't believe."

"But—"

"I'm armed and you're not, Noah. And I don't want anything to delay our getting away from the river. Besides, you'll be coming along right after me."

Noah didn't like it, but he abided by my wishes. He realized that if I encountered trouble of any kind, he wouldn't be of any great help without a weapon. Like Rebecca Brandon before me, I went up the creek in a hurry.

I found it unthinkable that the general's daughter had ventured this many miles from the safety of her father's station by herself. It was more likely that she had accompanied the armed escort descending the creek to meet us. And if that held true, she would be with them only if Brice Fowler was in command. I couldn't imagine the general allowing her afield with an all-male party otherwise.

At the first turn of the creek, I angled across the jut of the bend for a looksee ahead. The clank of metal on metal and chiding talk pricked my ears. I peeked from twixt two splotch-barked sycamores. Brice Fowler, astride his black gelding, with Rebecca now riding at his stirrup, led a procession of six men who marched in a ragged line at their rear. The two riders were immersed in a private chat, punctuated by much laughter. The six men following them, while armed with a mixture of rifles and muskets, joshed and shoved and pinched one another, often falling behind enough they had to run to catch up. Not a soul paid any attention to his or her surroundings.

The escort's lack of caution in dangerous country was unpardonable. Had the redsticks been laying in wait instead of someone friendly, they would all, to the man, have perished in a few seconds of terror and bloodshed. More lamentably, their disdain for their own safety endangered the woman they were obligated to protect. Was Brice Fowler so enamored with the Brandon daughter he had completely forgotten his military training?

How I longed to stun them out of their wits with a ball over their heads. But if I panicked them and they started shooting, I might get one of them or myself killed. Still hoping to startle an ounce worth of sense into the whole bunch, I let them march abreast of me, then stepped suddenly from cover into their path.

Rebecca's mare shied, nearly throwing her. Brice Fowler

recovered in a half second from the shock of my unexpected appearance. He spurred his gelding twixt the shying mare and me, yanking his sword from its scabbard. "Hold it, I ain't no redstick," I called out.

For a fleeting moment, he seemed intent on sticking me anyhow. Then Rebecca Brandon, her mare under control again, interceded. "No, Brice, don't! It's Mister Cooper!"

Regret tightened his narrow-lipped mouth. With a rapid flick of the wrist, he touched me under the jaw with the tip of his sword. "Lucky for you I hear well, isn't it?"

I nodded slowly so I wouldn't slice my own skin on the razor edge of his blade. Though I had managed once to wrest his sword from him, I didn't attempt it now. Unlike before, he had the advantage, and if I dropped the Bedford to free my hands or reached for a belt weapon, he would have the excuse he needed to cut on me.

The escort had gathered around us. Brice sheathed his sword. "Well, gentleman, if you'll take notice, Mister Cooper's pack animals are nowhere in sight. Once more, for reasons known only to himself, he has abandoned the freight for which he is responsible. This time, however, it's not household furnishings, but the foodstuffs bound for the mouths of your children."

He was lying, of course. He knew that in October I had gone in search of Michaela. The problem was, I had no notion how many of those listening to him were aware of the truth of my actions. Grumbling erupted among the members of the escort.

"Gentlemen, we are in dire need of the foodstuffs on those flatboats. That remains our prime consideration. You may rest assured I will address the general in regard to Mister Cooper's shortcomings. Form column single file and let us proceed."

I had to give credit where credit was due. I marveled how the sonofabitch could feather his nest at the expense of those who disliked him the most. He was a master at bending the truth and presenting it to his audience when they were hungry to hear it. Give him the slightest opening and he could ruin a man's reputation in a heartbeat. He was a relentless, unyielding foe lethal as the bite of a copperhead snake.

"Lead us to the Ohio, Mister Cooper," Brice barked. "With all of us watching, I doubt you'll stray away as before."

It was my doing he had the upper hand for now, and to defy him would only worsen the situation for me. With a gritting of my teeth, I spun and made for the river. It would help if I didn't have to look at him while suffering his snide insults.

At the river, Clay, with help from Knott's crews, had the stores aboard the horses and ready for the upcreek journey. He raised a bushy brow at my stormy countenance. "Don't ask. Let's move out."

As an extra precaution, the boatmen had been paid by the general to accompany his stores to Brandon Station. They were armed with a motley collection of weapons ranging from trade muskets to wide, stubby swords, belaying pins, and dual pistols. A proper officer would have glared down his nose at them, and Brice did. Me, I was tickled with them. Their eye patches, missing ears, crooked noses, broken teeth, and numerous scars told you they were a bunch of seasoned hard knots. They gave no quarter, dearly loved a fight, and on the march, foreswore the cavalier demeanor I had witnessed among the escort sent to meet us. Thus, I had no objection when Brice sent the boatmen to the rear with the pack animals.

Once we were under way, I gained the attention of Aaron Knott. With him giving the orders, we divided the boatmen into two details and placed them on either side of the horse strings. Brice Fowler and Rebecca Brandon, Noah walking at her stirrup, took the point. The escort dispatched by the general filled in the middle of the column.

We covered the five miles to Brandon Station in two hours, arriving there in the early afternoon. The winter sun, what little we had seen of it since dawn, lacked the warmth to melt the snow already on the ground, and more began falling as we followed the creek past the outlying settler cabins and angled up the bank to the main gate.

A bell pealed repeatedly and bodies big and small, young and grown, flooded from the cabins behind us as well as the interior of the Station. Those greeting us yelled and clapped and crowded so close we were forced to halt short of the main gate. Bedlam ensued till Brice rose in his iron stirrups and bellowed, "Give way for General Brandon."

The throng quieted and opened a path extending to the yawning gate. The general sallied forth, his gait uncertain. He lumbered along with the help of a hickory cane. His florid jowls were unshaven and he winced with each small stride. I realized then and there that Hugh Brandon was a mighty sick man, the core of his strength eaten away by the ravages of painful gout and his fondness for hard liquor. It alarmed me that if he became bedridden, overall command of the station would revert to Brice Fowler.

I followed the general's gaze as his bleary blue eyes swept over the milling settlers. I saw hungry and anxious faces, but no Michaela. Where was she? 'Lest she had gone deaf in both ears, she had to have heard all the commotion.

The crowd waited patiently for the general to address them, but he seemed uncertain of what he should say, like words were suddenly strangers to him. Laina Brandon, clothed in a woolen shawl, elbow-length leather gloves, and a bright green muffler, came to his rescue. She whispered in his ear, and spoke aloud as soon as the general nodded his head.

"We've had a long month of extremely meager rations. Your general and I, therefore, though Christmas is four days away, are declaring tomorrow a feast day. You are all invited to eat at our table in the big blockhouse, ten at a time of course," the general's wife proposed, drawing a brief laugh from her listeners.

"After the feasting, the men will stand watch so the young women and children can sled down the western slope. We'll light torches at dusk and you may enjoy yourselves until you're exhausted. Then on Christmas, we'll do it all over again.''

I was certain the cheering could be heard as far as the Shawnee towns miles to the north. To be invited to dine at the general's table once was a rare thing—twice in the same week was beyond comprehension. Hats and sundry garments sailed into the air. Two of our escorts touched off their rifles.

The general let the revelers carry on till they started to tire, then raised his hand for quiet. Though weak, his smile was genuine. ''My lady and I will welcome you on the morrow.'' New cheering erupted as Laina guided him through the main gate.

The crowd dispersed, allowing Clay and I to lead our strings into the Station. The provision shed occupied the center of the north wall twixt the cabins of Brice Fowler and Michaela Layton. Michaela's door was tightly closed. Smoke slipped from the mud-and-wattle chimney, indicating someone was to home.

Pratt came thumping from the blockhouse next to her cabin. The old roustabout was swaddled in enough clothing to keep three men warm. ''Howdy, Fell. You an' them vittles is a mighty pretty sight,'' he said, pulling his scarf tighter about his scrawny neck.

Too shy to ask after Michaela directly, I tried a different tack. ''I didn't see Hump or Breed in the welcoming crowd.''

''Naw, they ain't here. They left on a hunt an' scout in the upper reaches of the creek two days ago. Lookin' for meat and Injuns or so they said,'' Pratt related. ''His daughter's frettin' somethin' awful over ol Hump. But I told her only the devil hisself can kill her pappy.''

Thankful Pratt had opened the way for me, I nodded at the Layton cabin. ''Michaela's not ailing, is she? I didn't lay eye on her either.''

''Naw, she's hale and hearty as ever. Saw her just this mornin' curryin' that stallion of hers.''

Though I was convinced something unusual was afoot

where Michaela was concerned, I was forced to swallow my curiosity for a while, for at that juncture, Aaron Knott stepped next to Pratt. "Are we ready to off-load your supplies, young Cooper?"

We brought the horses to the door of the provision shed two at a time. With the boatmen forming a line, the work progressed at a steady pace. Whole barrels and half barrels of salt, flour, salt pork, smoked fish, and sugar, then kegs of molasses, rum, dried apples, and wine, followed by bundles of smoked hams, sacks of cornmeal, and crocks of honey disappeared into the dark confines of the shed. The prospect of any soul at Brandon Station suffering from hunger the balance of the winter was now the remotest of possibilities.

With the unloading completed, Clay and I led the pack animals to the creek bottom east of the Station. There we stripped the saddles from them, checked each for raw spots, swellings, and lameness, then watered them carefully. By the time we finished hobbling and picketing them, the day was almost gone.

We were enjoying a last drink from the creek ourselves when Clay, kneeling beside me, said, "Fell, there's a jasper been eyeballin' us from the trees yonder for better'n an hour. Sneak a peek 'thout his knowin', an' see if'n you recognize him."

Given the wiry black beard that hung to the middle of his chest, the knee-length canvas coat, and the tall feathers adorning his hat crown, identifying one of the Davies cousins was easy as telling oak bark from that of the beech. Pinpointing which of the cousins spied on us was considerably more difficult.

"He's in the hire of Brice Fowler, the gent who led the general's escort to the river today," I informed Clay. "He and his cousin came across the Ohio with Toby Wright last night."

Clay Kendall was no novice when it came to the scheming of his fellow men. "Was I you, I'd keep a damn close watch over myself. Wouldn't be any need to spy, lessen you're up to somethin' you'd rather do from behind rather than to a man's face."

We gathered our gear and rifles and made for the Station. The Davies cousin spying from the trees was gone, fading quickly into the winter twilight. "He's a dangerous one, Fell. He wanted us to spot him."

With my mind on what the Davies and Brice might be planning against me, I was almost to the blockhouse before I thought of Michaela again. Her door was still tightly closed. Smoke still flowed from the chimney. If she wasn't ill, why had she not joined the others in welcoming us? Was she still angry over my running out on her a whole two months ago?

I stepped toward her door, then halted. No, by damned, I would make her come to me. I started cowtailing to her, she would soon bring me to heel forever. Pratt, it was, always cautioned that a man on a short halter had about as much say in his own affairs as a pen-bound hog being fattened for market. Damned if Fell Cooper would ever "oink" on command.

So off to bed I stomped, where I lay awake half the night regretting I hadn't had the guts to just knock on her door.

21

Feast Day, December 22

Three inches of fresh snow mantled the yard and roofs of the Station upon my rising, and though the air was clear at dawn, the dark, leaden clouds hovering overhead promised more snowfall was in the offing. The absence of any kind of wind fooled you into thinking it was warmer than it was till exposed skin lost its feeling. I wasn't at the creek with the horses but short minutes before I was wriggling and kneading toes and fingers to keep my blood moving.

Being persistent by nature and headstrong as certain women I had recently met, the pack animals broke the creek ice with their forelegs and took to drinking without any urging on my part. The watering went quickly, and since we wouldn't depart for another day, I removed their hobbles and lengthened their picket ropes to allow them more grazing range. Enough freedom to move about and they would scrape snow aside till they had fed themselves.

Pratt joined me, bearing two steaming noggins of tea. He was so bundled up I could see only his eyes. To drink, he parted his layered scarves the slightest crack. No other borderer I had ever met hated the winter with as much vehemence as the old roustabout. Ask and he would recite how he had lost his foot to frostbite in excruciating detail—blackened nails, putrid flesh, and all. It was a yarn best survived on an empty belly.

"She wants you," Pratt said through the scarves.

Thinking I hadn't heard him correctly, I responded accordingly. "For chrissake, clear your mouth so I can understand you! Who wants me?"

Assured a captive audience, Pratt slowly peeled away the protecting layers of wool. And naturally, he had to clack those wooden teeth of his together a few times before saying, "I forgot to tell last night that Michaela wants you should join her for breakfast this morning."

"You're not joshing me, are you? Cause if'n you are," I threatened, "I'll wring your scrawny neck for you."

"Whoa, lad, don't be hasty with me. I ain't done you a wrong turn afore, have I?" the old roustabout retorted.

I let my temper cool while I sipped hot tea. "What if'n I say to hell with her invite? How many times have you warned me not to let any woman put a tight halter on me?"

Pratt's eyes widened. "This ain't just any woman, lad. This be the daughter of Hump Layton, an' for you to refuse her invite would be an insult to him as well he might not overlook. You understand what ol Pratt's sayin' here?"

I didn't have to ponder on it long. "Yeh, I don't need Hump Layton peeved at me if'n I have any desires on his daughter."

Pratt snorted and bobbed his head. "You got it figured straight, an' you best be on your way. She'll be gettin' anxious since she expected you at first light."

From the creek bottom to her door, I thought of a hundred excuses I might offer for why I had disappointed her in the past by running away. They proved, one and all, lame and indefensible. In short, I owed Michaela an apology on whatever terms she chose. That was, if I ever wanted to have her for a friend . . . or a lover.

The latch string was out. I stood on the stoop, bucking up my courage, then in a fit of pure bluster swung the door wide and stepped inside, slamming it behind me to keep out the cold air.

Michaela wasn't waiting demurely at the table, breakfast vittles spread before her. She was standing in a tub of water before a blazing hearth fire, naked as the moment she was born. I froze stiff as a tree, unable to speak, unable to move, unable to do anything except stare at the pure magnificence of her body. High square shoulders sloped to firm full breasts capped with nipples pointed and red. Her belly was flat as a board, the belly hole deep and intriguing. At the bottom of her belly, I was treated to long tapered legs that ended with ankles slim and finely hone.

As if my intrusion was as ordinary as sitting down to tea, she gave me a polite smile and said, "You might at least hand a girl a drying cloth and her robe. That is, if you intend to stay awhile."

Totally overwhelmed, I fled. I mumbled something sounding stupid and silly, backed for the door, missed the latch string, tried again, got a frantic grip on it. I jerked the door open, realized what I might be revealing to any chance passerby, yanked the door closed behind me with a hefty tug, and didn't stop running till I was in the creek bottom amongst my grazing pack animals. Legs spread wide, head lowered, I sucked air in huge gulps, fearing my heart might yet explode from the pure excitement of what I had just seen.

I thought Pratt had long since returned to the blockhouse, thus his voice jolted me upright. "You taken sick, lad? You're white as the snow."

"No, I'll be all right. Lost my wind for a moment is all."

Pratt didn't believe me, of course. But he had known where I was headed and respected Michaela's privacy too much to ask if anything had gone wrong. "Then let's hike on up to our quarters an' I'll cook us some breakfast. We old farts can't let you young bucks go without a proper start to your day, can we now."

Try as I might, I couldn't for an instant forget the sight

of Michaela standing in that tub. I ate and drank what Pratt set before me, remembering neither the taste nor the smell of it. Afterwards, I cut cane for the horses on the far bank of the creek, then passed the morning watching Emil and Shorty work at the forge in the southwest corner of the Station. They had little time to talk, and I was happy to be busy fetching wood for their fire.

The feasting began at noon. By then, the Brandon servants had beaten a path in the snow twixt the general's blockhouse and the provision shed. The first guests, arrayed in their best and finest, drifted through the main gate and Michaela emerged from her cabin to help with the serving. I watched her every step as she crossed to the blockhouse, the easy sway of her hips heating my blood to a boil. I couldn't convince myself beyond all doubt that she had deliberately shown herself to me. But if she had, she had made an impression on me that would accompany me to my grave if I lived a hundred years.

I lingered at the forge through the afternoon, watching the comings and goings. The last group called to the table consisted of the two smiths, Pratt, Aaron Knott along with five of his boatmen, and me. The river captain had hastily schooled his men in what would pass for acceptable manners. There was no rushing to empty trenchers, no eating with fingers, no rambunctious gulping of wine, no belching or swearing in evidence. Pratt remarked later that so long as Michaela and Rebecca Brandon were willing to lean over their shoulders and serve them, Aaron Knott's sailors would have done the angels of the Lord proud when it came to proper eating.

Michaela served the opposite side of the table from me and never once during the meal did she pay any particular attention to me. Her indifference infuriated me at first. But by the last sip of wine, I realized she had every right to ignore me. Hadn't I shunned an opportunity any other man would have jumped at had it cost him his very life? Love misery, I was learning, made damn poor company.

The sledding commenced at dusk. Bedford in hand, I

took the watch at the crest of the western slope. I did so because I suspected Michaela would stay the evening and roar down the slippery hill often as possible. After a few trips, she saw that the youngest of the children had their chance at the sleds. When the youngsters caved in to fatigue, she and Rebecca made the long run together a half dozen times, chattering constantly about male friends with whom they had shared sleds before leaving Virginia.

The increasing cold and the exhaustion of our supply of pine-knot torches curtailed the sledding after just three hours. The mostly satisfied gathering dispersed quickly to seek the warmth of a fire and a hot toddy. Clay and I reached the main gate last, where we met up with Hump Layton, fresh from his scout to the north. Noah Reem stood at his side.

"Fell, I have need of you, if'n you'll follow me. You, too, Noah. I don't plan on brookin' any dillydallyin' tonight."

Noah and I exchanged puzzled looks, but did as we were told. The big spy tromped through the gate and in a few steps we knew our destination—the general's blockhouse. We quickened our pace so as not to fall behind. If Hump Layton requested a parley at this late hour, he had news of paramount importance that couldn't wait till the morning.

The general, his wife, Rebecca, and Brice Fowler were seated in chairs in front of the hearth. Hump Layton, huge in his buffalo-hide coat, walked to the general's side. "Sorry to bother you at such a late hour, Hugh, but you best hear my report yet tonight."

"Not even a 'hello,' Captain. You must have much to tell. Pull up a chair and join us, why don't you," the general suggested, talking around his tongue. If he wasn't drunk, Hugh Brandon had a snootful of liquor in him.

"I'll stand, you don't mind," the big spy responded. "This shan't take long."

"Can't it wait until the morning, Captain Layton? 'Lest the Shawnee are at our very door, a few hours can hardly be that important, can they?" Brice Fowler interjected.

Hump Layton simply ignored him. "Hugh, Nathan and I found fresh sign in the upper reaches of the creek, half day's march away. Nathan stayed to see if'n he can ferret out what they're up to. It ain't ordinary to come on so much sign in one place in cold weather, particularly this far south. It may be just a large huntin' party, then again it may not."

"What is it you want of me, Captain?"

"We need everyone alert an' at the ready. We need to post sentries round the clock, an' work the fields an' the wood lot in pairs. We need to assign guards to the women when they're at the creek washing, an' when they're fetchin' water. No man goes anywhere without his weapon. Liken I said, maybe all that sign will amount to nothin', but we don't want to lose a single soul to the redsticks, not one solitary scalp."

Brice Fowler shot to his feet. "I must protest this foolishness. By your own admission the savages are nowhere near the Station yet, an' Nathan Breed has plenty of time to warn us if they truly are a threat to our well-being. General Brandon, it would be sinful to undo all the good your feast accomplished today with an Injun scare that never materializes. We don't want to discourage your charges unnecessarily. We must remember we are counting on more Virginians coming out in the spring. Your success, the success of your whole venture in this godforsaken wilderness, rests on that happening."

It was one fine speech, but Hump Layton wasn't buying a word of it. "Hugh, it would be just as ruinous if'n we let the redsticks surprise us. It's too late for anythin' when you're buryin' the dead."

Every eye was on the general, the women leaning forward in their chairs. To my disbelief, he rose to the occasion. Fat jowls shaking, he thrust his beefy chest forward, and for a few moments he was the staunch military leader who had won renown fighting the Redcoats. When he spoke, the slur was gone from his speech. "Brice, I'll not turn my back on the counsel of Captain Layton. Our first and foremost responsibility is the safety of every man, woman, and child. In the morning, you will implement the precautions the captain has spelled out, each and every one. That's an order, Lieutenant.''

Brice Fowler took his defeat with surprising calm, for now. "Yes, sir, it will be done the first thing," he promised, knuckling his forehead.

What the dandy didn't take calmly, at least not outwardly, was Rebecca Brandon's parting words to Noah at the door. "We will still walk in the forenoon. You may call anytime after nine," she said softly with a kiss to his cheek.

The annoyance flitting across Brice's hawkish features made his bleak eyes glitter like ice. He was confronting Rebecca about her planned walk with Noah as the door shut after us. The delighted Noah was unaware of what was transpiring behind that closed door, but he and I would have to talk soon about the danger of Rebecca playing him against Brice. Were I in his boots, Noah would do likewise, no matter how much hurt and disappointment might result.

"Don't think your presence wasn't worthwhile, young'uns," Hump Layton told us at the center of the station yard. "Hugh ain't so quick to forgo his proper duty when a few of the troops are on the scene." The big spy's capped head shook sadly. "Hugh just developed too great a liking for the cards an' the wineglass an' willin' women. It sparked a rot in him that's left him a shell of what was once a great officer. Hadn't been for Brice's daddy, the major, he would have gone under long ago. That's why he overlooks so much in Brice—he's payin' Asa back.''

Layton's sigh was a gush of spent air. "Let's just hope Hugh's blind loyalty isn't our undoing. Gentlemen, I thank you. Now I must say good night to Michaela before I turn in with you at the blockhouse.''

A warm bed was terribly enticing, but I had chores that required me to visit the creek bottom, so I went my separate way. My talk with Noah would have to wait till I returned or the morning.

The path descending from the bench on which the Station

rested to the creek was a pale span of much-tracked-over snow. Trees and brush grew close on either flank. I had the inkling if Hump Layton held sway, the cover surrounding me would feel the bite of the clearing axe come daylight.

The pack animals were bunched together just beyond the trees, well back from the creek and out of the wind. I divided the cane I had chopped and toted earlier amongst them while I took my head count. They were all there.

My ear caught the *zzzzzt* of compacting snow. I dismissed it at first, but then thought again. None of the horses had been moving or stomping at that exact same second, and the sound, coming from behind them, could only have originated in the trees toward the Station.

I was in the open with no real cover except for the bunched horses. Quiet as I could, I slipped twixt two of them, removed my hat, and peeked over their backs. The moon, what there was of it, hung in the western sky. In the dim light, I studied the trees and brush separating me from the safety of the Station. If anyone lay in wait for me, he was well hidden.

Beyond the horses, closer to the trees, I identified a large shadow as a tree stump tall as my waist. Fearing the person stalking me was moving to where he could have a clean shot at me, I gripped the Bedford with both hands, lunged into the open, plunged downward, slid on my face, and rolled behind the stump. No shot rang out. I dug snow from my ears and held fast.

By then, I was chilled through and getting mad. What if no one was there? Was I willing to freeze to death out of fear over nothing? What steadied me was an old contention of Breed's: Impatience was for dimwits and the suddenly departed.

I was lower to the ground now, and when I peeked around the stump, the moon was directly behind the trees hiding my assailant. I never stared harder or longer in my life. I missed it the first two tries but not the third. No tree had ever grown a branch so perfectly round and so straight up and down. Sure as rain was wet that was a rifle barrel.

I drug the Bedford up against my chest and slipped the cover from the lock. Knowing I might have lost my priming sliding and rolling around in the snow, I pulled the hammer back and recharged the pan with my horn by feel. I wasn't worried if snow had gotten down the barrel, it wouldn't melt in the cold anyway. Lord, was it better when you knew where the enemy was and held a loaded gun.

But what should I do next? If I waited too long to take action, he could gain the advantage again simply by changing position. I kicked it around in my head and decided I would risk the open ground again, eyes never leaving that rifle barrel, and make for the path up the bank. If that barrel moved to draw bead on me, I would fall to a knee and send a ball just below it. Whoever was out there had to realize a rifle shot in the still night would empty the Station in a flash. Whether I missed or not, once I fired, I was bolting for home and some help.

I sucked a deep breath and, knees crouched, slid from behind the stump. The rifle barrel didn't move. Heart trying to climb out of my throat, I took another smooth stride.

"Get down, Cooper, get down!"

Had I not taken orders from him before without thought, I would have hesitated. But when Hump Layton shouted an order, you damn well obeyed on the instant. I flung myself into the snow on my back side.

The shiny gleam of polished steel winked in the feeble moonlight. The thrown tomahawk passed over my prone body and buried itself with a sharp thud in the tree stump I had abandoned. That thud was still echoing in my ear when a black body hurtled from the night and landed atop my chest. Knocked breathless, I pushed up with the Bedford and squirmed sideways. I never saw the slash of the knife that laid my cheek open, missing my eye by the width of the blade.

Frightened and hurting, I shoved against the snow with my heels, desperate to get from under him before the knife struck again. He grunted, spewing spittle on my forehead, and his weight lifted from my chest. I rolled over and scrambled to my feet. I had my knife clear of its scabbard when the black body hurtled at me once more, landing at my feet.

I peered through the gloomy light and made out one of the Davies cousins. He was gagging on his own blood and tugging futilely on the handle of a knife buried hilt-deep beneath his rib cage. I jumped backward and looked wildly about. "There's two of them, Captain! They're always together!"

"Easy, lad, easy," Hump Layton said calmly. He leaned down and pulled his knife from lifeless fingers. "Next time they meet up, they can greet each other in the fires of Hell."

"You took the other one, too?"

"Yep, that's why that rifle barrel never moved. This one didn't know his partner was dead, so he stayed after you."

Wiping his knife blade on his leggins, the big spy stepped in front of me. "You hurt bad, lad?"

I swiped blood from my jaw and shook my head. "Slash on the cheek is all."

"Thank the Lord," Hump intoned. "That child of mine would never allow me a forgiving moment if'n anything serious was to befall you."

I didn't say aloud what I was thinking—that perhaps his daughter thought less of me than when he had left on his scout. "How did you come on to the Davies?"

"I saw them leave by the water gate next to Brice's cabin just as you went out of sight. I never seen either of 'em before, but not havin' any dogs to hunt with, they had no call to go off into the night so sneaky like. They was clever. They get on two sides of you, then one makes a noise. When you decide to move on that one, the one you ain't aware of kills you quick and easy. Injuns ain't any better than these two. What was their names?"

"Jasper an' Henlon Davies. They're Brice Fowler's hirelings."

"By damned, ain't this our lucky night."

"What do you mean by that?"

The big spy sheathed his knife. "Nothin' gets folks to

watchin' out for themselves like a freshly scalped body. You head up to the blockhouse an' have Noah sew on that cheek. I'll drag the Davies over where the women gather water an' lift their hair. There's so many tracks along the creek there, nobody but Breed could ever sort out it wasn't Shawnee that done them in.''

I gaped at him. ''And I thought Brice Fowler was the most devious soul I'd ever met.''

''Not hardly, lad. An' think about it, he don't dare say a word it was anythin' different or he'll have to confess he set the Davies on you. A sweet piece of meat pie all around, ain't it now.''

He stooped and retrieved my Bedford. ''Noah needs to see to that cut. Soon as I do for these two, I won't be far behind you.''

At the blockhouse Pratt and Askell still sipped toddies before the hearth. Noah answered my pounding, and soon as he saw my cheek he called for Pratt to stoke up the fire and sent Askell for his physician's chest. Once I was seated on a split-log bench, he tended to me. Awakened by the commotion, Emil and Shorty clumb from their rope beds to watch.

''Not a lot of swelling yet, which is good,'' Noah observed, pulling the wound open. ''Its deep, Fell, nearly to the bone under the eye. We'll have to suture it. Otherwise, you'll have a scar wide as my thumb that may turn the ladies' heads the wrong way. Give me some rum, Pratt.''

He tilted my head. ''Grab the bench, Fell, this will sting like the blazes,'' he warned just before pouring the liquor over the gash in my skin.

My senses reeled and my eyes watered, but I didn't cry out. Then it got worse. With Askell pushing the wound tightly shut for him, Noah employed a crooked needle and made his sutures with waxed shoemaker's thread, God forbid, explaining everything as he worked. ''It was Dr. Christiansen taught me to me to pass the needle the same distance either side of the wound as the depth of it and tie each ligature with a double knot.''

The pain was akin to what I had suffered cutting off my own finger at Big Three Mile Creek. I didn't swoon on him, but I was one happy fellow when Noah applied lengths of sticking plaster to hold his ligatures tight and declared himself finished. "There, that's as neat as I can sew, my friend. Some say to sever the thread after two or three days. Dr. Christiansen believes one usually suffices."

I couldn't contain myself any longer. "For chrissake, Noah, can I have some of that rum for drinking purposes now?"

Pratt howled, handed me the rum jug, and leaned close for a better view of my sewn cheek. "Feisty as ever, ain't he? Ain't no doubt about somethin' else neither. He ain't as pretty as he once was."

"Quit fussin' at him, you flip-crazy rumhead," Askell shot in. "Ain't it about time we asked who done the cuttin' on him?"

"Too many ears may be listenin' for that tonight," Hump Layton said from over by the door, nodding his capped head toward the ceiling above which slept Aaron Knott and his sailors. Not a soul present missed the blood staining his hide coat as he advanced into the firelight. "Gentlemen, the hour is late an' this might be the last decent night's sleep you'll have till the moon changes. Let's get in your blankets."

Askell's brows lifted, but even he lacked the gumption to challenge Hump Layton with the results of a fight in the dark glistening on the big spy's shoulder. So to bed we trooped.

"An', Cooper, put that rum jug back on the bench. Sore as your face will be in the mornin', you won't want your brain throbbin', too, will you now?"

22

Dull thunks brought me slowly and reluctantly from deep
sleep. I rose on an elbow and identified the sound as coming from the hearth. I shifted higher to peer over the chest
of the snoring Emil and saw a tall gray wolf adding wood
to the fire. The wolf turned and I saw that his jaws were
hairless and his cheeks painted in swirls. The sight of Nathan Breed in his wolf-pelt coat, home to report to Hump
Layton, brought me fully awake.

"Scoot out of that blanket, Pratt, and boil the man some
tea," Layton ordered from the far corner.

Pratt hung his steeping kettle on a hearth trammel and
beds emptied as everyone shucked their blankets and gathered close so as not to miss a word the scout said. Breed
slid his wolf mask back on his head and sat astride the half-
log bench on which I had suffered Noah's needle. "Captain, I'm feared we're in for a rough go of it."

"How would that be, Nathan?" Layton prompted.

"The Shawnee are still hanging about a half day to the
north. Yesterday, I crossed the tracks of three heavily burdened pack animals bound this way. I could never get to

where I could lay eye on them, not that I didn't try. But for the red devils to gather in large numbers and bring what must be a supply of powder and ball with 'em ain't ordinary.''

"What does it all mean?"

"Captain, I truly believe they intend to attack the Station. It don't make a lick of sense, though. They got no cannon and I can't figure how else they can breach the walls or gates. But damnit, I can feel it in my bones. They're gonna try to wipe us out.''

Hump Layton, leaning against the wall at the corner of the hearth, ruffled his straggly beard. ''It makes sense if'n they're hopin' to slow General Wayne's advance against them. How would it look for him and his legion if'n the redsticks show they can skirt around them anytime they please an' attack wherever they want. There'd be hell to pay for months, an' Wayne's whole campaign would be questioned. If'n you're right, Nathan, how soon will the Shawnee strike us?''

"Within the next two days or not at all," Breed determined. ''They ain't much for dallyin' in the cold, an' the weather can sour even more on them.''

"Maybe we should send for Kenton and his rangers straightaway, Captain," Pratt suggested as he passed Breed a noggin of boiled tea.

"They ain't there," I announced.

Heads turned my direction. ''Kenton and his boys are down to Lexington,'' I continued. ''The governor's hostin' a celebration for them an' presentin' them with the federal pay they're owed. They'll be gone two weeks or more.''

"That changes things a heap, Captain," Breed said. ''With Simon gone, I ain't trustin' to any outsiders for help. Maybe we should consider the women and children and pack them over to Limestone till we're certain the danger has passed. We could withstand a siege a heap easier without women and children afoot.''

"That we could, but the general would never agree to such a move. It would be admitting that it's not safe to settle above the Ohio, an' with that, everyone would desert him.''

"Would be bolstering, though, if'n we had a means of sparin' the women an' children," Breed persisted.

"We do, Nathan; it's ready an' waitin'," I informed him.

The scout was skeptical like the rest of those listening. "Speak up, lad."

" 'Lessen the Injuns cut them loose, the stores flatboats are still moored at the mouth of the creek. They'd hold all the women an' children easy, most all the men, too.''

"He's right," Aaron Knott chimed in from the bottom of the steps leading to the second story of the blockhouse. Knott walked forward and introduced himself to Breed and Hump Layton. "My men and I will follow your bidding, Captain. We hate the red heathen same as you."

The big spy stood silently, gathering his thoughts. "Listen up, all of you. I doubt I can convince the general to send the women and children off ahead of any attack. But with your help, Knott, we'll put a guard on your boats so we can be sure they're there if'n we decide to use them later. Detail a couple your men to march to the river with Fell and Askell Telow after breakfast. Fell an' Askell can bring back word the boats are ready and waitin'. I'll have no man out alone from here on out. Meanwhile Nathan and I will see that the Station is prepared for an attack if'n it comes."

Stepping to his sleeping place in the far corner, Layton secured his heavy-caliber musket. "It's nearin' full daylight, ain't it, Nathan?''

"Yes, sir!"

"Good, 'cause it's gonna bust a gut outside before long," the big spy asserted, ignoring the curious stares he drew. "Knott, you an' your sailors dig into that provision shed an' fetch some fixin's for your mornin' meal. Emil an' Shorty, you'll eat with Knott's crew. Askell and Breed, you come along with Pratt, Noah, Cooper, and me. Michaela wants us to breakfast at her table, an' I don't aim to see her disappointed. You can thank Pratt for remem-

berin' her invite. Bring your wraps an' weapons with you.
We'll get on with our business soon as we've et.''

Uncertain how I would be greeted, I was last through the
door of Michaela's cabin. She was at the hearth when I
entered, prim and proper and stunning in that familiar blue
dress, honey brown hair tied high on her head. Her hazel
eyes clouded briefly when she spotted the wound on my
cheek. Then she was caught up in the serving. ''The chair
at the end of the table is empty, Mister Cooper.''

She circled the table with a three-legged kettle, ladling
hot corn mush seasoned with molasses into our trenchers.
She greeted each man in person as she went, and I marveled
how men came alive in her presence. They hung on her
every word, her every gesture. Her warmth and charm exceeded her beauty. As I stared at her, mouth nearly hanging
open, I doubted I was right for her, but Lord, I surely loved
her with all my heart and all my being.

Platters of smoked ham and fried bacon made the rounds,
followed by freshly baked bread, then Michaela made a
final circuit, filling our noggins with a wonderful concoc-
tion, hot buttered rum spiked with chocolate. There wasn't
a soul at the table who wouldn't have sacrificed everything
for her then and there.

Yelling broke out within the station yard. The door burst
open and a bearded countenance, wild-eyed and panting,
yelled unnecessarily loud, ''Injuns scalped the Davies last
night, general wants you damn quick, Captain!'' The
bearded countenance then withdrew as fast as it had appeared, leaving the door ajar.

Hump Layton rose slowly from his chair. ''A fine breakfast, daughter. We thank you one and all. Fell, you an'
Askell need be off to the river. Don't let anythin' deter
you. Saddle two of the general's mounts, for I want you
both back here before dark.''

We all made to leave. Michaela scooted round the table,
halted Askell at the door, and whispered into his ear. She
then caught her father by the arm. ''Give Noah and me a

minute to smear Fell's wounded cheek with bear's grease, Father. It'll help against the cold.''

The objection about wasting time for no good reason I expected from the big spy was not forthcoming. Instead, he grinned happy as a fat child with a full belly and said, ''That's an order, Cooper.''

The door hadn't any more closed and she was in front of me with a crock of bear's grease. ''Perhaps you best sit on a chair.''

Noah, just one big smile, damn him, was only too happy to hurry and set a chair from the table before the hearth. ''Should have thought of it myself. Quite a clever girl, isn't she, Fell?''

I nodded and plopped down on the chair. Michaela slid beside me, tilted my head backwards, and applied the grease directly to Noah's ligatures, her touch light and smooth. ''Just stay still and I won't hurt you.''

She seemed to be at it overly long, but I really didn't mind for I could smell the flowery scent of her despite the stink of the grease. I swear I felt the rise and fall of her bosom though she was touching me with only two of her fingers. ''You know, Mister Cooper, if the proper lady is careless with her latch string, she can hardly hold others at fault. And if she were to be deliberately careless, then her visitor could rightfully assume, could he not, that she was quite willing to accept the consequences.''

It wasn't the swell of her breasts that turned my ears flaming hot now, and suddenly I was sorry we weren't alone, for even with Noah there I was about to come out of that chair and lay hold of her. But I hesitated for fear I would embarrass her with him being only a few feet away, and then Askell was at the door relating as how he had the horses saddled and waiting.

Michaela stepped back, the grease crock still in her hand. ''Go along, Fell Cooper. I had Askell bring Red Boy around for you to ride.''

I stopped halfway out of the chair. ''You know we might

run into Injuns. Perhaps you shouldn't be so generous with him.''

She never batted an eye. ''I understand that, but you take him anyway. Some things are more important to me than any horse, even Red Boy. Now, out with you,'' she cried, shooing me toward the door. ''I won't have you leave me in tears. I'll be waiting here when you return.''

With a last long look at her, I went through the door and up onto Red Boy's back, and as Askell and I rode from the station yard, I knew that whatever happened twixt us later that day, my life had forever changed over a few smears of bear's grease.

23

Hump Layton was in the creek bottom with Clay Kendall and the Henry pack animals. As Askell and I rode down the pathway from the Station, he waved us to him. Upstream, where the women collected water and did washing on the rocks, Nathan Breed in his wolf-pelt hood was examining the bodies of the Davies cousins, the discovery of which had alarmed the Station. The general was with him, wide girth bundled in a knee-length coat, legs looking like thin sticks. Brice Fowler, in his fancy cloak, tricorn, and high boots, watched from behind the general. I wondered what the dandy thought about this turn of events.

"Cooper, Clay here tells me most of your Henry horses will accept a rider," Hump Layton stated.

"Yes, sir, they will, but it's best if'n someone has a hand on their halter all the while. Having a rider up is not an ordinary haul for them."

"Any hay or fodder left on your horse boat?"

"At least two days' worth, sir," I informed him, curious as to exactly what the big spy had in mind.

"Lad, the Shawnee hit the Station an' we fort up, they'll

scatter the stock or kill it—horses, cows, everything alive. I'm gonna gamble the boats are still at the mouth of the creek. Clay an' Knott's sailors will follow you an' Askell with your animals. We'll stash 'em at the river, an' with Clay an' the sailors standin' guard over 'em, maybe we can keep them safe case we need to move the women an' children out in a hurry.''

I had no objection to relocating the packhorses away from the Shawnee point of attack. No matter what else transpired, the one certainty I faced was accounting for Ned Henry's property whenever I returned to Limestone. And if the Shawnee didn't attack, I had simply to load them and push off for the Kentucky shore.

My agreeing nod drew a brief grin from the big spy. "Good lad. Now, don't tarry. By the feel of the weather, a sizable storm is brewin' an' the redsticks may jump us before it interferes with their plans. Don't be surprised if'n Aaron Knott meets you at the river with his sailors. He fusses over his boats liken you do these four-leggeds.''

Askell and I rode south down Eagle Creek. The storm Captain Layton had predicted was definitely in the making. The air was damp and chill, and large banks of cloud hovered in the west, darker and heavier then the overcast directly above us. All that was necessary was a wind to stir the elements into motion.

I looked back from the spot where I had last seen Michaela in October and was struck again by the squat, formidable appearance of the Station. The blockhouses, the tall pickets, and three-inch-thick slab gates looked insurmountable 'lest the enemy had cannons to blast them apart. If properly supplied and provisioned, with enough barreled water handy, all of which the general had seen after, the only other serious threat to such a solid structure was that the Shawnee could take us by surprise and get inside before the gates were closed and barred. But where vigilance had been slack just a day ago, this morning two sentries manned the front gates, and a third sentry watched in all directions from the gun ports of the upper story of the main blockhouse, ready to ring the alarm bell. So thorough was Hump Layton's alert, even the cattle feeding in the canebrake on the far bank of the creek opposite the settler cabins were being overseen by two armed men.

I don't know about Askell Telow, but I paid attention to every sharp defile, stand of trees, and bend of the creek that lent itself to a potential ambush the entire ride south to the Ohio. Now and again I halted and studied what I would be seeing on the return ride, struck as always how differently the country shaped up depending on your direction of travel. In total, I found a half dozen sites where even with the trees bereft of leaves, Injuns could lay in wait.

We reached the river in early afternoon. The flatboats were as we had left them. Askell and I checked their mooring hawsers, then settled in the edge of the trees where we could watch both the creek and the river, to await Clay Kendall and the sailors. They showed an hour later, Aaron Knott and Clay in the lead.

While Clay and I picketed the horses along the creek bank above the boats and saw to their watering and haying, one of Knott's sailors built a fire in the metal hearth of the lead boat and brewed tea. We then gathered in the bow and sipped from two common noggins.

"I cannot believe the Shawnee will waste themselves trying to take the general's station," Aaron Knott put forth, twisting the tips of his bristling moustaches into points.

Yellow-eyed Askell nodded. "Me, too, but they ain't known for gathering away from their towns 'thout good reason. If they was huntin' meat, they would have shot everything with hair and drawin' breath within ten miles by now." With a deep frown, he reached and pitched the last few drops of tea in his noggin over the gunwale. "Fell, can you make the ride back by your lonesome? My belly has soured on me of a sudden an' I gots to heave somethin' awful."

With that small warning, Askell leaned over the gunwale and vomited into the river. When he turned around again, his face was white and strained. "I better get to the woods,

Knott. I'm gonna have to get my breeches down next, an' us Telows is plumb shy about our skinny bums.''

Askell was a blur of hat brim, long red hair, and flapping coattails as he vaulted the gunwale and lumbered behind the closest trees. The last we saw of him, one hand was clinging to his rifle barrel and the other was clawing desperately at the buckle of his wide leather belt. Aaron Knott couldn't forestall a wide smile. ''I'm afraid your friend is truly suffering, but never fear, young Cooper, we will guard his hiding place so the Shawnee do not catch him unawares. No man would want to meet his maker after losing his scalp with his pants on the ground.''

I had to smile, too. ''I appreciate that, Captain. Now I must be off. Hump Layton's expecting confirmation the boats are here before the end of the day.''

Rested, watered, and fed, Red Boy was anxious to run. I let him do so till we had gone a mile, then slowed him to a steady walk. His hooves still made enough noise in the creek bottom at that pace to prick at your nerves.

The wind from the west, the damp air began to stir at the midpoint of my five-mile ride. Those dark clouds hovering in the same direction edged closer. The storm might be hours off yet, but Hump Layton's weather eye was accurate: A heap of snow was building out beyond the horizon.

The afternoon light was winnowing rapidly when the lower reaches of the valley fronting the Station stretched before me through that familiar break in the trees lining the creek bank. Already guessing as to what Michaela might do or say when I saw her next, I abandoned the creek bed, guided Red Boy through the opening into the edge of the nearest empty cornfield, and aimed him straight for the main gate.

The signal bell in the upper window of the main blockhouse clanged. I reined Red Boy to a halt and stood in the stirrups, only to ease back down into the saddle. There was no alarm. The six settler families strolled calmly from their cabins, the men bearing weapons and lanthorns, their wives and offspring blankets and other bedding. The sight of the Davies scalped bodies preying on him, the general had summoned one and all to spend the night within the safe walls of the Station.

I was within forty yards of the walking settler families, a hundred of the Station, when cattle began bawling in the canebrake across the creek under the eastern ridgeline. I stood in the stirrups again and this time I stayed there. Besides us human folks, only troubled cows and disturbed watchdogs so loved to hear their own voices before suffering any actual hurt. The settlers paused to peer twixt their cabins. It was a most fateful delay.

Running cows splashed from the water of the creek. Directly behind them came a horde of screeching, howling, bloodthirsty Shawnee. Men shouted desperate warnings. Bug-eyed women and children screamed in panic. The station bell clanged a mad tattoo. But before the settlers could so much as move, the savages were almost to their cabins, leaving as their only escape the Station's main gate sixty impossibly long yards away. Almost to the man, the fathers and husbands sacrificed themselves in a display of unequaled bravery. They shoved their wives and children ahead and knelt to aim and fire directly into the oncoming wave of the enemy in a futile attempt to delay the inevitable.

Ignoring the fall of a few comrades in the front of their ranks, the Shawnee swept forward, hacking, chopping, and stabbing men, women, and helpless children with a brutal ferociousness that gagged me. And then, mortal danger or no, figuring I would be killed in the end no matter which direction I fled, I dug my boot heels into the flanks of the prancing, excited Red Boy and rode straight into that mass of screaming, sweat-smeared red bastards. Feet braced against the stirrup irons, I gripped the Bedford by the barrel and flailed left and right with the butt. Hands seized at my leggins, but the stallion's momentum shook them loose. An arrow whisked by under my chin, passing so close its feathers touched my skin. A dead cow blocked Red Boy's path, and as he gathered himself to leap, a Shawnee leaped on his haunches behind me, only to be knocked loose from his newly gained perch by a wild bullet or carefully placed shot, I never knew which.

Rifles cracked in the upper story of the blockhouse and savages tumbled head over heels. I was fast approaching the forwardmost Shawnee. Not a single male settler was left standing. Out ahead of the galloping Red Boy, over the bobbing topknots of the final redsticks separating me from the main gate, I spotted a lone white woman still upright and running, dragging after her a winded daughter of perhaps ten years. Hardly believing the stallion and I were still alive, I booted his sides again, determined to shield mother and child those last precious yards to safety.

A searing heat beset the top of my shoulder. I ignored it. Red Boy grunted and for one wild, awful second I feared he was hit, then he lunged and regained his balance from the stumble. The stallion was sucking wind in gasps and knew no quit. He would gallop flush into the jaws of hell long as you held the reins tight.

I chanced a peek at the main gate, and low and behold, Hump Layton slid through a crack twixt the opposing wooden spans and drew bead with his heavy-caliber musket. He pulled trigger, smoke and flame lanced from the barrel, and not one, but three heathen fell to my left. Calm as if he awaited the arrival of a passel of friends, Layton dumped an unmeasured amount of powder into the barrel, spat a mouthful of balls after it, and tapped the butt of the Brown Bess firmly on the frozen ground. Reaming the touch hole with a metal pick, the big spy primed the pan heavily, leveled his weapon, and fired a second volley. This go-round Shawnee faltered and went down on my right.

The leaders of the running Shawnee slowed and I booted Red Boy the hardest yet. Summoning some extra reserve of power and will, the stallion shot forward. I was within arm's reach when the fleeing mother lurched sideways and spun about as she fell, grabbing her chest with the frantic clutch of those dead before they land.

Holding the Bedford wide for balance, I leaned from the

saddle and wound an arm around the upper body of the
fallen mother's daughter. The shocked girl, believing the
Shawnee had caught up to her, screamed as her skirts billowed and her feet lifted into the air. I fought her efforts
to shake free, and my blunt ''Hush now!'' shushed her
tongue. Her eyes found my face and the next instant her
arms circled my neck. Through it all, Red Boy never broke
stride.

The explosion came with us a few leaping bounds from
the safety of the main gate. A thunderous, earsplitting boom
rent the air and I felt the ground quiver under Red Boy.
Yellow flame, brilliant in the dull gray light of the late
winter afternoon, plumed upward from the west wall of the
Station, trailed closely by thick, roiling black smoke and a
canvas-clad, twirling human leg severed whole from some
victim's body. We had no powder stored in that sector,
which meant the Shawnee were attempting to breech the
wood gate adjacent to the forge.

I reined Red Boy through the main gate held ajar by
Hump Layton and discovered the savages were pouring
through a gap wide as a freight wagon in the west wall.
Shots from the northwest blockhouse where we men slept
stalled the redstick assault for the briefest of moments and
Hump Layton screamed for me to get down.

I left Red Boy in a plunging dismount. Balls zinged past.
The stallion squealed with pain, spun, and retreated back
the way we had come, his hooves lashing at any savage
reaching for his loose reins.

''Give her to me,'' a demanding voice shouted, and with
a jolt I realized Michaela was outside the main blockhouse.
She yanked at the girl still clinging to my neck. I wrenched
the girl's arms free and Michaela pulled her, jerking and
heaving, through the blockhouse door. Hump Layton was
on their heels, yelling for me to follow.

The second explosion seemed to shove me to safety. I
missed the sight of the resulting fire and smoke, but the
blast was tremendously loud, absolutely deafening. In the
sudden gloom as the blockhouse door swung shut behind

me, a shaken survivor sounding a mile away mumbled, "The bastards blew the provision shed. That was our powder reserve going off."

Nearly dying for lack of breath, I rolled into a sitting position next to the barred door. I was delighted to discover my left hand still grasped the Bedford. A quick inspection revealed the weapon was intact despite all the bludgeoning I had done with it from atop Red Boy. "Upstairs, Cooper, get to a gun port upstairs," Hump Layton roared.

I rose shakily to my feet, confirmed that I somehow hadn't lost any of my own parts, and lurched to the stairs. A female was weeping and I desperately wanted to make sure Michaela was unharmed, but that had to wait. Pratt was there on the upper level, his beard a spark of white in the haze and stink of burnt powder. Nathan Breed was manning the ports overlooking the station yard and the main gate. "Need you here, Cooper."

I angled the barrel of the Bedford in the light of a gun port and could see no obstructions in the bore. Damned if I was gonna blow my face off unnecessarily after all I had survived to get safely inside. I primed the pan and ran the barrel through the six-inch opening of the gun port.

The view that greeted my searching eyes slackened my wind. Where the provision shed had been, smoke drifted from a blackened crater. The whole of the yard was a shambles, littered with charred wood, shattered tools, broken barrel staves, and Shawnee bodies. I had to look extra fine, but identified a lump impaled twixt two pickets near the northwest blockhouse as a smoked ham.

Live Shawnee, screeching and howling madly as ever, battered at the barred door of the opposing blockhouse with a length of thick log. Breed's rifle fired a fraction ahead of the Bedford. The loss of two of their fellows discouraged the heathen. They dropped their ram and sought shelter behind the blockhouse. They hadn't any more disappeared when a rifle cracked yonder, then another.

"Tells us one thing for certain, by damned," Breed surmised as he reloaded. "Emil and Shorty ain't breathed their last yet. They're shootin' through the ports of the over-hang.''

Just then, after twenty solid minutes of total bedlam and lightning death, the war whoops of the savages trailed off, and the sudden lack of frantic activity boggled the mind. I stared through the gun port. In the growing darkness, except for the blockhouses, the rest of the Station was afire. Pickets burned on every wall. Tongues of flame curled about the bottom of the door of Michaela's cabin, the roof of which had already collapsed. Wind fanned and brightened the spreading flames, and the first few snowflakes drifted from the sky.

Without turning from a gun port overlooking the valley, Pratt lamented that ''They've torched the settler cabins. Now they're cuttin' the hearts out of the dead an' eatin' them raw. I'm powerful glad we're forted up.''

''We ain't gonna be for long,'' Breed retorted. ''Snow's thickening, an' I think we best parley with the general.''

''Have you swallowed your pearl, Nathan?'' Pratt asked, incredulous over what the scout was proposing.

''No, I know exactly what I'm sayin'. We wait in here like penned sheep, they'll starve us out. Come along, you two can listen from the head of the stairs. We're gonna learn if'n there's still any backbone under all that fat on General Hugh Brandon's belly.''

24

Situated in his chair before the hearth, General Hugh Brandon poured wine into his pewter noggin and studied Nathan Breed's stern features. Behind him, Michaela and Rebecca Brandon helped the female servants heat tea and fry hoe cake in spider skillets in preparation for the eventuality we dreaded the most—a prolonged siege at the mercy of the redsticks.

At the general's invitation, Brice Fowler, Hump Layton, and Laina Brandon sat at the table for the parley Breed had requested. Three of Knott's sailors kept a vigil at gun ports looking east and south where the Shawnee continued to pillage and loot. Pratt and I listened from the head of the stairs, ready to man the upper story again if the sailors reported any threatening actions in our direction on the part of the enemy.

"Mister Breed, are you daft?" the general asked, no less incredulous than Pratt had been a few minutes ago. "Why would we choose to abandon a strong defensive position to flee amidst what you admit will likely be a blizzard by the middle of the night?"

Breed took no insult from the question. His dark eyes never left those of the general. "Way I reckon, our stores and reserve powder are blown to hell and gone along with our water barrels. If'n we're lucky, we've got no more than thirty rounds of ball and powder for each gun bearer. Our vittles won't last more'n two, three days, water an' spirits half of that. An' after the storm, when the cold sets in liken it always does, we'll be burnin' these walls to keep warm before any rescue party reaches us. We make off tonight or we stay an' be starved out."

"We'll never surrender," Brice Fowler contended.

"You will, young'un, when your tongue gets so big from thirst you choke on it."

"Mister Breed, how can you be so utterly convinced we must flee tonight or forget such a move all together?" the general continued.

"I know the Shawnee. They'll withdraw into the hills north of the station an' sit out the storm round a big fire, braggin' on what they've done an' fillin' their gullets with some of our dead beef. They'll figure we ain't crazy enough to try an' escape in the middle of a storm. They'll trust we'll be like every other station an' hunker down behind these walls till help comes. Storm passes, they'll post a watch clean around the valley, day and night."

"What are our chances of being rescued by a party from Limestone?"

Hump Layton gave the general the bad news about Simon Kenton and the ranger feast at Lexington. "We can count only on ourselves, sir," the big spy concluded. His eyes sought me at the top of the stairwell. "The boats are still at the mouth of the creek, Cooper?"

"Yes, sir," I sang out. "Askell Telow, Captain Knott, an' two of his sailors are guardin' the three boats an' my pack animals."

"I can presume then, Captain Layton, that you support our scout's risky proposal?"

"Yes, General, I do. I ain't anxious for any of us to end up dead or prisoners of the Shawnee. If'n we follow Nathan down the creek once it's snowin' full bore, we got as good a chance to survive as we're likely to have. We'll send someone ahead to bring the horses to meet us and ease the burden on the women an' children. A night march beats starvation and surrenderin' later.''

The weight of command and the enormity of the decision he, and he alone, must make, lowered the general's wigged head. When he straightened in his chair, he cleared his throat and smiled sadly at the big spy. ''It never behooves a man to think his responsibilities will lessen as he grows old and feeble, huh, Captain Layton? Mister Breed, your instructions if you please. We shall take advantage of your suggestion and flee while we can.''

Breed was terse, wasting not a word. ''Bundle in as many clothes as you can, but not so many you can't run if'n need be. 'Lest you can eat it or use it for a weapon, leave everything else behind. We hurry once we start, we'll gain the river in just three hours. Soon as we're aboard the boats, we'll have fires straightaway.''

Pratt giggled beside me. ''Makes a night march through a blizzard sound liken a walk to the spring in the middle of July, don't he now?''

Our preparations consumed the intervening hours. The women shared the entire contents of the Brandon wardrobes with each other—every coat, shawl, scarf, muff, and glove. These same ladies fried hoe cakes and filled muslin bags with them till the fixings ran dry. The menfolks checked and rechecked every gun lock and flint, counted each ball twice, and sharpened knife and hatchet blades to a razor keenness. Then we settled to rest and wait, the women at the table and on the floor in front of the hearth, the men at the gun ports. I did try once to speak with Michaela, but retreated to the upper story when I located her asleep on a blanket near the fire, her arms about the settler's girl we had spared.

Cold wind pouring through the gun port above my head brought me awake, or so I thought. ''Snap to, Fell,'' Pratt repeated. ''Breed says it's time.''

I stood and shook like an awakening hound. The gun ports were black now, indicating the Station fires had burned themselves out with the help of the wet, heavy snow. Pratt held his candle lanthorn steady at the top of the stairs till I reached him. His was the only light as we descended the stairs.

Breed confiscated Pratt's lanthorn and placed it on the table. The paint on his cheeks glowed in the flame of the wick. "I've alerted Shorty an' Emil. They're at the main gate or what's left of it. We'll line out right here. I've a rope for you ladies to hold onto so you won't get separated. Listen close. There's a guard at the washing rocks to the east that Hump will take care of. We're headed straight down the valley to the creek. Don't let the bodies of the settlers or the cows or other animals upset you. Whatever happens, don't cry out. We reach the trees at the end of the valley, we'll take a head count. Everyone understand? . . . Any questions?"

Nodding at our silence, Breed said, "Fell, you, Pratt, an' Brice will bring up the rear till the captain catches up with us. You sailors will walk with the smiths, Noah, an' the general behind me, an' break a trail for the women. Get in line, ladies, if'n you please."

Once we were assembled to Breed's satisfaction, he snuffed out the lanthorn's candle and Hump Layton opened the door for us. We trooped faithfully into the dark where the wind whipped and shrieked and snow drove from the sky. You couldn't see twice the length of your body. Past the charred post of the gate upright, Hump Layton veered to my left. He disappeared in two huge strides.

I brought up the very rear. My eyes adjusted to the dark in a while, and I had no difficulty identifying the snow-covered mounds Breed skirted by the number of legs each possessed. It was a disheartening start for such a perilous journey. I knew without hearing that some of the women would be fighting back tears. The wives and mothers of any station, whether rich or poor, always hung together. Theirs was a singular lot.

Black trees stark in the white flying snow signaled we were nearing the creek bank. Breed came down the line, actually counting heads. He leaned and spoke for my ears. "We're not waiting on the captain. He'll follow the creek bed an' catch us in due time. That was his choice. The women can only stand so much of this cold. We don't dare waste a minute. Understand?"

At my quick nod, the scout retraced his steps and the column jerked into motion again.

It was for me the reliving of a nightmare best forgotten. Running before the Shawnee was becoming a habit I could do without. I prayed earnestly there in the snow, the wind, and the dark, more than once, that for the sake of the women and the young girl with us, the Shawnee wouldn't snoop close to the Station and discover our absence. They had seen enough bloodshed for a dozen winters.

Breed called his first halt at the bottom of a sharp defile where the curving bowl of a cut bank at least sheltered us from the wind. Hump Layton caught the column then. He welled up out of the swirling snow, huge and limping. A bloody swatch of buckskin circled his left thigh. He plopped beside me without ceremony. It felt strange asking a man of his immense strength how badly he was hurt.

"I didn't kill him straightaway an' the sonofabitch stuck me with his knife. I had to break his neck with a forearm, an' he didn't die easy or quick. Much as he gouged with that blade, he didn't hit an artery or I'd've been a goner," the big spy explained, tightening the bandage on his thigh with a stick.

A new shadow forged past Brice and Pratt. It was Michaela, bundled in greatcoat, breeches, boots, and two scarves, one of which was tied under her chin to hold her hat on her head. She cared for none of the details of her father's wounding. Her sole concern was his ability to keep up with the column now that he had joined us. "Breed sent the sailors ahead for the horses. Can you walk another mile on your own?"

Hump Layton's affirmation that he could wasn't all that

comforting to her. Her face appeared at the end of my nose and her hazel eyes pleaded for honesty. "You'll see he doesn't fall behind, won't you?"

"If I have to carry him," I promised, though I knew I couldn't possibly achieve such a feat. With a kiss on my forehead, her face withdrew, and she spoke again with her father.

The next thing, the big spy's Brown Bess musket slanted twixt my knees and she helped herself to the Bedford. "Find him a tall staff. I'll tote your rifle; his musket's too heavy for me."

I realized Hump Layton was truly hurting. For him to willingly sacrifice his large-caliber gun for a longer crutch told how much the loss of blood had already weakened him. Pratt and I slipped into the woods opposite the cut bank and soon located a deadfall from which we snapped a limb thick as my fist and high as my chin. When we measured it out, it fit under Hump's armpit just dandy.

Breed got us moving again. It was nearing first light and everyone was excited that the sailors and the horses should be meeting us within the mile. We had been walking some while, me paying close attention to the staggering Hump, when I missed Pratt. He was smack on my heels all the time, then he was gone.

I waved Hump on ahead and turned back for Pratt. The snow had tapered off and visibility improved by the minute. I expected to find Pratt quickly. I didn't. Whatever had delayed him had occurred shortly after we departed the cut bank. Cursing my negligence, I broke into a near run. We were too close to escaping to lose the old roustabout now.

I scooted round a gradual bend in the creek and there he was, and he wasn't alone. Two Shawnee had him cornered against a black walnut trunk just off the ice of the creek. Pratt had his rifle at his shoulder, the barrel swerving from one advancing redstick to the other. They were closing on him slowly and surely, drawing within hatchet-throwing range. Both savages carried muskets in their off hands, but their choice not to bring them to bear bespoke faulty powder on their part. They were intent on dispatching Pratt nonetheless.

"Shoot the one nearest you," I yelled out, yanking the lock cover from Hump Layton's Brown Bess.

Pratt's rifle belched flame and smoke. The smaller of the Shawnee took the ball in the belly. As he toppled into the snow, his bigger companion spun to face me. I leveled the musket, centered front and rear sights on the redstick's broad chest, and gently squeezed the trigger.

I heard the flint strike the frizzen and saw sparks fly out of the corner of my eye, but there was no following boom, no harsh recoil. The flash in the pan took me completely by surprise.

The remaining Shawnee never hesitated. He screeched and went for Pratt, hatchet poised for the kill. Lacking the proper size ball to reload the musket, I clasped the Bess by the barrel with both hands and raced along the snow-slick bank.

Pratt had his rifle in front of him, muzzle first, jabbing at the advancing redstick. The Shawnee shoved the jabbing barrel aside, slid forward, and raised his hatchet high. The desperate Pratt flopped backwards and lashed out with his peg. The metal tip of the false leg speared the knuckles of the Shawnee and he lost his grip on the handle of the striking hatchet. The tomahawk whirled harmlessly in the snow.

I drew back and swung the butt of the musket at the Shawnee's plucked skull. He ducked at the same instant my foot slipped from beneath me. The stock of the musket whipped over his feathered topknot and shattered on the trunk of the black walnut, numbing my right arm.

A furred shoulder exploded into my exposed ribs. Off balance already, I sailed backwards and landed atop the frozen creek, my temple rapping hard on the ice. Stunned and nearly unconscious, I clawed at my belt for my knife and missed the handle. The Shawnee pounced on me, hands seeking my throat. I rolled and brought up a knee. He blocked the blow with his hip and locked powerful fingers on my windpipe. I felt his lower body lift. He was drawing his own knife.

I arched my back, grunting with the effort, and punched at the savage's jaw with my left fist. The blow landed bone on bone just before the plunging knife ripped into the sleeve of my coat and sliced through the outer skin of my arm above the elbow. The Shawnee's grip on my windpipe slackened and I squirmed from under him.

I rolled onto my knees, desperate to get my knife free of its sheath. Movement down the ice caught my eye. I glanced up and there, fifteen yards away, stood Brice Fowler, his rifle at his shoulder and pointed our direction. The fist-stunned, weaponless Shawnee froze at my hip.

"Shoot the red bastard!" I screamed.

The muzzle of Brice's rifle drifted sideways and suddenly he was aiming, not at the enemy, but at me. I looked wildly about for Pratt. He hadn't finished reloading. My eyes swept back to the major's son as his shot rang out.

No flame lanced from the muzzle of Brice Fowler's gun. Then, to my further amazement, a large round hole suddenly appeared in the center of his forehead. The hole came alive immediately with spurting blood. The dead Brice tipped forward and fell with a rush, and standing behind his fallen body, my smoking Bedford held firmly beneath her chin, was Michaela.

New movement at my side demanded my attention. The Shawnee was on his feet and coming at me, intent on retrieving the knife still imbedded in the flesh of my arm. A second shot echoed in the creek bottom. A black arrow caught the Shawnee in the lower side. He halted abruptly and rose up on to his toes. Air fled his lungs in a wheezing gasp and he collapsed against me, knocking me over backwards.

I shook my head clear and the first thing I noticed was that a black arrow hadn't finished the Shawnee. Protruding from below his ribs was the ramrod belonging to Pratt's rifle. The old roustabout had shortcut his reloading by firing without drawing the rod from the barrel. It was chancy, but the redstick was dead and I was still sucking breath with the living.

Pratt and Michaela arrived at the same time. The old roustabout pulled the body of the Shawnee off my legs and I hitched my feet under me and stood. A tear streaking her cheek, Michaela watched as I tugged the knife blade from the skin of my arm. The bleeding that resulted was slow in coming and I knew it was only a minor wound.

Crunching snow heralded a newcomer from down the creek. It was Breed, his eyes searching intently past us back up the waterway. He took in the scene with a nod. "Gentlemen, if'n you two are done with your killin', I suggest we be long gone right quick. Those shots may bring others." Breed motioned for us to go ahead of him, then paused. "Well, I'll be damned," the scout said, leaning and yanking at the neck of the slain Shawnee.

"What is it, Nathan?" Pratt inquired.

The scout reached toward us and dangling from his fingers was a strip of black pelt, the fur old and dry. "You two can brag real good over to Limestone. It ain't every morning you send off a warrior feared as Bear Hunter."

Breed tossed the neck garland to Pratt. "I'll let you be the one to tell Askell. Come along, the others will be at the river by now."

Not a one of us bothered to look back. We left Brice Fowler unburied and where he belonged—with the enemy.

The day was bright as it would get when we reached the Ohio. Only the horse boat awaited us, Aaron Knott having ordered the others to sail with everyone aboard except himself, Noah, Askell, Clay Kendall, and the nerve-strung Hump Layton. At the sight of her father atop the crew cabin, Michaela left me and raced up the gangplank to join him. The horses were already aboard thanks to Askell and Clay, and soon as my boots touched the deck, those two tied the gangplank fast and pushed us free of the bank.

Michaela insisted Askell and Clay could see after the pack animals, and once Noah had my coat and frock off me inside the cabin, he flushed my knife wound with whiskey and wrapped it with a bandage cut from his own shirt-sleeve. "I'd prefer I had my chest and could suture the opening, but that will suffice."

Noah was helping me button my coat when the door opened and Hump Layton surged inside the cabin one step ahead of an angry Michaela. "What do you mean, Noah, not having yet tended Father's leg?"

"He wouldn't let me anywhere near him till he knew you were safe," Noah offered by way of explanation.

An exasperated Michaela stared at the big spy. "That's no excuse now, is it? He's here and willing. Do you need help getting him out of those breeches?"

"Now, you wait a damn minute, girl," Hump protested. "I ain't shuckin' my pants with you watchin' even if'n you are my own daughter."

"Father, you can be such a child at times," Michaela scolded. "Come with me, Mister Cooper. We'll send Pratt in to help Noah. You won't object to that, will you, Father!"

The big spy merely shook his already lowered head. Michaela tugged my coat sleeve and I followed her from the cabin. She gave Pratt his orders, then led me around the horses into the bow of the boat. The Kentucky shore loomed a half mile to port. The other flatboats had already made their landings.

Knowing Michaela never did anything without a reason, I propped the Bedford in the corner of the bow and turned to face her. She sighed and stepped closer. Unsure what she expected from me, I held still and said, "Thank you for killing Brice. I would be—"

"Fell Cooper," she broke in, "if you don't take me in your arms and hold me, I'm going to scream."

I didn't need to hear any more than that. I grabbed her and pulled her tight against my chest. Shouts erupted atop the crew cabin. I ignored them, tilted Michaela's chin, and covered her lips with mine, and as I soaked in the warmth and smell and sweet taste of her, I realized I had not only kissed my first pretty girl, but also my last.

EPILOGUE

Lexington, Kentucky

May 18, 1834

To the Honorable Judge Hickersby:

Please accept my apology for my tardiness in forwarding the last pages of my feeble scratching with the quill. Since my return home from Louisville last autumn following the big commemoration, I quite honestly have had more poor days than good. But that is neither here nor there since you are preparing to publish the recollections you have so painstakingly gathered.

In response to your latest inquiry, I will relate as faithfully as I can what happened to those of us who escaped the Shawnee following the burning of Brandon Station. The demise of his Ohio venture was, of course, not the ruination of General Hugh Rolfe Brandon and his immediate family. The general, aided by Emil and Shorty, bore through the blizzard that black night a sizable leather pouch containing the last of his gold coins. After a week of rest at Monet's, the general, his wife, his daughter Rebecca, and their sur-

viving servants wintered here in Lexington. The following spring, he purchased land west of the village and returned to tobacco farming and horse breeding till his death in 17 and 99.

Rebecca Brandon was pursued by the bachelors of Lexington with the fervor of young hounds hot on the heels of the fox. None of them seemed to ever quite suit her, howsomever, and the chase continued for almost eight years. Then, one June afternoon, in response to a knock at her door, she found on her stoop my most trusted friend, Noah Reem, his studies under Dr. Christiansen in Virginia finally completed. I was not witness to their reunion, but did attend their wedding three days later.

As for yours truly, my biggest fear once the horse boat landed on the Kentucky bank that fateful December morning was how a man with no means could hang onto the girl he wanted more than his own next breath. I really had no other choice, so I left Michaela at Monet's with the Brandon clan and trudged to the Henry Yard with Clay Kendall, Pratt, Askell, the smiths, and the pack animals. In the course of my reporting to the boss man in his office all that had happened since he had watched Noah and me sail from Limestone just four days past, I couldn't stop talking and before I knew it I had told him of my plight. Not a moment of concern crossed Ned Henry's pox-scarred face. He merely leaned back in his chair and, while I listened anxiously, shared, for the first time ever, much of his own feelings. He had no wife, no offspring, no blood heirs, he revealed, and months ago had decided to someday offer me a stake in his business affairs. Well, by damned, if I intended to take a wife, he saw no reason why we couldn't launch our partnership immediately. About then you could have knocked me into my hat with a feather. I recovered enough that when Ned Henry came out of his chair with a smile big as the Ohio was wide, I done a decent job of stammering, "Thank you, sir," over and over and shaking the hand he offered.

I married Michaela a week later in the dining hall at

*Monet's, and from the very first night, my thirty years with
her was a constant whirlwind of excitement few men ever
experience. The one blemish on our initial happiness, her
loss of Red Boy, was rectified the following spring by Nathan Breed. He whistled from the yard one early evening
and called Michaela by name. Her squeal of delight
brought me outside and I found her hugging a gaunt, worn-
down Red Boy. The scout had for a second time risked his
life to steal him back from the Shawnee.*

*Late that summer Michaela took the stallion to race in
Lexington. The story of my ride through the Shawnee in
front of Brandon Station had spread throughout Kentucky,
and two nights of Pratt's enrichment of the growing legend
in the local taverns produced a huge crowd that included
General Brandon. The resulting victory and the purse that
accompanied it, augmented by Ned Henry's private wagers
with certain money-toting members of the cheering crowd,
launched the Cooper and Henry racing and breeding stable
that was eventually to make us rich ten times over.*

*The defeat of the Shawnee that same August of 17 and
94 by General Wayne spawned a new rush of settlers from
across the mountains into Kentucky and the Ohio back-
country. The Henry Yard flourished. Ned Henry purchased
General Brandon's Ohio land warrants on consignment
and gradually sold them at a fair profit for the both of them.
We opened a stage line from Limestone to Lexington at the
end of the decade. In 18 and 03, we built Cooper's Tavern
in Lexington, an establishment that rivaled Monet's in el-
egance and accommodations. The tavern provided us quarters for the racing season, and a place to consort with
fellow horse breeders and those who lived solely to race
and wager. After its formation in 18 and 09, on any given
evening half of the Lexington Jockey Club might fill the
tables at Cooper's. And my horse-loving wife was always
in the thick of the wheeling and dealing.*

*Amidst this continual growth and expansion, Michaela
presented me with a daughter and two sons and raised
Sarah Duncan, the settler girl whose rescue at Brandon*

*Station attracted the huge crowd to Red Boy's first race.
We were never separated, Michaela and I, till Nathan
Breed and I went north in 18 and 13 to help finish off the
Shawnee and the redcoats once and for all.*

A badly broken leg had kept me from joining the Lexington companies journeying north into battle the previous
year. But when news of the Shawnee massacre of helpless
Kentucky prisoners at the River Raisin reached us, a fresh
wave of war fever swept the city and every healthy male
but the coward signed up therewith. The announcement of
my enlistment sparked a tirade from Michaela the likes of
which I hadn't seen since that long ago evening when I
dropped her in Red Oak Creek. My leaving was not the
sole source of her upset. Seven winters before, in 18 and
06, her father, increasingly bored with what he called the
tame life of racing and planting, had taken the ancient Pratt
Jackson west of the Mississippi on a trapping and trading
expedition from which neither returned. Breed, who had not
gone with them due to illness, went searching for them at
Michaela's request, but returned by himself after weeks of
looking. It was as if the earth had swallowed the big spy
and Pratt Jackson.

That night before Breed and I marched north was the
only occasion I ever slept in a bed different from Michaela.
By daylight, her wrath had cooled enough she could talk,
though barely, and she saw us off with dry eyes and trembling lips. I was gone thirteen months. I survived bad officers, bad weather, bad vittles, and a determined enemy.
But, in the main, I survived because I had Nathan Breed
alongside me. I was aware he had secretly loved Michaela
forever, and if he couldn't have her for himself, he did the
next best thing and guarded those she loved. Breed was
there the foggy dawn the armed highwayman tried to take
my life and my purse on the Limestone road. He was there
when the freight wagon overturned and shattered my leg.
Most fortunately, he was there when we made the infamous
"Forlorn Hope" charge at the Thames River that doomed
Tecumseh, and slogging through the muddy marsh ahead

of me, shielding me, he took the ball that should have struck me dead.

I came home to Michaela shorn of weight, with an arrowhead lodged in my hip. She rushed me to bed and saw to my every need. We were inseparable for the next ten years, till I lost her in the spring of 18 and 23. She left my life as she had entered it—on the back of a horse. She was riding, our granddaughter seated in front of her, and put a descendant of Red Boy over the south fence, a crazy feat to attempt at her age, but that was Michaela. Her mount's rear hooves caught the top rail and he went down. Somehow she twisted in the saddle and threw little Laura safely aside before the animal landed, but in so doing forfeited her own life.

It was some comfort that Michaela was killed instantly and did not suffer. Her passing left a void in me that nothing can ever replace. Through all the sadness and tears, though, I was never angry with her for leaving me so abruptly, for my memories of our years together are powerful and vivid and temper my loneliness to where it is bearable most days.

I swear now and again I see her in my room at night, the lushness of her straining the cloth of her cotton shift, and I watch her snuff the candle, then wait for her to say in that soft, throaty voice so familiar to me, "Come here, my darling. Don't keep your Mike waiting."

Your obedient servant,
Fell Cooper